LAINEY LAWSON

Smoking Gun

This novel is entirely a work of fiction. The names, characters and incidents portrayed in it are the work of the author's imagination. Any resemblance to actual persons, living or dead, events or localities is entirely coincidental.

Lainey Lawson asserts the moral right to be identified as the author of this work.

First edition

ISBN: 9798870927022

Cover art by Sonia Gx
Illustration by Sonia Gx
Editing by Dani Galliaro

This book was professionally typeset on Reedsy.
Find out more at reedsy.com

Here's to me.
Here's to you.
And here's to the cowboys we love to screw.

Contents

Disclaimer

To avoid spoilers, the full list of trigger/content warnings has been included at the end of this book. If you prefer to vet these before starting the book, please skip to that section first. Happy and safe reading!

Chapter 1

Blythe

Until now, I didn't believe the feelings of achievement and dread could coexist.

I always imagined that one would cancel out the other. Despite my sense of pride in this moment, the voice in my head telling me that I'm far from where I want to be hasn't died.

Am I proud that I graduated from medical school? Yes. Am I one hundred percent positive that I want to be a doctor? No. Hence, the dread.

I gather the satin graduation gown in my hands, hoping its delicate softness can bring me back down to earth. People expect me to be happy right now, so I stifle my stoic expression with a smile.

"At this time, we'd like to recognize the winter graduating class's recipient of our research award. Please help me in welcoming her to the podium. Congratulations to Dr. Blythe Farrow."

Warm applause erupts from the crowd. I savor the moment

of praise, standing elegantly and gliding across the stage. I wonder if the audience has any idea how much I sacrificed for this.

For starters, the countless sleepless nights and I don't mean the fun kind. I can't even remember the last time I went on a date or had so much as a spontaneous hook-up.

On top of that, I've had few visits home and time spent with my family. Add in the lack of self-care, hobbies, travel, and relaxation? It's a little depressing really.

I miss spending time with my family. And I most certainly miss getting my rocks off from time to time. But I know what it takes to be the best in my field: full commitment and *no* distractions.

The executive director of the medical honor society waits at the podium to hand over my award. I graciously nod my head, shake her hand, and take the heavy black crystal that she extends toward me. Looking down, I see my full name engraved. Holding the evidence of my resilience is satisfying.

I had to rely on so many people to survive my early life. Coming from an impoverished home lit a fire inside of me to become more. More than just someone who is forced to depend on others. My greatest motivation has been making those people who held me up proud. This little award is proof that I haven't disappointed them yet.

I just wish I could say the same about not disappointing myself.

The director steps closer to the microphone and speaks a little too loud at first. "We're thrilled to present this award," she leans back a touch when the crowd winces at the volume, "to our most promising medical student of this year's winter graduating class."

I take a deep breath and keep my focus on her profile as she speaks. I don't dare make eye contact with the crowd. I know the moment I see my family; emotions will fully take over.

"Dr. Farrow has proved herself to our committee. Graduating at the top of her class while showcasing her talent and ingenuity for medical research made her the clear choice," she continues. "Her future in the medical field is promising. Selfishly, I hope that includes a career in academics."

She smirks and winks at me and that earns a chorus of laughs from the crowd. It's not the first time she's brought up the idea of my future in education.

"I can picture you teaching one day," she'd say. *"People respect you and listen to you. You'd be an asset as an educator."*

I'd need a whole lot more experience in the medical field first, but I can't say the idea of it isn't appealing. It's prestigious. Secure.

While the crowd claps again at the director's departure, I take a deep breath and step up to the podium. Intentionally, I keep my acceptance short and sweet.

"Thank you, Dr. Mullen. This is an incredible honor. And thank you not only to the committee but also to my professors and peers who have created a healthy level of competition and nurturing instruction here."

I pause, finally letting my gaze land on my parents and my brother in the third row. I make eye contact with each of them and sniff back my emotions.

"I want nothing more than to make you all proud."

They know I'm speaking directly to them.

They're the most important people in the world to me. My parents struggled financially throughout my entire childhood and adult years. They still do. But no matter what, they always showed me compassion and love. I may have hated the fact that we lived in a trailer house and never had new clothes or more than one reliable vehicle, but I never questioned the fact that my family cared for me and that they were good people.

It's been my life's mission to take care of them now. Nothing means more to me than to be able to help them live a more comfortable life.

To my surprise, my classmates give a standing ovation and the whole auditorium mirrors their gesture of respect.

I never went to medical school with the idea of chasing recognition. I wanted to save lives and help people, sure. But more than anything I wanted to never have to worry about money again.

I know you don't make great money right away as a Doctor. But eventually, it's a solid career choice in terms of potential salary. Since science was always my strong suit, I pursued a medical degree to lock down a career that would take me places. Places that felt a lot safer and more stable than a trailer park in the plains of West Texas.

The ceremony wraps up after they announce each of our names for the presentation of diplomas, we throw our graduation caps, and a string quartet plays joyful music as we parade down the aisle.

It's performative, sure. But seeing the gleaming pride on people's faces as we walk past seems fitting for the occasion.

Before I reach the end of the aisle, my heel slips and I falter a bit. My hand goes up to the side of my head and I fight back a spell of dizziness. I guess I should have eaten lunch instead of attending a skills lab and a gallery surgery today.

Chapter 2

Blythe

"What are you getting?" I ask my brother Warren as I peek at him over the top of my menu. He's seated across from me at the table I reserved for the four of us for a post-graduation celebratory dinner.

"No," he protests without even looking up at me.

"What?" I tease.

"I know exactly what you're doing and the answer is no. I ain't sharing with you."

"Fine you big grump," I slap his arm and he playfully rolls his eyes. "I didn't want to try the sea bass that bad anyway."

We give each other as much shit as possible, but at the end of the day, we're closer to each other than anyone else.

Since I moved from Texas when I turned eighteen to start college, he's called or at least texted to check on me almost every day. Since I didn't carve out much time to go down and visit my family, I treasured those moments talking with him. Getting the latest gossip around town, hearing what Mom and Dad are up to, laughing with him about his newest romantic entanglement.

The waiter comes to take our orders, and to absolutely no one's surprise, Dad and Warren both get big fat steaks and potatoes.

"Can I have the baked stuffed lobster, please? Oh! And the cheese and leak souffle. Thank you so much," I say.

"Of course. Excellent choice. And for you, ma'am?" He looks at my Mom.

"Let's see... I think I'll have the sea bass. Thank you." She hands him her leatherbound menu and gives me a wink.

She'd give me the shirt off of her back or order a dish for herself that she wouldn't have originally picked, just to share it with me without hesitation. I adore that woman.

Dad takes a small sip of his whiskey and clears his throat. "So... it's not much. But it's our way of saying just how proud of you we are. And something to remember us by when you become a world-famous doctor and all that," he chuckles.

He pulls a little forest green velvet box up from under the table and slides it across to me. I suck in a breath when I snap the top of it open and see a delicate chain. Dangling from it is a tiny gold prairie rose. The detail is gorgeous and exactly resembles the native flower that grows wild where I was raised.

Nostalgia doesn't typically hit me often. But this brings me back to a much simpler place in my mind when I didn't understand the struggles of the real world yet. When adult responsibilities and stresses didn't take over every fiber of my being.

I would pick these flowers from the pasture behind our house and bring them inside, soak them in the sink to rid them of any bugs, and fill a mason jar with water for them to be displayed in. It was rare that there wasn't a bundle of them in our kitchen on any given spring day. This little charm necklace gives me a sense of home.

I hand the necklace to Mom, sweep my long thick hair to the side, and turn away from her in my seat. She drapes it around my neck and clasps it with gentle hands. Before retreating, she touches both of my shoulders and leans in. I place my hands over hers and nuzzle into her embrace.

"We love you, sweetheart. So proud," she whispers.

"You know..." Warren starts, giving a break to the emotional moment, "When we talked this morning you mentioned you wouldn't be in Tucson for that interview until after the first of the year."

"Yes?" I say.

"Why don't you come down to the ranch for a bit? Harvest is over and things slow down around the holidays. Could be good for you. Spend some time away from all this for a while."

He gestures around the restaurant bustling with people in suits and fancy dresses. Classical music plays softly. Downtown Baltimore roars just outside the bay windows behind us. Nothing like home.

For a split second, I consider the idea. I expected this topic to come up. My family often requests I come and visit. I'm just always so busy. If I waste precious time that could be dedicated to job applications or networking, it negatively affects my career. That's not an option for me. I sigh and close my eyes, not looking forward to trying to let him down easy once again.

"Look..."

"We sure miss you, you know."

"Maybe if you did come, we could be together for Christmas

this year," Mom suggests. I hate how she sounds a bit defeated mentioning me being home for Christmas. It's been a while. A *long* while.

I meet my dad's eyes and notice immediately the sincerity there. Then the hope in Warren's. And the subtle sadness in Mom's. Heavy guilt weighs down my shoulders. I look down at my new necklace and rub the little rose back and forth.

My reservations about visiting home and staying for the holidays have nothing to do with my hometown or the people in it. In fact, the community of Westridge always felt comfortable and safe to me. Unfortunately, putting my schooling and future career on hold for longer than even a day hasn't been an option for me for years.

Remembering the last time I took a break longer than a singular weekend morning seems impossible.

Maybe I could take my laptop along with me, use the WiFi in town, and keep up with my work. After the first of the year, I'm scheduled to be in Tucson for a residency interview. But that's not for another four weeks. They're high on my list of preferred locations, and they've reached out several times wanting me to tour and meet with them in person.

Since I graduated in December, and Match Week is in March, I have a very limited amount of time to rank my preferred residency programs. There are a lot to choose from, but they're not all equally prestigious. It takes a lot of effort to perfect applications and set up and prepare for interviews. I refuse to lose focus now. Not after all I've done to set myself up for maximum success.

All of that considered, I certainly never planned on leaving the city to go home for the Holidays. But the look on my family's faces has me second-guessing that decision.

"You're tired Sis. I can tell. You've worked nonstop for so long. Surely you can hang it up for a little while. They say well-rested people are the most productive," Warren says. He sips his whiskey and quirks up an eyebrow at me, daring me to challenge him on this. He's not usually so insistent, normally the easygoing one.

"Pfft. No one said that. You made it up on the spot," I argue.

"Did not. It's a scientific fact. Right, Dad?" Dad rolls his eyes at Warren and Mom giggles but he continues anyway. "You're gonna run yourself ragged and crash and burn one of these days if you don't let loose. Hell, you can even stay with me at the bunkhouse since you know there isn't good service at Mom and Dad's. We have extra bunks *and* internet." He raises his brows to the top of his forehead waiting for my response.

Dad huffs. "You kids and your internet. Need to touch your bare feet to grass instead of burying your face into phone and computer screens all day for fuck's sake."

"Wade!" Mom whisper-shouts and smacks him on the arm. We all burst into a fit of giggles.

"Only kidding dear."

Mom smiles and kisses him on the cheek, unable to hide her amusement. He's always had a way of pushing her buttons and making her laugh at the same time. And she's all too happy pretending to get onto him for bad language or whatever grumpy statement escapes his unfiltered mouth. Their fire-and-ice dynamic has always seemed sweet to me.

It's part of the reason I haven't had a serious relationship. My parents have set the bar high and I can't imagine myself settling for anything less than someone who can go toe-to-toe with me and love me more than anything in the whole world at the same time.

I shake my head back and forth to stop myself from thinking too long about that. My career and taking care of my family are more important than any man I've dreamed up in my head.

"What is it you need, sweetie? Could we turn the kitchen table into a little office for you?" Mom asks. "Or maybe staying with Warren at the bunkhouse could be fun. They have WiFi like he said, and you could basically have the place to yourself while they work all day. We could visit the Harvest Festival next weekend! Oh, and—"

I cut her off before she gets too carried away.

"Mom. Think about it. What would happen if I missed a call or email from a potential residency program that I'm looking into? What if the applications I still have to submit end up failing to impress because I didn't take enough time fine-tuning them to their specific needs or standards? I can't afford to take time off right now."

"Well… but…" She struggles to come up with a good argument.

I feel like I've ruined the whole night of celebration with my reluctance to leave my comfort zone of constant work. Guilt settles in even deeper than before.

"Whatever it is that makes you happy, that's what we want for you Blythe," Dad reminds me. It looks like he and Mom are holding hands under the table and his arm flexes when he squeezes tighter. "If the idea of staying in Westridge for a while isn't that, we still support you. You know how much we love you and how proud of you we are. But we miss you."

"He's being too nice. What he really means is that you put too much pressure on yourself." Warren says with a scowl. "Stop overthinking and spend some time at home with your family. It's not that hard."

"Excuse me?" I scoff at his audacity. He has no idea what it's like to be in my shoes. The plans I have. The goals I've made. I refuse to let that all go just for a vacation.

"You heard me. You're not even thirty for another few years and you're already close to being burnt out. Don't deny it. I can tell by the bags under your eyes and the way you slouch when you think no one's looking."

Silence falls around us and Mom and Dad avoid eye contact with me. They're not arguing with him. They believe what he's saying is true.

I'm normally a chatterbox, but words escape me. I have a rebuttal swirling around in my head, but suddenly, it doesn't feel like a strong argument. The last thing I want is to make the conversation worse by refusing to see their side of things.

"I appreciate your concerns. The fact is that I've chosen this lifestyle and all that it entails. It's just... I want... I *need* to keep going. I can't stop now. Not when I'm so close to making sure we're all taken care of."

The sentiment slips out before I can stop it. I've never admitted to my family that the reason I ever went to medical school or chose to work myself so hard is so that I can help Mom and Dad retire. Help Warren achieve whatever wild dreams he's stashed away in that head of his. Give us all a better life.

Dad furrows his brows in confusion. Then his expression fades to shame as he realizes what I mean. I was afraid of this.

I only wanted to provide for us all, not make them feel ashamed that they couldn't do it themselves. Hell, it's been hard enough for them to see me take longer than normal to get through college having to pay for it on my own. They never would have been able to afford even one semester at the colleges I've attended.

I got the loans and supported myself completely through it all, while *still* sending money back home. That meant pushing back my graduation a few years in order to keep my weekend and nighttime jobs.

There's nothing wrong with not having a lot of money to your name. I don't resent the fact that my parents have worked minimum-wage jobs and lived in a trailer all their lives. Or that Warren never left our hometown and toils away working on a ranch day in and day out. I could be wrong, but I'm not sure that's what he envisioned for his life.

But I always wanted more for myself. For them. Us. More freedom and flexibility to worry about all the *little* things in life instead of how they're going to pay for insurance or rent all the time.

We're silent for a few minutes, all of us unsure what else there is to say.

Luckily the server breaks the tension when our food is delivered. The calm won't last. They're driving back to Texas first thing in the morning and I would never let them leave without making sure they understand where I'm coming from. After a few bites, I raise my glass.

"Let's soak in the night together and enjoy this gorgeous meal," I smile tentatively. "I love you three more than life itself and I'll give it some thought. Coming home for the holidays, I mean."

It's not a lie. I will certainly think about staying with them for a while. But I won't be able to actually go through with it.

They seem to accept the fact that I'll consider it and we clink our glasses together.

Chapter 3

Gage

"Look who decided to show up to work for once," I tease.

"Oh, fuck off. I was gone for one day and my best friend was graduating medical school," Warren shouts as he jumps off his horse and rubs the mare's neck.

"I thought it was your sister that was graduating?"

"Same thing," Warren beams.

"Right," I grumble.

The infamous Blythe Farrow. I've heard so much about her over the years that I feel like I know her. Warren never shuts up about his big-city smarty-pants sister. He's always bragging about her multiple degrees and how successful she is.

"That cuts deep man. I thought I was your best friend," Tripp covers his chest with a hand like he's in pain.

Heston huffs a laugh through his nose and shakes his head without looking up from the campfire he's putting out.

The four of us are pretty tight. We work seven days a week

on this ranch and all live in the bunkhouse. They're like brothers to me, and we've been raising hell together for years now.

Things didn't feel quite right without Warren around, despite him only being gone a day and a half.

"Man, seriously?! There's no coffee left," Warren turns the coffee pot upside down and one little drip falls to the ground.

"Snooze ya lose motherfucker," Tripp laughs.

"Pack up your shit and let's get a move on. These cows need moved before nightfall and we have a lot of ground to cover," I say.

Most mornings we have breakfast at the bunkhouse. But calving season is coming up in just a few weeks. Winter is setting in. Before it gets too cold and we're up to our eyeballs in baby calves, we like to camp out under the stars a few times.

Saddles for pillows, a fire pit to cook steaks on, and a few bottles of whiskey are our idea of a fun night out this time of year. Don't get me wrong, we go to the bar in town from time to time. We even have parties at the ranch. But nothing beats this.

"I'm getting too old for this. It's hard for me to sleep without a memory foam mattress and a plump juicy ass to cuddle up to," Tripp whines.

I tighten the cinch, put my foot in the stirrup, and swing my leg over the saddle. The leather reins feel rough in my hands, and the cool morning breeze whips by me as I pull the brim of my hat down a little lower.

"Quit your bitching," I yell over my shoulder as I ride toward the sunrise.

Heston lets out a sharp whistle to his blue heeler, Lucky. It only takes a few seconds for him to shoot out in front of us at a full-speed sprint. He's one of the best cow dogs I've ever been around. And he loves to run.

"Hes and Warren, y'all check this fence line all the way to the Bluff Pasture for any stragglers or posts that need fixed," I say. "Tripp, you're with me."

"Yessir," Warren sits up straight in his saddle and salutes. Smart ass.

Heston gives one quick nod and another whistle to Lucky, and they take off in the direction of the Bluffs.

A few hours and a couple hundred cows gathered later, Tripp and I stop the horses at a windmill water tank so they can have a drink. My phone buzzes inside my coat and I pull it out. It takes a whole second and a half to decline the call and stuff it back in my pocket.

"You gonna tell me who keeps calling you about this time every day and why you never answer?"

I ignore him and cross my forearms, resting them on the horn of the saddle.

"One of these days you'll get bored of not tellin' anybody shit," Tripp says.

Not a chance.

"Whoever it is makes your face twist up like you ate too many beans with your cornbread. Come on. Entertain me. Who is it? No, let me guess!" He's excited now and practically bouncing. "An old girlfriend that cheated on your grumpy ass but wants you back."

I shake my head and can't help but smirk.

"No?" He snaps his fingers. "Oh! Maybe it's the girl from the bar last weekend that wouldn't leave you alone. Jocelyn? Jaclyn? She was hot as fuck."

"Do you ever shut up? It's not some girl."

15

"See that's your problem man! You need to get laid."

Can't argue with that, but I won't admit it.

"Let out whatever else is bothering you while you're at it. You know you can talk to me right?" His face turns more stoic.

Tripp is the jokester of the group, always there to lighten the mood or make someone laugh. I've never seen him be the one to take the conversation into more serious territory. When I don't say anything in reply, he sighs.

"Seems like there's always a lot on your mind and you never talk about it."

I squint, scanning the field ahead of us. I'm not looking for anything, just deep in thought. I decide not to deflect for once.

"It's not easy for me."

"Yeah. Not trying to get all emotional on you or anything. Just saying you can trust me. I got your back you know? Best friends and all that."

There's a million things I wish I could tell Tripp. Hell, I wish I could tell all my friends. There's a lot I could get off my chest right now.

He holds his arms outstretched on either side of him, "Look at me. I tell you everything and I feel as light and free as a bird!" He caws like a hawk and flaps his arms.

I chuckle and shake my head again. I knew the seriousness wouldn't last for long. He couldn't keep that up for more than a few sentences without acting like an idiot.

What I *should* say is that his friendship means a lot to me and that I trust him with my life. And thank him for being someone that I can talk to and confide in if I wanted to. I *should* say that I've been dealing with some shit no one knows

16

about. Thank him for the support. Let him give me a little advice and stop secluding myself. Stop going through it all alone in my head.

But I don't.

"Whatever's stopping you, man, let it go."

I hear him loud and clear, but I pretend I don't by not taking my eyes off of the horizon. "Oh, and we're going out tomorrow night. You may not want to tell me what's bothering you, but you can't stop me from setting you up with a pretty girl that'll suck the sadness right out of ya." An evil grin spreads across his face.

Let it go. Ha. Easier said than done.

He may have a point, though. I've been so closed off for so long that it's second nature to deflect my feelings and emotions. I rarely, if ever, participate in any sort of serious conversation with my friends. And they're well aware of that fact.

There's too much of me that I want to keep hidden.

Once upon a time, I reinvented myself. I hate the fact that the only way I could do that was to keep secrets. But I've never once regretted it. Not yet.

The pain of not letting anyone close to me is a lighter load to bear than the weight of my past.

As long as I keep my head down and focus on what keeps me grounded and sane, I'm fine with a private personal life. It's... isolating at times. Nothing I can't handle though.

"I don't have time to fuck around at the bars."

"Oh come on. It's the *weekend*. As long as the work's done I know Boss won't mind," he argues.

I quirk an eyebrow. "Oh yeah? And how do you know that?"

He taps the side of his head and smirks "I know everything."

17

Cocky bastard.

I can't help but laugh. No one knows better than me whether or not *the Boss* would mind.

I shake my head and lean down to pat my horse's neck under her thick mane.

"No such things as weekends on a ranch, shithead."

Chapter 4

Blythe

I need a piping hot cup of tea, a ridiculously soft blanket, and to take off this god-forsaken bra.

I slam the door to my apartment shut, instantly dropping my bag and kicking my shoes off. Normally, I'm insanely organized and clean in my living space. But today I don't have the extra energy to neatly place my things where they belong.

Before I make it past the entryway, I can already smell the Chinese food and a candle burning. That can only mean one thing.

"Kee?!" I yell down the hall while I shrug off my coat.

"In here!"

There's one thing that has kept me afloat during medical school: my best friend Keanna. She knows no boundaries and I gave up on not letting her into my place at all hours of the day and night. I finally made her a key a few months into my first year here.

"You wouldn't believe what I got to do today," she mumbles,

19

mouth full of fried rice. She points at her takeout box "You want some?"

"I'm not hungry. Thanks though. What did you get to do?"

"The chief of surgery let me scrub in on a transplant. A transplant, B! With the chief! She's amazing. I wish this internship didn't have to end. If they don't accept me into the residency program I might cry."

Keanna is a year ahead of me and has been a surgical intern for the last nine months. I wish I had her energy and enthusiasm. She's always so full of light when she speaks about her job. No one on the planet was more meant to be a doctor than her.

"Wow that's amazing," I say.

"Well don't sound too excited," she laughs.

I rub at my temples with my thumb and forefinger. The light on the tea kettle flickers as I turn on the switch. I turn back around, wrap my arms around her shoulders, and squeeze.

"I'm sorry. I'm excited, I promise! I love that you got to do that today."

She pats my arm and lays her head back on my shoulder.

"I'm worried about you, you know?"

"Here we go." I groan and move to pick out a teacup from my extensive collection. A creeping heat starts in my chest and I rub it absentmindedly.

"Heartburn again?"

I scowl and take a deep breath wishing away the pain.

"Yes. It's this damn bra I think. It's way too tight," I scoff as I unhook the clasp behind my back and pull the straps through the sleeves of my shirt.

"You want to know what I think?"

I shoot her a questioning look.

20

"It's not the tight bra. And I'm beginning to think it's not heartburn either. I think it's your anxiety. Your body is telling you to slow down and be calm for longer than a second."

What? I know stress can sometimes trigger things like acid reflux, but I never considered that to be the case with me.

"Maybe," I admit.

There's a soft and concerned look on her face, but the room falls silent. So quiet I can hear the rapid beating of my pulse.

Isn't every medical student tired and stressed? This has to be normal. Common, even. The fact that I've been getting random bouts of heartburn, barely keeping my eyes open on the ride home from school, or tanking up on energy drinks to work on my computer late into the night is not that concerning. I'm just a hard worker. Dedicated to my studies and my future.

Kee toys with the straw in her cup and avoids eye contact. She's letting me think to myself for a beat. That's something I've always adored about her. We communicate well with each other in our friendship, and she always leaves me space to gather my thoughts.

It's then I realize how tight my jaw is. How bunched up my shoulders are. My back aches, there's tension between my eyes, and a loud voice in my brain won't shut up about how long it's been since I've checked my email.

The room starts to spin, and at first, I think there might be some sort of earthquake happening. Instead, I fall forward and my face lands straight on the island countertop.

* * *

The pungent smell of a hospital is unmistakable. Before I even

21

muster up the strength to open my eyes, I know exactly where I am.

"She's doing fine. Just resting right now," a voice whispers.

I crack an eye open to see Keanna facing the window on the other side of the room. There's a steady beep of the vital monitor next to me, but it doesn't tamp down the deep throbbing happening somewhere on my face.

When I reach up to feel where the pain is coming from, I rustle the covers and it causes Kee to whip around and face me.

"Oh! Well, actually, she's awake!" She rushes to my side and shows me the name on the phone screen before putting it back to her ear.

Warren. Great.

"Can we call you back? Yeah, I promise," she nods her head and hits the end button.

I look for a hint of panic in her expression when she pulls the chair up next to the hospital bed. Even when she grabs my hands and meets my gaze though, she doesn't look too worried. A little pissed off maybe.

"They had to put the IV in your hand you know? You were so dehydrated they had to find a vein elsewhere."

I look down at my hand where the sting of the needle is coming from. I was eating and drinking enough, wasn't I?

"I know that look. You're about to argue with me." Her hand squeezes mine a little tighter. "You're smart, B. So smart that it scares me sometimes. But one thing I think you've forgotten about in all of your constant focus on school is to take care of yourself."

I rub the side of my nose like I have an itch, but really I'm just trying to sniff away oncoming tears.

22

"It's not that I'm going to argue with you. I understand. It's just that…" For the first time in a while, words escape me. I don't know how to describe how I feel at the moment. I'm overwhelmed by the fact that I've landed myself in the hospital. If I wasn't so tired I could probably think straight. I lay my head back on the abysmally thin pillow and close my eyes. "You're right."

Most friends would tease you to repeat that phrase or write it down for them so I'd never forget admitting that she has a point. But Keanna doesn't. She just wraps her free hand around my shoulders and leans in for a hug.

I release a long-held breath into her hair and decide to stop fighting my emotions. The waterworks start flowing free and fast. Admittedly, it feels good to let it all out.

"Can I make a suggestion?"

I sniffle and nod my head.

"Let's get out of here. Classes are over, you've graduated, and programs around the country will still be knocking down your door in a few weeks to offer you a residency position." Her hug tightens as she tries to convince me that what I swore I didn't have time to do is actually what I *should* be doing. Going home.

"You're the best. And that's not going to change if you go home and take a little break. I don't have to work this weekend," she goes on, "so I'll go with you for a few days. It'll be fun!"

She's never steered me wrong, and I've backed myself into a corner this time with no choice but to follow her sound advice.

"These sheets are itchy," I whine and we both break out into a belly laugh. This conversation is too serious and emotional and I had to break the tension somehow. Then, I pull back to look her in the eye. "Alright," I whisper. "I'll go."

Chapter 5

Gage

"You can't miss it. You'll see the big hanging sign over the cattle guard on the side of the road. Turn your camera around. Let me see where you are," Warren says from where he sits on the arm of the couch in the bunkhouse living room. He brings his phone screen closer to his face, trying to see better.

It looks like he's on FaceTime and judging by the giggles and pop music coming from the other end of the call, he's got girls coming over. Fantastic.

"There! Turn there!" he stands up and shouts.

"I know where it's at dummy. I grew up down the road, remember?" a female voice says through the phone.

Grew up here? Who is he talking to? I keep listening in on his conversation but don't bother looking up from the computer. I have too much data to enter into this spreadsheet to be worrying about what girl Warren's got on the roster.

"Right. Did you stop by Mom and Dad's?"

"Yes. They sent a huge loaf of bread. It smells amazing and

I might have taken a few bites already," she laughs.

A smooth, sultry, incredible laugh. I smile to myself then shake my head back and forth to right my expression. Cracking my knuckles, I try to focus back on what's on my laptop and not whoever is on the phone.

Focus is hard to come by around here. The bunkhouse is more like a madhouse most of the time. Myself, Warren, Tripp, and Heston all live here. But other guys that work at the ranch part-time come over quite a bit as well, sometimes for breakfast or just to hang out. Not to mention the girls Warren and Tripp always have over.

I could tell them to stop having girls over. They'd respect it if I made it a rule. It's annoying when there are articles of girls' clothes strewn down the hallway or I have to pound on their door to get their asses to work instead of laying in bed with a naked chick all morning.

It's not too bad though. Especially with Tripp. He usually kicks them out before they fall asleep anyway. At the end of the day, the friend in me is happy to see they're having a good time.

I haven't felt a connection to anyone enough to bring them home in… well, almost ever. I've had plenty of hookups over the years. But with strict rules and never here at the ranch where I live.

I'm not jealous of my friends enough to cock block them though.

"We'll be there in a minute, I can see the lights at the barn up ahead! We're hanging up now, bye!" A different female voice sounds through the phone.

I hear the tone signaling the FaceTime ending and against my better judgment, decide to pry a little.

26

"Big plans?" I smirk knowing he's always got big plans.

"About that…" Warren runs a hand through his dark blonde almost brown hair, and gives me the look he always uses when he's about to ask for forgiveness instead of permission. My eyes narrow.

He looks back and forth between me and the front door. "My sister and her friend flew into town and they're planning to stay."

"Okay?" I question.

"Here."

"Here as in Westridge?"

"Here as in," he clears his throat. "The bunkhouse."

"Uh…"

"It's not a big deal. My sister is really great, and, well, my parents' place is a little rundown at the moment. I told her she could stay here. I didn't know her friend was coming until last night. I figured they could just crash in the loft right? Maybe even help out around here a little?"

"Right," I deadpan. He can't be serious. "Just how long are we talking here?"

"Her friend is just here for the weekend. But I'm going to try and get Blythe to stay longer. Maybe until after Christmas at least," he admits.

"You want your sister to live in the bunkhouse for a month?"

"Well. Yeah," he laughs. "Seems a little crazy now that I've said it out loud."

I hate the idea. But I'd bet cash money she'll be packing her bags once she's slept here for more than a few nights. I doubt she'll enjoy being woken up at 5 AM when we're all putting our boots on and heading out the door.

I don't have more time to think about it or talk to Warren

27

though, because gravel crunches outside to announce a car's arrival.

Tripp pokes his head out from around the corner. He's got a bottle of beer in his hand and his hat on backward. "Who's here?"

"Buckle bunnies," Heston grumbles as he makes his way down the hall toward the living room. Black felt cowboy hat and all.

"They're not buckle bunnies," Warren corrects him.

Tripp lets out a whistle as Heston walks by him. "I'll be damned! Hesty's coming out tonight boys!"

Heston's boots track loudly on the hardwood floor as he makes his way to the fridge for a beer. He pulls one out and holds the top against the edge of the counter, smashes it down with his fist to pop the top off, and takes a long swig.

"Hell yeah," Warren clinks his bottle against Heston's and then chugs what's left. "This is going to be great. Gage, you got the first round at the bar right?"

"Not going," I say, turning back to my computer.

As usual, Heston completely ignores the peanut gallery and plops down on a bar stool at the island.

The front door swings open and a girl with jet-black raven hair storms in. Her bright red lips tip up in a grin.

"We made it!" She skips over to Warren and gives him a big kiss on the cheek. They look nothing alike and I have to assume this isn't his sister. He smiles and hugs her back in a friendly way.

Then a new set of softer footsteps sound in the doorway and I turn to look.

Now this is definitely Blythe Farrow. I'd know that dark blonde hair and golden tan skin anywhere. The same as her brother's.

"Hey," the voice I recognize from the phone call earlier says. Her hand raises just barely above her waistline in a small wave.

She's quite a bit shorter than the first girl that walked in, and not quite as cheery. Warren walks over to her and lifts her into his arms.

"You're. Choking. Me," she grunts.

"You won't regret this sis," he says as he puts her back down on the ground. He holds her at arm's length like he's checking to see if she's injured or something. "I'm so glad you're alright and that you're here."

Was she hurt? She looks fine to me.

In more ways than one.

"You look like you're about to go out," she speculates.

She smiles and deep dimples appear in each of her cheeks. They're cute as hell.

"Like *we're* about to go out," he replies, rubbing his hands together with a devilish grin.

"I don't know if that's such a good idea," her friend suggests.

"Oh hush Keanna. I told you. There's nothing wrong with me. I thought you wanted me to have some fun?"

"It's been a long few days," the girl whose name is apparently Keanna says.

"I took a nap on the plane. And I'm sick of drinking the endless water you've been forcing down my throat," Blythe fights back.

"Ladies," Tripp croons as he walks in the room. He holds his arms out on either side of his body. "I have a good feeling we're—"

He doesn't get the chance to finish his sentence. I throw a pillow from the couch that lands square in his face.

"Shut up Tripp."

"I was just going to say," he throws the pillow back at me and rubs his jaw, "that I have a feeling we're all going to have some good clean fun tonight."

"Right," I say.

"This is my sister, Blythe, and her friend, Keanna." Warren tentatively announces. He looks in my direction and I just shake my head. I don't hate the idea of playing host as much as I did a few minutes ago. "Girls, these are the buddies I work with. Gage, Heston, and Tripp."

I stand and put my hands in my pockets because for some reason I'm too nervous to know what to do with them, and nod in their direction.

They both smile. I think. I haven't exactly taken my eyes off one of them long enough to notice what the other is doing.

"I gotta make a stop. You riding with me?" Heston says to Tripp, then starts toward the door.

"Yeah, wait up." Tripp tosses his beer bottle in the trash and runs after him. Before he makes it out the door he turns around, takes his hat off, and winks in the girls' direction. "Nice to meet you ladies."

The laugh that bursts out of Keanna's mouth is hysterical. "He really thinks he's hot shit huh?"

"You have no idea," Warren and I say at the same time.

"Well, we doing this?" Keanna looks to Blythe

"Might as well. You lectured me the whole way here about having some fun, remember? Don't chicken out now."

They both squeal and jump up and down.

"Warren can you get the rest of our bags? There's still a few in the rental car. I'm taking the world's fastest shower and then getting ready! B, pick an outfit for me!"

Warren nods, turning on his heel and heading out to their car for the bags. Keanna opens a few doors in the hallway before finding the guest bathroom. It only takes a second after she steps in and closes the door to hear the water starting up in the shower.

Blythe and I are alone now. I look down at my phone to check the time for no reason. Try to act casual or like I'm busy or something.

"I like your beard."

Her sexy voice directed at me makes me flinch, and my phone drops to the floor.

Fuck.

I bend over to quickly pick it up and wipe the nervousness from my face before I right myself again. One hand lifts my hat while the other runs through my hair.

"Thanks," my mouth hangs open like an idiot. I'm not even making full-on eye contact with her.

I've had normal conversations with pretty girls before I swear.

"You're welcome."

She leans a hip against the island counter and laughs, soft and amused.

My eyes slam shut at the sound.

"I wish you wouldn't do that," I blurt out loud. Accidentally. Where's my brain-to-mouth filter when I need it?

"Do what?" She asks and tilts her head like she has no clue about the effect she's having on me right now.

Laugh like that. It makes me want to cover the sound with my mouth.

"Nothing. Never mind," I shake my head. "I'm Gage." I'm not usually so formal, but I don't know what to do other than introduce myself and stick my hand out towards her.

Her palm slides into mine and I squeeze it.

I've heard people talk about an electric zap or a current that shocks you when you touch someone for the first time. Someone who interests you. Someone you seem to have a new and unexpected draw to.

They must have been lying though. It's not some sort of shock that I feel. It's more like a pull. Like if I move my hand away from hers, it would just find its way back. Like my hand *wants* to keep touching hers. Like I've discovered something.

But she takes her hand away from mine and brings it to her chest, fiddling with the string on her hoodie.

"Blythe." She says her name like I didn't already have it stuck in my head.

I nod, swallow hard, and look down at my hand that's throbbing from touching her.

The voice in my head asking how soon I can touch her again is a moron.

"Are you coming?" She asks innocently.

I snap my gaze up to hers and widen my eyes.

"To the *bar*," she clarifies with a knowing smirk.

Right. She's not wondering if I just nutted in my jeans from a fucking handshake.

"I wasn't planning on it," I say. Although I may reconsider going now. "It seemed like your friend was worried about you. Are you sure you're good to go out?"

I don't know where the sudden concern for her is coming from, but I'm curious as to why Warren mentioned he was glad that she was alright. And why her friend questioned whether or not she should be going to the bar.

"Oh. I'm good as gold," she waves her hand in front of her face. "Nothing to worry about."

I don't buy it. There's more to the story.

I've only known her for a few minutes, but I get the idea that she's not about to crack open like a book and spill all her secrets.

That makes two of us.

"You should definitely come," she says.

Gladly.

But *please*. For the love of god stop saying the word come. If she says it again I'm going to have to go take an ice bath. I don't remember ever being this flustered around a girl before. I'm just tired. That must be it.

"To the *bar*, Gage." Her smile is sneaky and knowing. Oh, she's good.

"Anyway," she goes on when I can't bring myself to say anything out of fear that she'll make another innuendo and I'll spontaneously combust. "You're the big boss around here huh?"

"Who told you that?" I demand.

She jerks back a little at my defensive reaction. *Fuck*.

"No one," she speaks softly now. "From what Warren's told me I just assumed you were the general manager."

Most people around here know better than to ask me specific questions. I'm used to them just talking to me about the weather or simple things like that.

"Sorry. No. I'm not the boss. I mean... kind of? It's complicated. I'm sorta in charge but I'm not—" I stutter and fight to find the right words.

Her expression changes to one more sympathetic. Like she's reading my struggle.

"You don't have to explain," she says.

I stare at her. She probably has no idea, but no one's ever

33

said that to me before in a situation like this. People that aren't around me on a regular basis are always pushing my buttons. Trying to get more information. Waiting for some long elaborate story or reason. Getting too personal.

It feels different to have someone I just met clearly state that I don't need to explain myself. She recognized so quickly that it was something I didn't want to have a conversation about.

A strange comfort washes over me. One simple little sentence and I'm more relaxed than I've been in a long time.

I tilt my head and squint, studying her.

"How about a drink instead?" she perks up and suggests.

Without answering, I walk to the fridge and open it up. It's an old vintage one complete with a shiny silver handle and olive green exterior. It was here when I first moved in and it keeps the beer cold so we just never got around to replacing it with something newer.

"We have bottled beer. Beer in cans. And… a couple tall boy beers," I chuckle. Not much variety around here I guess.

"I always hated tall boys," she scrunches her nose.

"Oh yeah?"

"The beer doesn't stay cold. By the time I get halfway through, it's already warm ya know?"

"Makes sense. Or maybe you're just drinking it too slow," I smirk.

"Fair enough," she says and there's that laugh and those dimples again.

Make it stop.

I turn back to face the open fridge, adjust myself below the belt, pull a few long necks out, and pop the tops. She takes one from me and our fingers brush.

Is it cold in here? Because I'm pretty sure she just shivered.

34

"These towels on the floor smell like they came from a hockey team locker room!" Keanna yells from the bathroom. "I need a clean one!"

I take a big step back when Warren bursts through the door with their bags.

"Guys? A little help here?!" Keanna shouts again.

Blythe wraps her slender long fingers around the cold bottle of beer and brings it to her lips. I need to look away before Warren catches me staring.

"There's some clean towels in the dryer. I'll grab them for her," I say.

I disappear into the hallway and distract myself by digging through the clean laundry for a towel.

Is there some sort of switch I can flip in my brain that will keep the heart eyes from showing up in my irises while she's here?

It doesn't matter how beautiful she is or how addicting it was to touch her for even a few moments. She's my best friend's sister. And I can't be into a girl I just met less than ten minutes ago, right?

Chapter 6

Blythe

Being able to fit all of my clothes into one suitcase seemed like a smart traveling decision. But now that I'm staring down at a pathetic assortment of stretched-out T-shirts, leggings, a few pairs of jeans, and several hoodies? I wish I'd thrown in some more options that weren't so comfort-coded.

I wasn't expecting to go out the first night we were here and I certainly never planned on needing a cute dress or two. Not that I'm trying to impress anyone.

I *definitely* don't care what type of outfit Gage would drool over.

When I used to visit home more often, I'd stay with Mom and Dad. Their small trailer house didn't leave much in the form of privacy or space, but I was used to it from growing up there. Still, I'm glad that Warren invited me to stay here at the bunkhouse.

Now that I'm going to the bar with everyone, it's a good thing that I don't have to stumble up the porch steps of my parent's trailer at two thirty in the morning.

Warren already mentioned that he wants me to stay for Christmas and through the end of the year. We'll see how long I last, but right now the decision to let loose tonight feels great. If I was back at my apartment in Baltimore, I'd already be four hours deep into working my life away.

Now that I think about it, maybe I'll pull my laptop out for a few minutes before I get ready.

"Oh no you don't," Kee warns from the doorway of the loft.

The whole upstairs of the bunkhouse is an open room with several beds. There are also a few couches, oversized chairs, and a huge TV. It's almost like a second upstairs living room. I remember Warren talking about it before they renovated the downstairs to have four separate bedrooms. The guys all lived up here at one point. I wonder which bed was Gage's?

My head whips in her direction. "What? I wasn't doing anything," I say as I try to casually slip the laptop back into my tote bag like I wasn't about to plug it in and hook up to the WiFi.

"You're a terrible liar."

"Fine. But I don't have anything to wear and it didn't look like Warren was in a huge hurry. I have plenty of time to—"

"B. Look at me." She grabs both of my shoulders and shifts my body to face her directly. "No working. And turn the notifications on your phone off too. This is going to be good for you if you stick to the plan. All play. No work. Deal?"

"Deal." I link my pinky with hers and lift our joined hands to face level. We kiss our thumbs and high-five our free hands above our heads. It's a silly secret handshake, but we've always used it when making promises to one another, no matter how big or small.

"Now," she whips her towel off and fluffs her glossy wet hair up. She's never been shy and it makes me laugh out loud. "As far as an outfit goes…"

"I did bring these," I hold up a pair of jeans that I haven't worn in years. I'm not even sure why I still have them. I'm not nearly the same size that I was when I started college eight years ago.

Pulling them on, buttoning, and zipping them up is a fight for my life. But when I lift my hands and turn in a circle, Kee gasps and squeals like a little girl.

"Holy shit. Those are hot as hell. They're practically airbrushed on!"

I look down and see that they're *definitely* tight. They don't leave much to the imagination. Hugging the curves of my hips, thighs, and ass.

"Put this on."

She hands me a cropped tank top and I take off my hoodie to slip it over my head.

"I might as well stay home. Not a single person is going to be talking or looking at me with you walking in like that."

I playfully slap her on the arm and roll my eyes.

"Won't I freeze to death? It's not that cold out, but it's not exactly tank top weather," I say.

"First of all, did you forget that bars are hot as hell on the inside? Second of all, it doesn't matter what time of the year it is. When you're going out, you wear whatever you want. You might shiver on your way to the taxi, but you'll look like a million bucks doing it," she laughs.

She whips out a sinfully short and flowy baby blue dress with sleeves that flutter and ruffle over her shoulders. When it's on, she spins around the room.

Before I raid her makeup bag and do my hair, I hook my phone up to the Bluetooth speaker that I brought for a time just like this. She smirks when she hears the first song. We dance and float around like there isn't a care in the world.

Having something fun to look forward to is a whole lot different than dreading a deadline. The natural blush flushing my cheeks is from excitement this time, not anxiety. My smile feels more easy and honest. Less forced.

I made the right decision coming here and I'm so grateful to Kee for tagging along. And to Warren for pushing for it. Not everything in my life is perfect. But I have a group of people who love and care about me, that much is obvious.

I've never taken that for granted. After all, the countless hours I spend dedicated to making a successful career have all been for my family. I love them more than my own happiness and health. I need to knock it out of the park as a doctor. I need to make enough money to retire my parents, get them out of the trailer park, and allow them to enjoy the rest of their lives in comfort and safety. Stop Warren from holding back. Give him enough money to allow him to go chase whatever wild dream he's been unable to go after. I have a sneaking suspicion that working here on this ranch isn't it.

For now though, in this moment, I'm forgetting all of that self-inflicted responsibility. I'm going to live and make decisions for myself and no one else for a change.

I smile to myself as I look in the mirror to put in my earrings. My smile has *everything* to do with being excited about a night out with my best friend and my brother. *Nothing* to do with the grumpy cowboy downstairs who all but sent me into cardiac arrest when he touched my hand. Nothing at all.

Chapter 7

Blythe

"Wipe the scowl off that ugly face of yours," Warren teases Gage. He wraps his arms around Gage's neck and rubs his knuckles on the top of his head. His face is anything but ugly, but I don't dare make the correction out loud.

I laugh at the way the two of them give each other shit. I haven't even been here a full day and I can already see how close they are. One of the rarest things in life is friendship. Real camaraderie. I can sense that they trust and respect each other. They wouldn't poke fun so much if they didn't.

"I agreed to go because…" Gage puts a hand in his pocket and looks like he's unsure where he was going with that sentence.

"Because you love me and living and working with me just isn't enough time together for you. We know," Warren suggests.

"Just shut up and get in the truck," Gage shakes his head and bites back.

"And how's this going to work exactly?" I ask.

The four of us - Warren, Keanna, Gage, and myself - stare at the single-cab truck sitting in the driveway next to the bunkhouse. It's gorgeous. Looks like it's had a new coat of paint, possibly new tires, and an immaculate detail recently. But there's just one long bench seat and apparently, we're all supposed to pile in there to drive to the bar.

"My truck's in the shop and that little rental car y'all showed up in is basically a two-seater. Gage's truck is our only option," Warren says.

Keanna flinches but surprisingly catches the ring of keys tossed in her direction.

"You're driving. The rest of us have all had drinks already," Gage directs to Kee.

She shrugs and walks straight to the driver's side door and hops in. Warren and Gage follow close behind, Warren jumping in the passenger side first. From where I'm standing, I can see him slide across the seat to the middle. He flicks the pine tree air freshener hanging from the rear-view mirror and yells out. "You coming or what, sis?"

Hesitantly, I walk up to the passenger door and look inside. I've never really been good at Tetris, and I for damn sure don't see any way I'm going to fit into the cab of this truck. There's not an inch of seat open.

An outstretched hand enters my line of vision. It's big and strong and belongs to the mountain of a man on the edge of the bench seat. I look up to meet his gaze and he gives me a smirk.

"I don't bite," he says.

"Somehow I highly doubt that."

"You don't even know me."

"Exactly! I'm not about to sit on your lap. I just met you

41

today!"

The truck starts up and a billow of exhaust fills the air. Music blares through the speakers and it convinces me to throw caution to the wind and take his hand. Fuck it.

I wish I could say I was prepared for how deliciously rough and warm his hand felt completely wrapped around mine. We touched earlier, but this was complete and total hand-holding.

What am I, a teenager?

What is it with this guy that is driving me crazy?

Either sex is dripping out of his pores or it's been way too long for me and I just need to get laid. Maybe it's both.

The cab of the truck is higher than I'm used to, so I hoist one foot up to settle on the running board. Gage's grip on my hand tightens and suddenly I'm flying up toward him like I'm as light as a feather.

My landing is graceful somehow. It took all of a few seconds for him to perfectly place my ass directly on his right thigh. It was unavoidable that he had to wrap an arm around my waist to keep me from falling backward into the door. I'm sure of it.

Now I just have to hold my breath and stay completely still for the entire 15 minutes it takes to get to the only bar in town.

I'm finding it hard to breathe, so I reach over to the door to roll the window down. Where's the fucking button?

"Old truck. It's not an automatic window," a deep voice whispers behind me.

I wish he would have just used his regular voice. He just *had* to lean in and whisper it in my ear.

If I could stop the hairs on my arm from standing straight up and the chills from running up my spine, I would. It's no use though because a literal shiver works its way through my entire body and he chuckles. *Chuckles.*

"Are you okay?" Warren asks me from his seat next to us.

"Yep!" I reply a little too high-pitched.

He nods and smiles at me, then turns the music up. He and Keanna seem to be having a great time in their own little bubble on their side of the truck, just jamming out and screaming the words to whatever headache-inducing song he's playing.

I look down at my wrist, feeling something wrapped around it. It's Gage's hand lifting it toward the moonlight shining in through the window.

We stare at it for a moment and then I turn my face toward his. His brow quirks in curiosity.

"Burn scar," I explain.

The white patch of skin is about the width of a ruler and runs half the length of my forearm. It's decades old and I'm so used to it that I hardly ever notice or think about it anymore. I'd rather not dive into details about it right now. Not with Warren sitting right next to us.

Luckily, he doesn't proceed with any questions. His thumb runs the length of it. The touch is so light and tentative that I can barely feel it. Like a light breeze.

The urge to pull away is strong. But I don't. It feels too good.

He breaks the connection for me and lets me lay my arm back down in my lap. All of a sudden he feels more rigid and tense beneath me.

If I was brave, I'd place my hand on his knee. Soothe both our nerves. Maybe lean back into him a little. Shoot him a mischievous look over my shoulder. Admit to him how handsome and alluring I think he is.

I'm not brave though. Not *that* brave anyway.

I have no business feeling up my brother's best friend anyway. That feels like a recipe for disaster.

Chapter 8

Gage

Warren's a great guy so it shouldn't surprise me so much to find out that his sister is just as cool.

I don't know much about her yet, and it feels weird to admit, but I want to. Over the years I've heard endless talk about her.

"My sister's the best."

"Blythe just got accepted into Johns Hopkins Medical School. She's so smart."

"Look at this playlist my sister sent me, she cracks me up."

"My sister sent me the new hat I wanted. How cool is that?"

I felt like I halfway knew her before she even showed up here. The one thing in all of Warren's ramblings that he so conveniently left out is how fucking cute she is. She's more than cute, she's... flat-out stunning.

Of course I noticed how thick and sweet-smelling her hair is. And the dimples and the light freckles and the button nose. But it was her voice that about knocked me off my feet. When she laughed I swear my heart stopped. There was a rasp to it. The type of sound that could hypnotize you. Calming but sultry.

And I was hanging on every damn word out of her mouth like a lovesick puppy dog.

I'm pathetic.

Horny and pathetic.

"You have no game," Tripp says next to me.

"Excuse me?"

"That girl in the purple shirt over there?" He points his beer bottle in the direction of the bar. Our high-top table is towards the back on the other side of the dance floor. I spot the one he's talking about and she winks and waves. Good grief. "She's been giving you fuck me eyes for a solid five minutes."

"I didn't notice," I say honestly.

"Apparently," he scoffs. "You wouldn't know what to do with a woman that wanted you if it was written in a handbook that you kept in your back pocket, you old grump."

"Yes I would. And how the fuck would you know?"

"Let's see it then," he smirks and holds his hands out, waiting for me to make some sort of display of performance. He knows I won't play his little game. I have no interest in that girl. I wouldn't go hit on her and get her number just to prove that I could. "Your dick's gonna fall off if you keep ignoring every girl panting in your direction."

"Wh-what?" The laugh that's been stuck in my head all night sounds behind us

"Gage is scared of girls." Tripp deadpans as he takes a long swig of his beer.

Blythe slides between us and takes a look at the water in front of me.

46

"Well?" She smiles. The neon lights dance off the highlights in her hair and the apples of her cheeks. "Are you?"

The answer is no, I'm not scared of women. I'm just a lot more discreet about my hook-ups. Tripp trots around like there's some sort of prize to win for taking a girl home for the night. Not my style.

But right now? Yes. Hell fucking yes. This woman next to me, almost leaning against the side of my arm, scares the shit out of me. I like her way too much already and I've barely even talked to her.

I shift my weight from one foot to the other a few times and cross my arms in front of me to lean on the table.

"Absolutely not," I say.

"Confident," she raises an eyebrow.

"Totally," I add several nods.

"Oh my... GOD! You're lying," she squeals.

"Am not," I huff.

"You are," Tripp chimes in.

At this point, I can only hope she doesn't see the beads of sweat forming on my forehead. I wipe at it with the back of my hand and realize that was probably the dumbest thing in the world to do. Now I look nervous.

She makes me nervous.

She grabs my glass of water and downs a few gulps of it. The tiniest drop of water escapes and falls from the corner of her mouth. What I would give to lick it off of her chin. Instead, I wipe it with my thumb and instantly regret that decision.

She freezes and I jerk my hand away entirely too fast. Now the jitters?

Fuck me.

At least it makes her smile.

"So practice," she suggests.

"Huh?" I ask.

"Practice! On me."

"No fucking way. And I don't need practice. Because I'm *not* scared of girls," I shake my head and chuckle.

"Oh come on you big baby!" She's beaming now and asking for trouble wanting me to *practice on her*. Whatever she thinks that means, trust me, my version is a whole lot filthier.

"Yeah." Tripp is enjoying this way too much and it makes me want to punch him in the nuts. "Practice on Blythe, Gage." He turns toward us completely to give this debacle his full attention. The slow grin that lifts one side of his mouth is nothing but devious.

"I don't do cheesy pickup lines," I tell them.

"Clearly," Blythe jokes.

"And you're tipsy."

"So?" Her eyes are big with anticipation like she can't wait to see what a fool I make of myself trying to hit on her. *Fake* hit on her, I mean.

I rub the short scruff along my jaw and look around the bar. It's usually pretty low-key, but with harvest over and slow farming season starting for folks around here, it's packed.

"Well, offering to buy you a drink right away is off the table since you've already had plenty."

"Okay," she urges me to go on by raising her brows and stepping closer.

"And I'd probably notice that you're here with a group of friends. But I would rather talk to you without them eavesdropping." My voice lowers and I lean toward her. "But I wouldn't want to make you uncomfortable by pulling you away from your friends just to talk to a stranger alone. So I'd ask you to dance instead. Only when a slow song comes on. So I can concentrate on your eyes. Ask you a few questions and commit your answers to memory. Study your reactions. Wrack my brain with ways to make you smile again because it's the most captivating smile I've ever seen. And it'd be the perfect excuse to get to hold you."

Her lips part but otherwise, she's still as a statue listening to me. I lean in even closer, brushing my lips right against her ear.

"It'd be hard to stare at your perfect lips the whole time and not kiss them, but I'd hold back."

Her breath hitches and she sucks in a breath and holds it.

"When the song ends, I'd wait to see what you do. Maybe you'd run away from me to get back to your friends. Maybe you'd stay in my arms for a second hoping I'd ask for another dance or your number. What would you do, hmm?"

I pull back. Barely. Just enough to see her reaction and wait for her answer. Her focus moves back and forth between my mouth and my eyes. A throat clears behind her.

"Uh, guys?"

Blythe jerks back and nervously laughs.

"Not bad," she admits and pats me on the arm. Her hand freezes right on my bicep and her eyes dart to where she's touching me. She dances her fingers along the tattoo peeking out from under the sleeve of my shirt. "What would I do?"

I nod waiting for her answer.

"I'd probably unbuckle your belt," she says.

Oh shit.

Her hand trails down until it's gripping the top of my belt buckle. Painfully slow, she unfastens it and pulls my belt about halfway off. I look up to see Tripp with his jaw on the floor.

Did I die and go to heaven, or is this really happening right now?

I need to start thinking of anything that will make my dick go down, like the time I got completely covered in afterbirth helping a cow while she was calving. We're in public for fuck sake and she's literally taking off my belt. At least it's dark in here.

She reaches both arms around my waist to the back of my hips, loops the belt back through all the way, and buckles it again in the front.

Huh?

She stands on her tiptoes to get her face close to mine.

"You missed a belt loop in the back," she whispers and slaps her hand twice right on my ass.

As if nothing happened, she grabs her drink and walks off.

If I could turn around to watch her leave I would. But I'm frozen on the spot.

I look down at my belt where her hands just were. Then back up again, looking around to find out how many people just saw that. If there was ever a time I'd been this turned on and stunned at the same time, I can't remember it.

"Dude," Tripp finally says. "What the hell was that?"

Believe me, I wish I knew.

Chapter 9

Blythe

Flirting with Gage is harmless right?

I mean, he was totally messing with me about the whole asking me to dance thing. That was just a silly little game. But it felt like he was being honest for some reason. Like the things he was saying he would do… were real and he *wanted* to do them. To *me*. And he had already been thinking about it.

He may have been playing the game, but he was flirting too. I *think*. So I flirted right back.

I loved seeing the look on his face when I went for his belt. Laughing to myself, I swing open the door to the bathroom door. I had to break the tension somehow. When we were walking to the truck earlier this evening, I was totally staring at his ass. It's just so nice. But I noticed that he missed a belt loop and I was just wishing for the chance to give him shit about it.

Turns out, the perfect opportunity arose. Right in the middle of the bar no less. I wish I would have pulled out my phone and took a picture of how shocked he was. If I'm not mistaken, the crotch of his jeans was suspiciously tight, too. Did he like it?

The idea of Gage being into me seems too good to be true. Here I am, taking some personal time to have fun and relax. It's the ideal situation for a hot fling. What are the chances that on night one I meet an insanely tall and manly and funny and sweet albeit grumpy man with dreamy facial hair and tattoos? And one that seems to be attracted to me as much as I am to him?

I must be even more exhausted than I thought. Delusional. Overthinking things again.

I'm sure in reality, he's just being nice out of obligation seeing as how I'm his friend's sister. Harmless. Indifferent toward me.

Speaking of exhaustion, I'm starting to get tired. I get that way when I drink a few beers. Makes me want to go to sleep every time. If I took a shot and danced around with Kee for a little bit, I'd be ready to rage all night. But I don't know if I want to push it just yet.

I look down at my phone and see that it's already midnight. I wouldn't turn down the idea of heading back to the bunkhouse and crashing for the night.

After washing my hands and walking back out, I find Kee and the rest of the group we came with all huddled around the side exit door.

"What's going on?" I ask.

"There's a party down at the river," Warren grins.

I try to hide the hesitation on my face. I think I do a pretty good job of it until I feel a large hand at the small of my back.

"I'm done for the night. Y'all got a safe ride home later?"

Gage asks the other guys.

They all nod and look excited to go. I remember hearing about river parties growing up. I was never partying or sneaking out to drink though. I was too focused on my grades and getting into a good college.

I should be feeling nostalgic about the "good old times" and jumping at the chance to make more memories there. Maybe it's the alcohol, but sadness is the only thing I feel. I didn't realize it until now, but I missed out on a lot of fun experiences when I was young.

Hell, I'm *still* young. And yet here I am missing out on even more. Living inside the same strict bubble I created for myself so long ago.

Maybe I should consider going. It's late. And I'm tired. Barely recovered from the chaotic week that I've had between graduation and the hospital visit. But if I just pushed through it I could…

I wobble a little bit and lean on the body closest to me. It's hard and somehow soft and warm at the same time. I'd love to close my eyes and lay on top of it for a twelve-hour nap.

"If you're not up for the party, you can ride back to the bunkhouse with me," Gage says. "I have to be up early and planned on leaving anyway. It's no problem."

Somewhere in his voice, I detect a hint of concern and I have to admit it's tempting to let someone else worry about me for a change.

"I'll go, too. Make sure you get a glass of water and take your makeup off before you pass out on the bed," Kee teases. She's always willing to be there for me and I appreciate her more than she knows. I hate that I've been reluctant to accept her help in the past.

53

Right now, I could take her up on her offer, but I can read her like a book. And before Gage mentioned the idea of me riding back with him, she was all too giddy about finding out what the river party was all about.

She shouldn't have to call it an early night just because of me.

"I promise I'll hydrate and wash my face." I grab her hand and give her a reassuring smile. "Go have fun and tell me all about it in the morning. Not early though. I haven't even gotten to lay down yet and I already have the urge to sleep in."

She laughs and nods. "Alright, if you insist! Love you." She kisses my cheek and gives me a swift but tight hug.

Warren nods in Gage's direction and they do that three-second clasp hands, hug, and slap each other on the back thing that guys always do.

The short trip to the truck in the parking lot is silent. When Gage walks ahead of me and opens the passenger door, I step into the cab and plop down on the seat. As I lean my head back, I hear the seat belt being pulled. Is he... buckling me in? My eyes widen in shock but I still don't say anything.

He checks me over, grabs a water bottle out of the glove box, unscrews the top, and holds it out to me. On instinct, I take it from him. When he's satisfied that I've accepted the bottle of water, he backs up and gently closes the door. I take a long drink and put it down in the cup holder.

I know the ranch is only about 10 miles outside of town, but it feels like so much longer right now. The gravel road underneath the tires is creating white noise inside of the truck and I'm fighting for my life to keep my eyes open.

"You good?" his gruff voice asks.

"Yeah. I'm good," I sigh. "Are you? I mean you're not going

to get arrested if we get pulled over for some reason right?"

"Nah. I've just had water since we left the bunkhouse."

I shift in my seat to get more comfortable. I'll just close my eyes and rest for a second.

"Oh. Why?"

"Just wanted to make sure you made it home safe."

Chapter 10

Blythe

I should check my last grocery store receipt. Whatever detergent I grabbed off the shelf is incredible. I make a mental note to buy the same exact one for the rest of my life. My sheets have never smelled this good. Like green earth and clean air and man...

Man?

My eyes snap open and I feel around. There's a mountain of pillows and a thick down comforter on top of gray jersey sheets. *Jersey* sheets. They're incredibly soft and comfortable but definitely not the silky cream Egyptian Cotton ones I splurged on for my birthday this year.

And why are my clothes still on?

I groan as I sit up slowly. Rubbing my forehead and squinting my eyes, I take in the room that is very clearly not mine.

My brain finally decides to catch up, and I remember that I am in fact not in Baltimore right now, but at the ranch where my brother works.

The only problem is that I distinctly remember Kee and I bringing our bags up a flight of steep stairs to a loft full of bunk beds. This... is not the loft.

I fall back down on the pillow and close my eyes again, hoping I just need another minute to wake up. When that doesn't work, I turn my head to the side and spot a yellow legal pad with a steaming to-go cup of coffee on top of it. I pick it up and inhale deeply. Still hot. Mmm.

On the pad, scribbled in barely legible handwriting, is a note.

Drink this. Painkillers are in the drawer in the bathroom. Your phone's plugged in on the counter in the kitchen. You should really put a passcode on it.

-G

My head snaps to the other side of the bed. It doesn't look ruffled or slept in. There are no pictures around the room or any solid proof, but this is Gage's bedroom. I can feel it. I put the note back down and decide to snoop around.

There's a collection of hats hanging from a wood plank shelf on the far wall. Some are perfectly shaped and clean, and others are older and worn in with evidence of sweat and dust around the band. Underneath, there's a neat stack of records next to a black turntable. I flip through them, almost every one being classic country or rock. I laugh when I see one where Tanya Tucker's got a mic chord in between her legs on the cover.

Everything in here feels rustic in a charming way. Simple. Unique. I run my fingers along the wooden table that holds the record player and vinyls, taking slow steps as I go. If there were a bottle of cologne on his dresser I'd shamelessly inhale it until my lungs burst. But there isn't one. I guess he naturally smells as intoxicating as he does. I let out a strong breath and shake my head.

So, I slept with Gage last night, put all of my clothes back on, and somehow completely have no memory of it? Highly unlikely. Something tells me a night spent with him in his bed and I'd never be the same. Not something I'd have a hard time remembering.

After several panicked sips of coffee, I peek my head out the door and into the hallway. The coast is clear. I'm not above tiptoeing into the open and up the stairs to avoid someone here finding out I slept in Gage's room last night. Not a conversation I'd like to explain to my brother.

Finally safe and in the kitchen, I wander around looking for something to eat. I refuse to take painkillers on an empty stomach. Is that my phone?

I recognize the purple silicone case right away. It's tucked into the corner next to the coffee maker and plugged into a charger. The screen lights up when I lift it from the counter.

There are several new email alerts (shocker). A few app notifications (uninterested). And one unread text message that catches my eye from a contact I didn't know I had. G (gasp).

G: You alive?

I stare at the text with a mixture of confusion and excitement. When my brain connects to my fingers, I type out a response.

Me: Barely.

Me: About last night…

G: ?

Me: I woke up in your bed?

G: I slept on the couch.

Me: Right.

Me: Still confused.

He doesn't text back right away, and I bolt up the stairs to the loft. I debate waking her up to freak out with her, but Kee is sleeping like a rock. There's mascara smudged on her cheek, her mouth is wide open, and she's full-on snoring. We hardly ever get the chance to sleep in, and I imagine she had a wild late night, so I leave her to her peaceful slumber. Without thinking, I find my way back to the new comfiest spot in the bunkhouse. Gage's room.

I didn't realize the room smelled so strongly of leather and musk until I walked back in and retrieved the coffee on the nightstand. Now I understand the dramatics of old movie actresses who would put the back of their hand on their forehead and faint. I'd probably do it too if it wasn't for the coffee offsetting the aroma of the room just enough to keep me on my feet. Either I drank more than I thought last night and it's still in my system, or his scent is *that* good.

Deciding to ignore the fact that I shouldn't lay back down in Gage's bed, I jump back in. The stained concrete floor is freezing on my feet, and I need to burrow back under those heavenly-smelling blankets. After taking a few more sips of the coffee in bed, I shamelessly inhale the pillows and bring the comforter up to my chin.

I'd like to say that I didn't throw them off and reach for my phone at the speed of light when I heard it buzz with a new text. But that'd be a lie.

G: You fell asleep on the way home. I could tell you were pretty tired yesterday and I didn't want to wake you up by climbing the stairs to the loft, so I carried you to my room.

G: Did you sleep well?

Well, this is a far cry from my normal day-to-day life. I'm usually overwhelming myself with studies and work. Constantly worrying about the well-being of my family and career, never just about myself. Now Gage seems genuinely interested in whether or not I'd woken up or slept alright. Brought me to his bed last night. Left coffee for me. Plugged my phone in.

I pinch myself on the bicep. "Ouch," I hiss.

Nope. Not a dream.

I wonder if this is what life is supposed to feel like. Someone checking in on you and caring for you, and you doing the same for them. Waking up well-rested and not immediately jumping into work clothes or firing up the computer.

Once upon a time, I thought the workaholic lifestyle was the only option for me. I've been determined to provide for my family and establish a high-paying stable career in order to do that. Now I'm second-guessing that a little bit. Knowing my Mom and Dad are just down the road and that I can visit them today warms my heart more than I thought it would. Having friends around. A simple life with the things that truly matter.

How did a few gestures from Gage get this big realization out of me? I shake my head. This is all crazy talk.

I moan and fling my arms out on either side of me while collapsing back on the pillows and staring up at the ceiling. I'd like to forget the last 24 hours ever happened. Like this man wasn't concerned about me. And I wish I didn't like it.

Me: I did.

Probably would have slept even better if my legs were wrapped around you all night.

G: Good.

Chapter 11

Gage

I need to hurry through the rest of what I need to get done this morning so that I can make it back to the bunkhouse before Blythe gets the bright idea to wash the sheets she slept on in my bed last night.

I could have easily walked her up the stairs to the loft. She was out cold and it definitely wouldn't have woken her up. But the idea hit me that I could just carry her down the hall to my room and tuck her into my bed. The possessive side of me won over. I *wanted* her in my bed.

I wanted to climb in next to her too. I had to take a cold shower and force myself to settle for the couch. When I woke up early this morning and went in to check on her though, I thought I was having a heart attack.

My chest physically hurt at the sight of her. Dark blonde hair strewn every which way. Her whole body was covered but I could see the outline of her curves that I wanted too badly to feel. Her breaths were slow, even, relaxed. Like she was content and happy to be fast asleep right there in my bed.

I'd always been intrigued by this girl, even when all I knew of her were the stories her brother told me. When I met her in person yesterday, I could have sworn that some sort of cupid sent her to me.

I don't believe in love at first sight by any means. But I've never seen a woman so smart, kind, and gorgeous at the same time. Add the car ride to the bar on my lap, her taking off my belt in the middle of a crowd of people, and then her sleeping in my bed?

When it comes to Blythe Farrow, I'm good as gone.

She just doesn't know it yet.

As if perfectly on cue to ruin my day, I feel my phone vibrate and see that it's another unknown number. I get this call, never from a traceable source, at least once every day. Sometimes more often than that.

I used to answer every once in a while, but I never stayed on the line for too long. I don't want them to be able to track my location. They want to dig up the ugly parts of my past. But refuse to let them.

I've known from day one that moving to Texas was a risky move. Not as risky as staying in New York though. My so-called father made sure of that. Fucking crook. I couldn't get out of there fast enough once I realized the situation that he'd put our family in. The corner he backed me into. The lies he told me.

It changed the entire trajectory of my life when I finally realized that the life I was living wasn't the one that I wanted anymore. I had the power and the resources to get out, so I did.

I just wish it wasn't continuing to affect me even thousands of miles away and years later. The shadow of that previous life threatens to come into the light all too often. And I've been fighting like hell to keep it hidden.

I tighten my fists inside of my leather work gloves and close my eyes. It's ironic that I left because I wanted to be a better and more honest man than my father, yet here I am keeping secrets like my life depends on it. Maybe it does.

My unwillingness to get close to people has made that possible. Something about Blythe makes me want to throw that philosophy right out the window. I'd love nothing more than to be close to her. *Insanely* close.

* * *

By the time I make it back to the bunkhouse, it's a ghost town.

Normally I'd enjoy the quietness that this time of day usually brings, but I find myself wishing there was a certain laughing blonde skipping around putting a smile on everyone's face. Mainly mine.

Seeing as how it's Saturday night, I'm sure the other guys have some sort of plans again. They don't always stick around on the weekends like I do. At least half of the time, I make sure all of the animals are fed and the rest of the chores on the ranch are taken care of while they trot around town with friends or family doing whatever it is social people do.

Well, I'd hardly consider Heston to be social. Not sure where he goes exactly.

There's a back door to the bunkhouse that leads right into a mudroom. I don't want to trudge my dirty boots and jeans all over the living room, so I enter through here instead of the front door.

Once in the mudroom, I strip everything off but my briefs.

We keep an old washer and dryer back here so I throw my clothes in, toss in a detergent pod, and start the load.

I'd like to take a long hot shower before I open a beer and grab my computer to do some end-of-the-year ranch bookkeeping. But I stop short of my bathroom when I see steam rolling out from under the door.

I walk as quietly as I can to get close and press my ear up against it. Just barely, I can make out a sweet humming sound and the spray of the water. I furrow my brows. Looking around to investigate, I see Blythe's phone and a pillow with a pink satin case on my bed. An entirely too-large purple water bottle sits on my nightstand. A black hair scrunchie is on top of my dresser.

I smirk and huff out a breathy laugh. Shaking my head, I turn back to the door and slowly turn the knob so as not to make a sound.

One foot after the other, I carefully walk toward the shower and stop anytime I think I may have made too loud of a step. It smells like a meadow of wildflowers in here. The floral scent wafts out of the sides of the shower curtain and I inhale deeply.

The groan that escapes me is a mistake because Blythe gasps and a plastic bottle falls. Realizing she probably doesn't know who's in the room with her, I clear my throat.

"There's a guest bathroom you know."

An adorable squeak rings out and yet another plastic bottle crashes down. Just how many products did she bring in there with her?

"Umm…" A nervous giggle. "I thought maybe you wouldn't be back until after dark sometime."

"Mm-hmm." I cross my arms and lean my hips back on the

64

edge of the sink opposite the shower.

"I'll just... well... can you give me five more minutes? I have to rinse out my hair mask."

"I think not," I answer. It's a rush flustering her like this. I want to pull back the curtain just to see the flush in her cheeks. Maybe to see a few other things too.

When she grabs the edge of the curtain and pokes her head out I let out a deep laugh. A genuine, cleansing, all uninhibited *laugh*. The mean look she's trying to pull off is more cute than it is intimidating.

"Why?!" She protests. "I'm almost done. You can't wait a few minutes?"

It's obvious the moment she realizes I'm in nothing but my briefs because she rolls her lips in and her mouth forms a tight line. I don't think the sudden flush of red in her cheeks is from the hot shower either.

I right myself to stand. The shock on her face becomes even more animated as I close the bathroom door. I take the two strides of distance between us, calculated and steady.

"There's a drought in Texas, honey." My voice drops dangerously low. "Wouldn't want to waste water when we could just shower together instead."

My brain is short-circuiting. Misfiring. Shutting down, because what the hell am I doing? Trying to scare her off? This is by far the most unhinged spur-of-the-moment decision I've ever made. And I'm just stupid enough to not stop.

Her lips part and her gasp is barely audible. She could slap me or immediately shoot down the idea, but she doesn't.

I hook my index finger and thumb onto her chin.

"Don't be shy. Scoot over."

65

Chapter 12

Blythe

He's kidding.

Every bone in my body with a shred of dignity or common sense melts and swirls right down the drain with the flow of the water.

My eyes flick down in a flash. His hand is still latched onto my chin, but I've seen enough. He's almost completely naked and it's a glorious sight.

This man is *hot* and he knows it, or he wouldn't be teasing me about hijacking my shower. Well, I'm going to call his bluff.

Tentatively, I take a few steps out of his way, expecting him to retreat and not go through with it. My prediction skills must be rusty though. It only takes a few seconds for him to shove the black underwear off of his hips. His thighs are so thick, it's a wonder his tight briefs didn't just bust off themselves. Like we've done this sort of thing together before, he casually moves the shower curtain to the side and steps in right next to me.

Oh. He wasn't kidding.

Mayday. Mayday! Naked cowboy entering the shower.

The tiny detail I forgot to consider in this situation is that I too am naked and in the shower. I smash my lips together in a hard line and look around for a hiding spot. My hands whip up to cover my breasts, and I stand awkwardly in the corner while he moves toward the shower head.

It's a nice shower that I would guess was updated not that long ago. It's more luxurious than the guest one, and far cleaner than I expected. But it's fairly small. This space is not designed for two people, especially when one of them is built like he fought in the Roman army.

I hear a shampoo bottle open and shut. Out of the corner of my eye, I see his muscular arms raise above his shoulders to wash his hair. I haven't been able to take my focus away from my direct line of sight though—his bare chest. Don't look a gift horse in the mouth is taking on a whole new meaning.

The deep tan of his skin is a stark contrast against the white tile of the wall. I want so badly to reach out and touch a pec, just to see if it's as hard as it looks.

I'm too nervous to do it, yet unable to look away all at the same time. I just know that if I moved my gaze even an inch, it'd go straight down and I wouldn't be able to stop myself. Or my hands.

His muscles ripple with every movement, splashing water in every direction each time he lifts or lowers his massive arms. It's mesmerizing.

"Do you make a habit out of taking showers with girls you just met?" I ask although I can barely hear myself over my pulse pounding in my ears.

His shrug is subtle, and I can't believe he's being so nonchalant right now. He's not unaffected. Right?

At that moment, I decide to look down. Oh, he's affected alright, and *oh my God*.

The bigger the hands analogy suddenly makes a whole lot of sense to me, although I never believed it was true until now. My mouth drops open. Is that a stray droplet of water on my chin or drool?

"Do you make a habit out of foaming at the mouth every time you see a boner?" He quips back.

I redact everything I said last night while teasing him that he was scared of women at the bar. When Kee told me that I needed to have a little fun, I think this was exactly what she was talking about. Randomly shared showers with hot guys. If I can rein in the shock a little bit first.

I'm drawing my brows together trying to come up with a believable defense. I was ogling and he knows it.

"If you think any harder, your head's gonna explode," he says.

The sound of his deep voice echoing in the small space jolts me out of my trance. How is he acting so casual right now?

"Switch?" he asks.

I'm cold now, so I nod. He shoulders past me, and maybe I'm imagining things, but I could have sworn I saw him shiver when the surfaces of our skin slicked against each other.

I move to stand under the spray of the water, facing toward it. The heat feels amazing. You don't realize how cold it is in the shower until you're just standing there with no hot water falling on you. Before I turn around to rinse the conditioning mask out of my hair, I feel a hand swipe across the nape of my neck. Gently, he grips and turns me to face him.

"I don't want you to hide from me," he says while he drops

his chin to look down at me. His hands move to my arms and gently bring them down to my side.

"Close your eyes," he demands. On my best day, I'm still a stubborn woman. But for some reason, I stop overthinking and follow his bold order.

Involuntarily, my lids shut and he gently cradles the back of my head to tilt it back. When both of his palms move up to massage my scalp, I slip into a state of such bliss that a long sigh makes its way out of my parted lips. I don't even flinch when I feel the brushes of his erection and the rest of his body up against mine. It's erotic and unexpected. And I don't hate it at all.

His touch is so slow and firm, relieving the severe tension I've been harboring in my head for so long.

Every last brain cell that I have is working overtime to suppress the moan stuck in my throat. It feels so good... until one of his hands leaves my scalp and his index finger runs down from the center of my forehead, between my eyes, and to the tip of my nose.

"The little wrinkle between your brows disappears when you're like this."

"Like what?" I whisper.

"Calm. Relaxed."

His finger continues down, the tip of it leaving goosebumps on my skin in its wake. My entire chest inflates to capacity when he reaches the top of my collarbone. But he pauses and hooks a finger around my necklace, lifting it off my chest. He turns the charm on his finger.

"It was a gift from my parents. A prairie rose," I say.

He nods and continues down, tracing the curve of my breast and lifting his index finger and replacing it with his thumb

69

when he reaches my nipple.

We're both breathing heavy and looking down, watching intently as the pad of his thumb glides over it. Back and forth.

We're out of our minds and I don't care. Not one single bit.

I take one step closer, trapping his hand between us so that it can no longer move. I'm just deranged enough to skim over the deliciously deep V shape of muscle between his abdomen and hip bone with my hand. His tongue runs across his bottom lip, and his top row of teeth bite down on the same spot a second later.

I almost slip and fall when a loud banging echoes around the bathroom. My hand flies back to my side, and Gage's head whips toward the direction of the door.

"You're gonna use all the hot water again!" The muffled voice yells.

I let out a gasp, and Gage steps toward me again with a finger to his mouth.

"Warren," I squeak out.

He pushes my back up against the wall and brings his hand up to my mouth to cover it. I moan when his full body presses against my front, caging me in. My brother is shouting for Gage to get out of the shower and here I am moaning from the feel of his best friend's naked body. My eyes close and I let out a breath through my nose as I realize how ridiculous this is.

"Be out in a sec," Gage yells.

The door swings open. My eyes widen as far as they possibly can and our bodies go rigid against one another. I hear the toilet flush and instantly, the shower turns freezing cold. I wince and Gage turns his body to block me from the spray of the cold water.

"Serves you right, motherfucker!" Warren shouts and laughs on his way out.

His footsteps grow quieter the farther away he gets, and when there's no sound at all, Gage removes his hand from my mouth.

He blows out a breath and shoves back the wet hair on his forehead.

"We should—" I start.

But he cuts me off as he slides to get out. "I'll let you finish." He moves the curtain and steps onto the rug, yanking a towel from the nearby hook. The corner of my mouth jumps up in a mix of surprise and amusement at his words.

"Your shower, I mean. Finish your *shower*," he twists his face. Steam rises from his skin and I snicker at the sight of him stumbling around. Big strong Gage is *flustered*.

He flicks the lock on the door from the inside so that no one can barge in again, then steps into his bedroom and shuts it behind him.

I don't think I've ever experienced anything so exhilarating. I blow out a breath and blink slowly several times, working to slow down my body's release of adrenaline. Turning the knob in the shower to make it hotter, I move to stand under the falling water.

I always wished I could feel the type of desire that most girls only dream about. The kind where you forget about everything else in the world, it's impossible to fight your urge, and you melt from just a look or simple touch from him. But that's exactly what just happened.

Transfixed by the flutters still floating in my chest, my hand finds its way to the places on my body that he touched. Each spot is hot, left burning from his contact.

71

My eyelids flutter closed when instinctively, I reach farther down to the throbbing that won't quit. My clit was furiously pulsing, begging for his touch before we were so rudely interrupted. It still is. I don't know exactly where things would have ended up going, but I know where I wanted them to.

I tilt my head toward the ceiling and my lips part as my middle finger flutters down through the slickness. I brace my free hand against the wall, then picture Gage's hand, so rugged and rough, between my legs instead of my own. Maybe he'd be standing behind me, head buried in my neck, one hand on my breast, and the other teasing at my opening. He'd moan in my ear about how much he likes how wet I am just for him.

The image is fucking mind-blowing. I can almost feel him rubbing back and forth. Alternating between a whisper of a touch, and then more unrestrained pressure.

The crest of an orgasm starts to build and my heart rate skyrockets. It's not just the friction I needed so badly that finally sends me over the edge. It's the visual. I picture the veins in Gage's arms straining and popping as he'd work in and out of me. The scratch from his scruff against my cheek. The gusts of his breath in my ear.

"*Fuck. Gage,*" I moan out in a hushed breath. My entire body detonates from head to toe. My vision blurs, my lungs seize, and I curl my toes into the wet shower floor.

It takes a few minutes of controlled breathing to get a hold of myself, but I finally manage to bring myself back down to earth.

I turn off the shower, grab a towel on my way out of it, and slump against the vanity. I'm trying not to smile, still rolling through the high of that orgasm. I should probably wipe the grin off of my face before I walk out of this bathroom that's attached to Gage's room, he takes one look at me and realizes that I just got off to the image of him.

* * *

A finger snaps in front of my face.

"Earth to Blythe," Keanna singsongs.

My eyes blink rapidly and I turn my face up toward her. I'm sitting on the edge of one of the beds in the loft while Kee gets dressed. Apparently, I fell into a trance remembering the shower debacle while trying to fill her in on what happened. I just can't stop picturing it. The insanity and spontaneity of it all? The stuff daydreams are made of. Ones you never think would actually happen. A fantasy.

He's crazy for jumping in like that right?

Maybe I'm crazy too, then. Because I can't lie to myself and say it wasn't the hottest thing that's ever happened to me.

"Sorry," I smile. It's one of those smiles that appears all on its own. I couldn't wipe it off of my face to appear more indifferent if I tried.

"What happened next?!" Kee squeals as she balances on one leg to pull a sock on her foot.

"Nothing. He got out."

"What?!"

"Yep," I laugh recalling how jumpy he was trying to dry off and make himself leave. "Enough about that. What were *you* up to last night at the river party?" I lean back on my hands and wiggle my eyebrows.

"It was a blast," she giggles while she puts a few dainty rings

73

on her fingers. "I mean, I drank *way* too much. And possibly danced on a tailgate," she cringes. "No one carried me to their bed and then violated me in the shower the next morning, so maybe it was a little disappointing now that I think about it."

"He did not violate me!"

"*Okay*," she mocks and rolls her eyes.

"Whatever," I scoff. "How long did it take for Tripp to hit on you?"

She puts a hand on her hip and one finger on her chin. "Let's see… about fifteen minutes I think."

I fall backward on the bed and grab my midsection in a belly laugh. I figured he wouldn't be able to help himself. Kee is unbelievably pretty and Tripp seems like a shameless flirt.

"I banged the top of his beer bottle with the bottom of mine. It exploded in his face. I think he got the hint," she howls in laughter.

I wipe under my eyes and sit back up. I hate that I wasn't there as a buffer for her, but I know my best friend. She can certainly handle herself, and she has a thing for older men anyway. I'm pretty sure there's a shirt in her closet that says *Do DILFS, Not Drugs.*

"Come on. Up." She takes both of my hands and pulls me to my feet. "Go put something cute on."

Chapter 13

Gage

Hey, it's me. Your brain. What the fuck is wrong with you?

I don't know what's gotten into me. I can't *think* straight around her.

I shake the leftover water out of my hair as I towel off and find some clean jeans and a T-shirt. Too bad I can't shake off the hard-on under my towel too. I need to get out of this room before I go against my better judgment and jump back in the shower with Blythe. My dick immediately swells even more thinking about her naked.

I don't know whether to thank the universe for saving me from making a rash decision with her in the heat of the moment or cuss it out for leaving me with the world's worst case of blue balls.

The women I've been with in the past have all been beautiful in their own way. But seeing Blythe all wet and naked just inches from me about brought me to my knees. I'm not usually that affected. But I also don't usually come face-to-face with

75

the sexiest face and body I've ever laid eyes on. Those tits were so round and soft, I didn't know whether I wanted to squeeze them, suck them, or fuck them.

All of the above.

It was the way she seemed shocked that I'd get in there with her, but curious and excited at the same time that really got me though. The restraint it took not to haul her up against the wall and touch every part of her was almost impossible to hang on to.

I'm good at reading people. It's why I don't have to say much around them. Not a whole lot of questions are needed for me to figure them out. I knew the second the idea popped into my head to get in with her that she'd be down.

It seems childish, but I couldn't go another moment without finding out whether or not she was as attracted to me as I was to her. We're not in middle school, so I couldn't exactly pass her a note to see if she had a crush on me.

I never planned on trying anything when I got in there with her. I just wanted to catch her off guard and see her reaction. By the way her breaths quickened and she had a hard time taking her eyes off of me, I'd say it was mutual.

The way she smelled. How soft her skin was. Her nervous laugh and her bright blue eyes bigger than the damn Texas sky. I wanted to sink into her and stay there until the sun came up.

I pull up the clean pair of pants that I found, groan, and adjust myself. Someone get me an ice pack.

Warren might have mentioned when she was leaving, but I was so distracted by her that I can't remember. I don't even know if she'll be here for long. The thought makes me panic. Maybe if I ask in the group chat it'll seem less obvious, so I pull my phone off the side table.

Me: How long is your sister going to be living here again?

Warren: Til the end of the month hopefully. If I can keep her around that long.

Interesting. When she and her friend first got here, it seemed sudden. Like it was a last-minute decision to come and stay here. Her friend seemed oddly overprotective like something had happened recently too.

After putting my clothes on and heading to my computer in the living room, I hang my head and hold it with both hands. If I could just stop thinking about her for two fucking seconds I might be able to get some work done before this place is crawling with people. It never fails that we have a few get-togethers or parties on the weekends. Going to the bar last night was rare for me. But I always join in on the fun if we keep it at the bunkhouse.

Tripp: That reminds me, I spilled coffee on my comforter this morning. I might need to shack up in the loft until it's washed.

Warren: Not a chance motherfucker

Tripp: Kidding ;)

Tripp: We still busting bottles here tonight?

Warren: Idk I'm still hungover as hell.

Me: Pussy

Now I'm thinking about pussy. Just *great*.

Maybe we could hook up to get it out of my system and it wouldn't be a big deal? If I could keep Warren from finding out, that is. I have no doubt he'd have my ass on the floor if he knew I was fantasizing about his sister. Worse if I was fucking her. Not that I couldn't take him. He's strong, but I'm taller.

Then there's the issue of making sure she knows I don't

want a serious relationship. Or any sort of relationship for that matter. It's never bothered me before to know that I need to be upfront with girls about not dating before we hook up. But for some reason now, it twists my stomach.

No way would I be able to taste her just once. I just know it. Everything about her is addictive. And everything about this predicament screams complicated. I'm already thinking about when I could get her alone again, and we've barely even touched. The best thing to do would be to stay friends. Don't cross that line.

I just don't know if I'm capable of that when it comes to her. I've never wanted someone so badly like this before.

Warren: I'm not a pussy

Tripp: If the boot fits.

I chuckle and shake my head. I'm used to it now, but these guys used to drive me up the wall. It's crazy to think that now I consider them my best friends. We trust and respect each other and I know firsthand how rare that is.

Warren: Fine. I'll pick up the keg.

Tripp: Yeehaw bitches

Me: Just have your asses to the barn by six tomorrow morning.

Heston: Y'all are annoying as fuck

* * *

I walk out the side door in the kitchen to the grill and throw the steak burgers on. They sizzle and I push up the brim of my hat to lean over the charcoal to give it a stir. Somehow I always end up as the designated griller, but I don't mind.

It's peaceful out here. I like being able to look across the land and watch the sunset. It's not the only reason I moved down here, but the beauty of the wide open country on a night like this is my favorite thing in the world. I couldn't imagine living anywhere else.

It's not full-on winter around here yet. It stays pretty mild in the South, and we've been lucky to avoid any cold temperatures so far. Calving season is coming up in a week and I know I'll be thankful the first batch of calves won't be freezing their ears off.

I make my way to the battered old rocking chair on the patio. It's not the most comfortable thing in the world, but it's got character and I like that about it. It creaks as I lean back, in unison with the sound of the door behind me opening and closing.

"Beer?"

Blythe.

I clear my throat and look up at her standing next to me. "Thanks."

I grab it by the neck of the bottle to avoid her hand.

I was hoping that having people over tonight would help me avoid her but apparently, that's not the case. It's not that I don't want to be around her. It's that I want to be around her too much.

She looks over at the grill and bites her bottom lip. Fucking adorable.

"You look hungry," I instantly close my eyes and regret that sentence. Real smooth.

"Guilty," she laughs.

I down a few gulps of my beer and stand. "Sorry, all the other chairs are out back around the bonfire from last weekend.

"Oh, I'm fine. I'm used to standing," she waves me off like it's no big deal.

"Right. You're a doctor."

"Kind of. I just graduated."

"You always wanted to be a doctor?" I don't know why I think to ask such a personal question, but her answer surprises me.

She shrugs. Her hands are buried into the sleeves of her hoodie as she looks out to the sunset. "I like it. I'm good at it," she sighs. "I never really considered doing anything else with my life."

"You'd make a great news anchor."

She coughs and laughs at the same time. It makes me smile.

"Sorry, what?"

"Well, you're smart. The sound of your voice is like... honey. So smooth and warm. And you're beautiful. Millions of people would turn on the TV every morning just to listen to you and see you. I would." What the fuck am I saying? I'm not even trying to hide the fact that I'm into her. It's pointless. My brain has no filter around her.

She turns to face me with a smirk. "Real funny."

"I'm serious," I say as I take another swig of beer.

"That's so random and specific," she laughs again, harder this time. After a minute, she looks back at me. "You think I'm beautiful?"

Now I'm nervous that I'll say something cheesy and cliché like *"You're the most beautiful woman I've ever seen"* and she'll roll her eyes. No matter how true that statement is.

"I don't think. I know you are." I lean down closer to her. I can't help myself. "And I've seen all of you."

The blush that spreads across her cheeks matches the hot pink of her fingernail polish. I take her hand to inspect closer like I know shit about a girl's choice of nail polish color.

"Cute."

She smiles. "I painted them earlier. I usually don't have extra time to do my nails."

I nod my head. Looking back up at her, still holding her hand, I want so badly to lean in an inch closer. Instead, it's her that takes the step to close the distance between us.

"I can't figure you out," she says softly with her eyes narrowed.

"Don't waste your time trying to figure me out."

"Ha!" She jumps and points her finger at me. "That's it!"

"What?" I laugh.

"Your type."

"My type? And what type is that?" I ask her.

"Prickly Pear. Pretty to look at." She fiddles with the top button of my shirt. "But I bet you're tender and sweet on the inside." I quirk a brow and she pops open the button.

What is it with this girl and undoing articles of my clothing out in the open? And how do I get her to keep doing it?

"Lots of sharp needles on the outside to keep everyone from getting in," she goes on, her finger trailing down my chest. I can't keep my fucking heart rate down. "You feel like you need to hide and protect parts of yourself. Even with the people closest to you."

Nailed it.

"And what type are you?" I ask her, failing to mask my shaky voice. Her hands are on my bare skin and I can't speak right.

"Lucky for you. We're the same," she whispers as the second button of my shirt pops open between her fingers.

Chapter 14

Blythe

Where this bravery came from, I will never know. But touching and teasing him like this feels too good to stop.

When I couldn't get the image of him in the shower out of my head this afternoon, I knew I wanted to see him with his clothes off again. Preferably with more touching involved this time. Unfortunately, my brain doesn't care that this isn't the most ideal time or place to be unbuttoning his shirt. There's a party happening just behind us inside the bunkhouse.

But I have a career to get back to in a few weeks that will take over every waking moment of my time and every ounce of my energy. If this is my chance to have some fun, I'm going to take it.

"Say something to convince me that this is a bad idea," Gage says in a low voice. His eyes are trained on my hand where it touches his skin.

"This?" I answer as I trail my finger down the ridge between his abs.

He swallows hard and gives me a *"no shit"* look.

I shrug. "Maybe it is a bad idea. But we're on the same page, you and me."

"I don't know about that," he says.

Oh.

He takes my hand and lifts it to his mouth. It tickles and sends a shiver up my arm when he softly kisses that tender spot on the inside of my wrist. He groans and closes his eyes, tilting his face up toward the darkening night sky.

"I want to let these burgers burn to a crisp while I sneak you to my room and lock the door. Is that what page you're on?"

The butterflies in my stomach race around in a flutter.

"Buns and cheese!" Tripp howls from the door and we jump apart from each other. I brush my hair back and Gage turns to fix his shirt and adjust the problem behind the zipper of his jeans.

I move to look busy and give the burgers a flip. "Couple more minutes on these," I say like I've been watching them the whole time and not exploring Gage's irresistible chest.

"Master griller huh?" Tripp teases me and puts an arm around me casually.

Gage steps up next to us, and I peek at him out of the corner of my eye. He looks none too pleased. I snicker to myself because if he's trying not to appear jealous, he's doing a terrible job.

I'm a warm-blooded human, so of course I've noticed that Tripp is attractive. Between the full tattoo sleeve on his one arm, the ridiculously chiseled features that could cut glass, and his witty and infectious life of the party personality, I have no doubt most girls flock to him like vampires at a blood bank.

83

But from the moment I met the boys in the bunkhouse, I wasn't drawn to him like I was to Gage. It's harmless and fun, nothing serious of course. But the way I want him is impossible to ignore.

The burgers are done, and the guys carry them inside on a platter. I follow in behind them, pretending I didn't just go over a list in my head of ways to flirt with Gage again.

Music plays from the retro jukebox in the corner and several people I haven't had the chance to meet yet mingle around the pool table in the corner. From the looks of it, they're other guys who might work here. The jeans and boots are a dead giveaway.

I turn toward the dining table where the cheers are coming from. Warren holds the top of his hat down while he chugs a cup full of beer. He stands across the table from a guy whose name I don't know, then flips it upside down on the table. The four people in a line next to him jump and yell, slapping him on the back.

Another group in the kitchen clinks their shot glasses together, taps them on the counter once, and then tips them all back in unison. I smirk at the surrounding chaos and laughter.

A football game plays on mute on the TV and I spot a stack of red plastic cups on the coffee table right in front of it. Before moving to grab one, Kee slides up next to me and bumps my hip with hers.

"There you are!"

"Hey," I smile at her. "Having fun?"

"Totally. This is great isn't it?"

It is. There's warmth all around and it's not just from the fireplace. It's familiar to me. I can remember nights like this when I was growing up. It wasn't the same type of party, but it was a group of people who gathered together to chat and eat and watch or play games. We didn't have much in the way of money or material things, but there were always people around that we loved. People that worked together, played together, and would do anything for each other. It's a part of this community that I've always loved and missed.

It's a whole different lifestyle compared to the cutthroat world of medical school. In Baltimore, I'm constantly surrounded by competition. People who are simply courteous out of obligation, not caring and friendly out of love.

I like to pretend that it's a good thing I didn't have close friends like this in school and that I need to be pushed out of my comfort zone to reach my potential. And maybe it was that way for most students. But in reality, I took it too seriously. Like my life and my family's lives depended on it. I was sacrificing friendships and other life experiences just to get ahead.

I still believe that I need to do whatever it takes to take care of my family. And I will. I'm just beginning to see what I've been missing out on by taking the path I chose.

This is exactly what I was afraid of when I agreed to come stay here. Questioning myself. Regret. Longing for the type of life I haven't allowed myself to have.

I've been nearly killing myself through medical school as a means to an end. But looking around, these people are happy and thrilled regardless of whether their bank accounts might be bursting at the seams. That's not what's important to them. Their circle of people? That's what they value.

They're living in a place that makes them happy. Doing what fulfills them. Not what earns the highest paycheck possible. It's a way of life here. I can respect that. And honestly? I envy it.

"I'm glad you brought me here," I confess.

She wraps an arm around my waist and snuggles into my side.

"Me too. I want you to be happy, B. I knew coming home would help you figure that out."

"You did?"

"Yes," she smiles. "The way you avoid this place like the plague? You're just scared you'd like it too much, call it all off, and come back here for good."

I swallow hard and my spine goes rigid. I do miss it here, but I could never do that. I mean, I could. Technically.

But job options are just so limited around here. I can't let go of my goals in favor of frolicking around the wildflower meadows. Poverty is not an option. I want better. I *need* better.

"I'm having a great time and all, but I'm going to lose my job if I don't go back to work on Monday," she blows out a huff and takes a drink.

My shoulders slump and I sigh.

"Well," I raise my glass toward her in cheers. "Here's to tonight then."

She taps her drink to mine, and we smile while we tip them back and drain what's left of them.

A burst of laughter sounds from the couch and I turn to see a woman with copper-red hair covering her mouth and throwing her head back in a fit of giggles. Gage is facing her and chuckling as well. What are they talking about that is so damn funny? I scowl.

Warren walks our way with too many drinks in his hands. The smile on his face is infectious and I can't help but mirror it despite my frustration with Miss Redhead sitting right next to Gage.

"You good?" Warren asks when he reaches us.

"I'll take one of those," I answer and take a drink of the cold beer.

"Did you meet Amy and Keith yet?" He points to the girl I was just scowling at. "Keith works here part-time and they have their own place down the road. They're getting married."

I look where he's pointing and see the couple he's referring to. A kind-looking man sweeps and tendril of hair off of Miss Redhead's shoulder. Oh. False alarm.

I wasn't that jealous of her laughing so comfortably with Gage anyway.

"Oh, how lovely! Can we come?!" Kee squeals.

"I'm sure you can. I'll ask," he laughs. You know Kee is buzzing when she starts inviting herself to weddings. She *loves* weddings.

"By the way, I'm heading out pretty early in the morning to check cows," Warren says to me.

"No problem," I say. "I was planning on stopping by to see Mom and Dad tomorrow anyway."

"I think they're working."

"Oh. Well, I'll go early then."

Of course, they're working. They're hardly ever not working. That reminds me. Work.

I noticed a few new residency interview invitations in my email earlier today when I had a moment to check my inbox. I shouldn't wait too long to confirm and schedule those. Maybe I should stop daydreaming and shift my focus back to that.

"I'm going to head to the kitchen for a water actually," I announce.

"There's some right there in the cooler by the couch, sis." Warren nods to the oversized white ice chest next to the couch in the living room.

"Okay. I'll catch up with you guys later."

I wind my way through a few groups of people eating. drinking, and in deep conversation to make my way closer to the living room. Gage spots me and stands. He pulls his hat off and runs a hand through his hair. It's vaguely disturbing how hot the air in my lungs feels every time he does that.

"Hey."

"Hi," I say back sheepishly. I don't feel as confident as I did earlier when were out on the patio alone. I reach down to open the lid of the cooler and pull a water out. Is the heat on in here? I fan my face and twist off the cap of the water bottle.

"Come with me," Gage says in a whisper.

It's pathetic how I snap to attention and do exactly as he says. This man could tell me to get on my knees and crawl and I'd probably fucking do it. I silently chastise myself.

Get a grip girl.

He leads us out the back door but doesn't stop when we're outside. Curiously, I try to peek around his big frame to see where we're going. After a few short minutes of walking, I see a line of trees and a wooden fence. On the other side is a group of chairs and a campfire surrounded by big cinder blocks.

He effortlessly places a hand on the top of a fence post and swings his body over the top to the other side. Tentatively, I secure my foot on the lowest picket to climb over. I need to remember to pick up my old boots from my parents' house tomorrow. These chucks aren't going to last long out here if I'm climbing freaking fences every day.

As I bring my other foot up and begin to swing it over the top, two strong hands grab my hips on both sides. Gage lifts me high in the air and I gasp at how quickly I'm brought back down to my feet directly in front of him.

He brings his hands back to his sides and leaves a burning where they were just on my body. His throat clears and I'm beginning to realize that must be a nervous habit of his. We walk toward the chairs and when I sit down, he picks up a quilt and offers it to me.

I gladly take it and bring my legs up to my chest, wrapping it around my whole body. He takes the seat right next to mine and sighs.

"Thanks. I needed the fresh air," I admit. "It's a little overwhelming in there."

He chuckles. "Yeah. I don't notice anymore because I'm so used to it. But it's a lot of people."

"Is it always like that? A lot of people around, I mean?"

"Nah," he shakes his head. "Just on the weekends and during the slower parts of the year. There are a lot of guys that come in and out of the bunkhouse though. For breakfast or to hang out or whatever. I—" he clears his throat again. "*We* have several part-time guys that crash there on nights where we have an early morning the next day."

I nod and take another sip of water.

"It feels good to be around people that you're not working with or competing against for some type of accolade or position," I say.

"Is that part of why you don't want to be a doctor?"

"I never said I didn't want to be a doctor."

"You didn't have to."

I turn my head towards him to see he's already looking at

me. He holds my gaze like I'm made of glass and he can see right through.

"I want to be successful."

"Doesn't everyone?"

"Sure. But we all have different definitions of that. For me, it's being so good at my job that I feel secure in never losing it. And working toward a salary that could provide for my entire family. I wasn't born rich. Unlike some people, I have to dedicate every fiber of my being to achieving the success that I want."

He shifts uncomfortably for some reason and the tension in the air between us thickens.

"Sorry, I went off on a rant. I'm just saying that things like this," I wave my arm out to the wide expanse of the beautiful ranch in front of us, "mean something. The work you guys put in here every day to make things run? I respect that. It wasn't handed to you."

"That means a lot to you?"

"Yes. It does. I've met too many entitled people who walked around with a silver spoon in their mouth before they even learned to talk. It's partly why I wanted to go to medical school. It's challenging and rewarding."

Gage rubs his jaw. He looks deep in thought.

"What's wrong?"

"Nothing. I agree with you. You have ambition. I like that about you."

It makes me smile to know that he appreciates that part of me. A lot of guys might be intimidated by a woman who's as driven as I am. I study his profile while the flames light up the contours of his face. It makes me squirm in my seat seeing how handsome he is.

It hits me that we're in the middle of a pasture sitting around a campfire just talking in the comfortable peace of the countryside. It feels natural. The subtle breeze is clean and crisp. The crackle of the fire is like a soothing white noise to my normally overstimulated mind. I inhale the air around me and let it out slowly.

"I grew up here you know."

"I know. Warren talks about it all the time. He's missed you I think."

A pang of guilt hits me in the stomach. I'm well aware of how excited my family is to have me here and how much they've missed me while I've been gone. They're supportive of my decisions. I know deep down they wish I was here though. Family was everything to us growing up. It was all we really had.

"I missed him too. I've missed everything about this place actually."

"Yeah?"

"Definitely. You can take the girl out of the prairie but you can't take the prairie out of the girl," I laugh.

"Country girl at heart huh?" He beams and crosses his arms over his chest like he likes the idea of that.

I laugh harder and rest my head on the back of the chair that I'm snuggled up on.

"I'm not waking up at five in the morning to help you feed cows if that's what you mean," I tease.

"That's fine. We don't get up til 6 on Sundays," he says with a smirk. "So you've graduated. What now? You're probably moving soon for a job?"

I look up at the night sky dusted with bright stars.

"Yeah," I whisper. "I have a lot of work to do where that's

91

concerned. But after getting lectured by my doctor and Kee a few days ago about taking care of myself, I decided to come here. Forget about all of that stress for a while."

I swivel my head towards him again. His head is leaning back on his chair like mine, but he turns it to look at me too. Our smiles match. Soft and comfortable. Curious and perceptive.

We soak up the easy silence for a few minutes. I'm content to just sit here all night even if it meant I'd fall asleep and need to be carried to the house again. *Especially* if I fell asleep and need to be carried to the house again.

I can just barely hear the music and laughter coming from the bunkhouse. A yawn escapes me and I start to wonder what time it is. That's when I realize I don't even have my phone on me. That's a first. I haven't given a second thought to my emails or notifications all evening.

I don't know whether to be worried or elated about that fact. This place has reminded me of my love for simpler things. Genuine conversation and down-to-earth people.

The one thing I wanted to do over winter break was to stay focused on my career. But I'm beginning to think it wasn't so that I could get into the best residency program. It was because I knew that if I let my heart open back up to the idea of coming home someday, I'd never want to leave again.

Chapter 15

Gage

Heston leans back against a stack of hay looking down at his phone when I drag my ass out of bed and to the barn. Tripp and Warren show up on time, but Hes and I are always early and up before the sun.

"Food bank today?" He asks.

"Yeah, I got the truck loaded up. Probably head that way first thing. Think you can handle hauling hay with one rig for the day?"

He nods and takes off toward his truck. The drought this year has been one of the worst in decades. We usually have plenty of pasture to get us through the winter, but with so little grass this season, we've had to feed more hay. Having so many cows to feed usually takes more than one truck, but I have some errands to run.

I check the bed of my truck to make sure everything is secure. The door to the bunkhouse opens, and who comes striding out toward the barn but Blythe. She's got a hat and a big coat on that makes it hard to tell, but I'd know that walk anywhere.

"Morning!" she beams.

"Morning. You sleep good?" I ask her.

"Honestly? Not really. Those mattresses up in the loft feel ancient."

I cross my ankles and lean back against the tailgate.

"It's called roughin' it. Bunkhouse initiation rules," I say with a chuckle.

That earns me an eye roll. I'd like to say she can sleep in my bed instead, but I keep that idea to myself.

"What's all this? Need any help?"

"Uh. It's nothing," I say. I stand and flip the tailgate up, then turn to walk toward the driver's side door.

"Where you headed?"

"You ask a lot of questions," I reply.

"And you rarely give answers." She crosses her arms and quirks one eyebrow up to challenge me.

I sigh and turn back toward her, one hand still on the door handle. She pops one hip out to the side and stares me down. I look away, trying to convince myself to blow her off and tell her to mind her own business. But those are the last two things on earth that I want her to do.

There's something about being around her that is so addicting to me. I couldn't make myself push her away no matter how hard I tried. It's not even how pretty she is that makes me so crazy, although that alone knocks me out of my fucking boots. It's the way I have to constantly wipe the smile off of my face to avoid looking like a damn Cheshire cat when I'm near her. The things she says, the *way* she says them...

Inviting her along is a terrible idea. But I can't help but want to spend more time with her.

Fuck it.

"Hop in then, nosy."

She squeals and I expect her to run around the front of the truck and get in on the passenger side, but she slips underneath my arm just as I open the driver's side door.

I watch with amusement and shake my head when she crawls across the bench seat and clicks her seat belt in place, excited smile and all.

It's a short drive to Miss Lynn's kitchen, one I know by heart because I make it every Sunday morning. She set up a food bank a while back. I started packing up coolers of frozen meat, keeping some vegetables from the garden, and taking them to her every week. I leave money too and that always seems to put a tear in her eye.

It's not easy in this economy. Especially not around here. Westridge is a town with a lot of struggling families. After the oil industry took a downturn not long ago, a lot of people lost their jobs. The major oil company based out of this county went bankrupt and left them all out to dry.

Miss Lynn never asked for my help, but she did have a close relationship with the previous owner of the ranch. When I learned that her food bank was on the verge of shutting down, I stepped in to give as much as possible.

"Can we stop by my Mom and Dad's real quick? I need to grab a few things."

"Sure. But we don't have a whole lot of time," I answer her.

"I'll be fast I promise!"

A few minutes later, we pull into their humble driveway. I helped Warren out fixing their front porch one time. It's an old trailer, but they take good care of their place and it has a charm to it. There's a welcome sign in the middle of a wreath hanging from their front door, and it swings back and forth when Blythe pushes through and runs inside.

When she skips down the porch steps a minute later with *very* worn-in pink boots on and an overflowing duffle bag, I laugh.

"What?!" she says nearly out of breath.

"Those boots look like they've seen better days."

"Speak a word against these babies and I'll shave off your left eyebrow while you're sleeping." She lifts her foot, slaps the side of the boot a few times, and dust flies everywhere. We both crack up and I rest my hand on the back of the seat to look out the back window and back up out of the parking space.

My fingers graze her left shoulder, and I decide not to move my hand even when I'm finished backing up the truck.

"You'd have to sleep in my room to accomplish that. My door is way too loud. I'd hear you sneak in," I challenge her.

"I will then!"

I lift one brow in interest. "Promise?"

Judging by the slap she gives my bicep, I'm guessing that's a no. Damn. I'd let her shave both of my eyebrows off if it meant having her back in my bed. Just the thought of her skin lying on my sheets all night gets me hard.

I sneak a look over at her when she doesn't answer. She's got her nose scrunched up while she thinks. I can see the moment she knows what she wants to say because a little smirk makes her left dimple show.

She kicks off the dusty old boots and turns toward me. Both of her feet are tucked under her now and she leans toward me with her upper body.

"What is this?" she asks.

"What is what?"

She points to me, then to herself several times back and forth. "This. You know what I'm talking about."

I *do* know what she's talking about. But I want her to come to her own conclusion before I blurt out what I think *"this"* is.

"I'm not sure that I do," I lie.

"Oh, come on." She lifts both of her arms into the air and then drops them back to her lap dramatically. "You're really gonna make me say it?"

"Yep." I grip the steering wheel a little tighter as I take a turn down a side street.

"You got into the shower with me. You touched me. Hell, we almost…"

"And?"

"And you flirt. And ask me things. And you took care of me the first night I was here."

"I don't flirt. And you stare at me when you think I don't notice," I fire back. She crosses her arms and rolls her eyes. But I can see a hint of amusement there. She thinks for a minute, then blurts out exactly what I wanted her to say.

"We are mature adults. We can be honest, move past the games, and say that we want to fuck."

Wildfire heat blooms in my chest just hearing her confess that. I knew our chemistry was strong. There was no way she didn't feel it too. But the satisfaction of her saying it out loud about sent me off the road. I rub the back of my neck and try and focus on not wrecking the truck. Or pulling to the side of the road and taking her right here and now.

"You want me to fuck you?" I ask slowly, barely able to keep myself under control. Each word lower and more unhinged sounding than the one before it. I *need* to hear her say it again.

97

I need to hear it like I need air to breathe.

I watch the road ahead of me while driving, but still catch the single syllable word that comes out as a whisper from her sweet mouth. "Yes."

I inhale deep through my nose. Pull my hat down farther on my forehead. Rub the top of my thigh. Bend and straighten my left leg. Anything to keep me from reaching out and pulling her into my lap before I've even stopped the truck.

"Rules," I manage to say. It comes out more like a grunt than a discernible word though. "I don't date." I wait for her reaction hoping she doesn't protest my demands.

"Neither do I," she assures me. Her voice is higher pitched than normal now, a mix of nervous and elated. The fact that this is exciting to her and that she might want me as much as I want her is going to make it hard to get through the rest of the workday. And it was still early morning. *Christ.*

"And Warren would strangle me within an inch of my life if he found out," I add.

"He doesn't have to know," she smirks mischievously. I can feel the seat dip as she scoots closer to me. "And what about me? Don't I get to lay down some rules too?"

I chuckle at that. She has no idea how little control I plan to let her have once she's under me. But I'll let her believe she has some semblance of power anyway. "And what rules would those be?"

"We stay friends even after this is over. No awkward avoiding if we ever see each other ever again."

Blythe is sure of herself. Confident. It's one of the things that makes me so drawn to her. She knows what she wants. I try to picture this playing out the way she wants it to. Unfortunately, I have no intention of being friends with her.

I could never pretend to just be her friend after this, and that internal realization scares the shit out of me.

Big bright burning red flag, dude.

Turn back now.

I don't respond to her. I just narrow my eyes and stay focused on the road as other cars pass by. We come up to a stop light, one of only three in town, and it turns red. My head turns to face her. Luckily, she jumps right into another rule without waiting for me to verbally agree to her first one.

"And no kissing," she demands.

I twist my expression, jerk back, and huff out a quick breath. "Yeah right."

"I'm serious. We can't kiss."

"And why the fuck not?" I hiss my disapproval. Now all I can do is stare at her perfect lips. So pink and full. *Dammit.*

Her chin tips up and she crosses her arms with determination. "I don't want it to feel like anything other than what it is."

"And that is?" I'll respect her wishes if she doesn't want me to kiss her. I'd never make her do anything she wasn't on board with. I can't lie and say I'm not dying to do it though.

"This is… no strings attached," she unfolds her arms and makes an ex in the air with her two pointer fingers. "You might forget that if we get too smoochy. Better to avoid it all together."

My shoulders shake with laughter. "Alright, *buddy*." I refuse to say friends. Buddy will work for now. "No kissing."

I'm a strong-willed man, aren't I? I can keep a few tiny little rules.

Chapter 16

Blythe

S queezing my thighs together to dull the ache between my legs is the only thing keeping me glued to my seat for the rest of the drive.

The needy impatient side of me is begging me to see what Gage would do if I pounced on those strong thighs of his, looped my arms around those hard round shoulders, and set the spark between us aflame right this second.

The more realistic and cautious part of me is glad I won't get the chance because the truck comes to a slow creep down a narrow driveway.

A weathered sign that looks like it used to be white, but is now brownish, with the words Westridge Food Bank on it comes into view. Right behind it is a brick building. Gage pulls around back and I realize this is our destination.

Instead of asking questions, I pull my boots back on and follow him out to the bed of the truck to start helping him unload it. There are various Styrofoam coolers to carry inside. And they're *heavy*. When Gage goes back outside for more, I lift the lid of one of them and look inside. There are stacks of frozen meat in a variety of different cuts. The label says S Ranch. Gage walks in a second later with a crate of overflowing vegetables. I leap forward to catch a few that spill over the sides.

"This is a lot of food," I say.

"It's not much, really. We usually bring more than this in the spring and summer. Not as many fresh produce options this time of year."

My eyes widen. "And you donate all of this? How often?"

He clears his throat and looks away. "The ranch donates it. Every week."

"Well, who do we have here?" A tall woman with short brown hair walks into the kitchen. There's a welcoming warmth to her voice and the cream-colored apron she's wearing has little baby blue polka dots all over it.

"This is Blythe Farrow. Warren's sister," his hand finds the small of my back, severing my last bit of resolve. As much as I'd like to sit here and chat, I'd rather leave and see what it feels like for his hands to make their way elsewhere on my body.

I fix my expression and respectfully reach out for a hand-shake, but she goes in for a hug instead.

She's still squeezing me tight and she says, "I'm Miss Lynn." When she pulls back and holds me at arm's length, I smile. "It's nice to meet you dear. Warren's sister? I just met your mother at book club last month. She bragged about you two until her throat hurt," she laughs.

That sounds like Mama, always letting everyone know what her two kids have been up to. Whether they asked or not. I can't even imagine how insufferable she'll be to strangers when she has grandchildren. Endless unsolicited baby pictures and videos.

"How is she by the way? You know with all of the…" Miss Lynn has a concerned look on her face and waves her finger in a circular motion around her mouth.

I'm confused. "With the what?"

"The sleep apnea? The surgery?" Miss Lynn clarifies.

A phone rings and Gage reaches into his back pocket. "I need to take this, sorry. Be right back." He leaves the kitchen before answering.

My head snaps back to Miss Lynn and I want to scream and quiz her for every detail. I haven't heard a single thing about my mother dealing with sleep apnea or some sort of surgery. My mind whirls and goes in every direction of the possible worst-case scenarios. She notices the worry on my face and instantly places a hand on my forearm.

"Oh dear. I am mortified that I just blurted that out. I assumed you knew."

That's a punch to the gut. Of course, I should have known. She's my mother.

"It's not your fault. I haven't been home in a while." A *long* while. "I just got into town a few days ago." It sounds like a perfect excuse as to why I'm not up to date on all of the happenings around here. But to me, it's an embarrassment. I pride myself on how much I care about my family. My whole life is based on being able to take care of them. Why would she hide this from me?

Miss Lynn seems like a sweet and affectionate woman. It's clear that she's someone my mother must trust. I let out an unsteady breath. "I—" I shake my head and start to explain myself, but she cuts me off.

"Have a seat," she suggests with a soft hand on my shoulder. I sit on the tall stool next to the counter, and Miss Lynn shuffles over to the fridge to grab a soda and offer it to me.

The cold fizzy drink helps. "Thank you."

"Of course dear. Now I know we just met. But I can practically see the steam of stress rising out the top of your head," she laughs. "Want to talk about it?"

Bravery is a tricky thing to conjure when you need it most. I dig deep down to find mine. But it won't budge. I can't seem to lift my eyes to meet Miss Lynn's. To word vomit all of my worries and stresses and problems. She knows it too, because her calm voice coaxes at least one sentence out of me.

"Blythe?"

"Everything's a mess," I whisper. Tears pool in my eyes and I hate it. I hate it with a fiery passion because when I start to let my emotions pour out, they're hard to stop. And I'm here with Gage, who I just agreed to have a no-strings-attached friends-with-benefits situation with. Talk about embarrassing.

Now, this lovely woman that I've barely just met gets to see the ugly head of my despair rear up and be on full display. Just my fucking luck. I'm not sure what I'm more emotional about - the mortification of this very moment, or the fact that apparently my mother needs surgery and hasn't bothered to tell me about it.

A ruthless burn starts in my chest. I rub at it to will it back down.

"Are you okay?" Gage's deep voice asks from across the room. He's not far away for long though, because in a moment's time, he's standing next to me with a hand on my shoulder.

"My mom…" I sniff and reach again for the soda Miss Lynn

handed me. After a drink and a shake of my head, I stand and smile.

"Thank you," I say. My bravery may not have shown up, but my brain still works. And I'm not about to apologize. Thanking someone for their kindness instead of apologizing for my weakness is my favorite way to take back my power in a moment like this.

"I'd love to come back another time and help however I can. Would you mind giving me a ride back to my parent's house again?" I look to Gage. He might see right through my calm facade, but he doesn't show it.

"Of course," he says. Then he takes me by the hand. *Holds* my hand so warm and firm. It's infuriatingly comforting. I should give in to the urge to lean into his side and wrap my other hand around his arm. Leaning on someone for support, literally, is taking things too far though. I'm not about to wobble my way out of here clinging to this man no matter how good he's making me feel right now.

I force a tight smile on my face and drop his hand when we take a step toward the door. He looks over at me for a split second, but I catch it. The disappointment. Then the realization. It was an instinctive move, taking my hand.

The ride back to my parent's house is completely silent. We both know that asking questions or confiding is dangerous territory.

I pull out my phone to text Kee and let her know that I won't be back until later. I know she was planning on a long bath, a face mask, and reading her book today before I helped her pack tonight. I don't know how long this is going to take, but she might have to start without me.

When I open the door and get one foot on the ground, Gage

finally speaks up.

"Hey." He keeps one hand on the wheel and the other on the gear stick. His hat's been pushed hastily back and a thick tendril of dark hair lays across his forehead. Instead of answering him, I just meet his gaze and raise my eyebrows in wait for whatever it is he wants to say.

"Just... text me." He tries to mask it, but there's no missing the concern in his tone. The clench in his jaw makes it seem like he's holding back. That makes two of us. Because in a perfect world, I'd have already let him hold me the whole way here. Told him my whole life story. Vented about how worried I am about taking care of my family. Invited him inside for moral support. Asked for his advice. Then let him kiss it all better when we got home.

But we aren't doing any of those things. So his jaw stays clenched and my spine remains rigid. Not the least bit relaxed or soothed like it could be if I let it.

Chapter 17

Blythe

Me: Can you pick me up?
      Warren: Pick you up? Where are you?
      Me: At Mom and Dad's. You might want to come inside when you get here.
  Warren: ??
  Warren: Is everything alright?
  Me: I guess so. Idk.
  Warren: I'm at the feed store. Be there in 5.

"The weather is lovely, isn't it?" Mom says as she sets down a plate of brownies on the coffee table.

Dad's in his favorite chair, the one perfectly situated in front of the TV for football season. I'm leaning back on the old floral couch that I've never managed to convince them to take to the dump. We had some chili and talked over Mom's little health-related secret.

Warren comes through the front door a few minutes later and kicks off his filthy boots so they don't track dirt in the house. He plops down next to me and grabs two big gooey brownies. "So what's going on?" He mumbles through a mouth full of chocolate.

Mom pulls at her dangling earring and looks to me.

"Mom has sleep apnea but hasn't visited a doctor to treat it for the past year. When it finally got to where she couldn't sleep at all, she made an appointment and they suggested surgery on her soft palate to fix it," I blurt out in a single breath.

Warren chokes for a second and brings his fist to his mouth until he can swallow his brownie. "Excuse me?"

"Told you they'd freak out," Dad mumbles. He's half asleep after working all day and then eating half his weight in Mom's cooking.

"It's not a big deal!" Mom defends herself. "I didn't want to worry you two. You both have better things to do than fuss over your old Mama."

"Are you getting the surgery?" I demand.

She looks off to the side and squints her eyes.

I hold my hand out toward her but look at Warren. "A little help here?"

"Mom what do we need to do to help?" he steps in and asks.

"We're saving up for it is all."

I see Dad rub his temples from the corner of my eye. I realize that this isn't a life-threatening sickness. Her doctor has suggested a solution, and it will help her get back the quality of life that only sleep can achieve. I should be happy that it isn't anything more serious. But I know that surgeries aren't cheap. I cringe inwardly at the thought of them having to pinch pennies or wait to do something that is going to help her so much.

I've seen my parents work their tails off all of my life. I'm incredibly proud of that. We've never gone without food or a roof over our heads, and they've always done whatever they could to provide the necessities. But they don't have high-paying jobs. They don't come from wealth and they've never acquired it either.

I look down at my arm where the burn scar is. A chilling reminder of the night I left a candle burning in my new room. In our new house. In a new neighborhood. It all went down in flames because of me. Insurance was no help at all.

Mom and Dad were left with a mountain of debt, a loss of all their belongings, and a dead dream. They gave everything to get that house. And I not only put my family in danger that night, but I cemented their fate. Back to the trailer we went.

Since that day, I made a promise to them and to myself that I would get them out of here. Buy a house, pay their bills, let them rest. Live the remainder of their lives in peace and absent of financial stress.

"I will pay for the surgery, and you will call your doctor tomorrow to schedule the soonest appointment. Maybe they can do it within the next few weeks? I'll be here and I'll take care of you."

"B—" Warren cuts in. I hold a hand up to him and he sighs. He knows better than to argue with me on things like this.

No protests from my parents. They learned a long time ago when I started sending little bits of money here and there that I *want* to help them. And I won't take no for an answer. I haven't been able to help them as much as I'd like to yet. Being a full-time student brings a whole new meaning to the words *dirt poor.*

I don't know how, but I'll figure it out. I always do.

I'm happy that my mom seems to be in good spirits and that there's a way to help her get better sleep. Hopefully soon. But right now, it's getting late and my nerves are shot.

I stand to give her a big hug. Being able to hug her is one of the things I miss most about living here. It's been way too long since I've gotten to do this whenever I feel like it instead of having to hop on a plane and pause my entire life just for a hug. My Dad reaches his hand out for me, I take it, and he pulls me in to give me a wink and a kiss on the cheek.

"Love you," he says.

"Love you more," I smile.

"Not possible!" He yells as Warren and I make our way to the door.

Mom leans against the door and touches both of our faces before sighing. "I don't know what I did to deserve you kids, but I want you to know how happy I am to have you both here." *Me too* I want to say back to her. But I don't want to give her false hope and risk her getting used to the idea.

Warren puts his arm around my shoulder. "You ready?"

I nod. "We'll stop by again tomorrow to check on you, Mom. Get some rest if you can."

When we pull into a spot next to the bunkhouse, Warren checks his phone and wrinkles his brow.

"I need to check on this water tank. The sensor says it's not running. Might be a while if it needs fixing. You good?"

"I'm fine. Do you need help?" I ask.

"Nah. Go up and go to bed. I'll see you tomorrow."

I give him a quick smile and shut the door behind me.

The bunkhouse is completely dark with the exception of the light above the stove. I drag my feet to the stairs leading up to the loft and go up to get ready for bed. If there's one thing I will never do, no matter how tired I am, it's go to sleep with makeup on. If my face isn't clean before I hit the sheets, I know I'll regret it the next day.

"Hey," Kee says in a soft voice. She sits up slowly in her bed and rubs her eyes.

"Hey," I answer back as I sit down next to her.

"Is everything okay?"

"Everything's fine. I think I'd like to just get ready for bed and talk about it tomorrow," I sigh.

Maybe it's a terrible personality trait to push down my emotions, but when things weigh heavy on my mind, I like to keep them to myself for a while. Sit with my feelings. Make a plan. Kee knows that about me, though. I'm sure she'll have a million questions for me when I'm ready to talk about it in the morning.

"Alright," she says as she yawns and lays her head back down on the pillow. "Are you sure?"

"Promise. Go back to sleep."

I move to rummage around in my bag for my favorite crew neck and my skincare bag. Then, I multitask using a makeup wipe to take off my mascara and shuck off my clothes at the same time. I'm about to change, wash my face, and moisturize when I stop in my tracks.

It's then I realize my face wash is in Gage's shower.

Chapter 18

Gage

Counting sheep doesn't fucking work.

I'm desperate to turn off my brain that won't shut up, so I snatch my phone from the side table and Google ways to fall asleep. The first result says to get comfortable.

No shit.

I roll my eyes.

I scroll down and see a breathing exercise where you inhale for four seconds, hold for four seconds, exhale for four seconds, and repeat.

It doesn't help in the slightest. I scroll down further, hoping to find some revolutionary way to fall asleep without using a tranquilizer when I hear the patter of footsteps down the hallway.

I sit up and look toward my door. In the crack between the door and floor, a shadow passes. A second later, it passes back the other way. There's no way it's one of the guys. They're all too loud. These steps are delicate and quiet. I move the covers and walk towards the door.

When the shadow underneath passes a third time, I decide to open and see for myself instead of waiting. Blythe whips around to face me when I creak the door open.

"Oh!" She puts her palm on her heart and takes a step back like I startled her.

"Need something?" I ask.

"Yes," she answers way too fast. "I wasn't sure if you were awake or not." She stares with wide eyes as she scans below my neckline.

Maybe I forgot to put a shirt on before I opened the door. Maybe I stayed shirtless on purpose, secretly hoping it'd be her on the other side.

"I am."

"Yes I can see that," she laughs.

She doesn't have the slightest clue what that sound does to me. Every time she laughs, another piece of my control shatters.

"Is your Mom alright?"

"She'll be fine."

"Good," I say. I nod my head and try and think of some small talk to keep her here.

"Can I come in?" she looks around and whispers.

Abso-fucking-lutely.

"Uh, sure." I step aside and let her through the door, closing it behind her. I wonder what she'd do if I locked it and then asked her what she wanted me to bring her for breakfast in my bed tomorrow morning.

"I think I left my face wash in your shower the other day when..."

"When we took a shower together?" I step closer to her.

112

She's got her back to the door now and flattens herself against it. Slowly, she lifts her head. Her gaze travels from my chest to my neck, to my lips, and finally to my eyes.

I raise my arm to place a hand against the door. Right next to her face. My other arm fists the baggy pink sweatshirt she's wearing. It's big enough on her that I can't tell if she has shorts on or nothing at all underneath.

"Did you come to my room just to get your face wash in the middle of the night?"

"Yes."

I shake my head and smirk. "Liar."

There are no lights on in my room, but moonlight spills in from the bay window. It's reflecting off of her hair and I can't help myself. I take a strand of it between my fingers and twirl it.

She sucks in a breath and when her chest inflates, it closes what little distance was between us. Feeling her right against me for even a second is more tantalizing than I could imagine.

"Gage?"

I move my gaze up to meet her eyes.

"Make me forget about the awful day I just had," she breathes out.

Holy shit. Mentally, I'm doing a fist pump in the air. On the outside, I try to keep my composure.

I study her. She's flushed, inhaling quicker with every passing second, and she's looking at me like I could take away whatever pain she's stuffed deep down inside.

I lift the bottom hem of her sweatshirt up to her chin and lick my lips when I see a lace pair of black panties. No bra in sight. She lifts both of her arms in the air, and I swear my heart fucking stops. I've seen her naked before, but not like

113

this. Knowing I'm about to do a hell of a lot more than just look.

In one swift motion, I have the sweatshirt over her head and tossed on the floor. She doesn't bring her arms down. Instead, she wraps both of them up and around my neck, pulling me in as close as I can get without smashing her.

"*Fuck*," I whisper.

I lean my head down and bury it between her jaw and collarbone. That first swipe of my tongue across her skin is slow. Intentional. This isn't just licking, it's tasting. My mouth closes around her pulse point and she lets out a moan that sends shock waves through my entire body.

She's got a death grip on the hair at the base of my neck, and the pain of it sends me into overdrive. I bend my knees, grip both hands under her ass, and lift. I don't have to tell her to wrap her legs around my waist, she just does. I turn and walk us to the bed, but stop short of it. I don't want to put her down just yet.

"Stop moving your hips like that," I growl against the shell of her ear.

"Why?" She's panting softly and wrapped so perfectly around me, I think I'll never put her down.

"Because it makes me want to bury my dick inside you. But I want to taste you first." I kiss down her neck. "*Really* taste you."

"*Yes.*" She closes her eyes and tilts her head to the side giving me better access.

Reluctantly, I break our close contact and bend down to lay her on the bed in front of me. As much as I love looking at how sexy she is in her cheeky black thong, I waste no time taking it off and hiding it under my pillow.

Blythe Farrow is a vision. Her long hair is strung out all around her head. She arches her back the tiniest bit like her body misses the connection of mine against it. How can someone be so graceful? So gorgeous?

And the thought comes to me before I can stop it... so mine.
Fuck.

I need more of her. Now.

Things can be awkward and uncoordinated the first time. Not with Blythe, though. When I yank her toward me by the tops of her thighs, she throws her head back and lifts her hips off the bed. She all but screams when without wasting another second, my mouth lands right on her clit and I take one long hard suck.

My hand shoots up to wrap around her throat.

"Shh," I whisper between sucks.

"Oh. Oh my God."

I squeeze tighter around her throat, hoping it'll remind her to keep quiet. My hand is going to move from her throat to her mouth soon if she can't control herself. I peek up to see her reaction. Her eyes are closed and her mouth is open but tipped up at the corners.

I thought nothing could ruin me forever, but I was wrong. Blythe smiling while my hand is around her throat? That'll do it.

She moans and hearing her bursts of pleasure is driving me wild. I want to know what she sounds like when she comes. I flatten my tongue against her clit, working it hard and slow back and forth. She rocks her hips and pulls at the sheets underneath her.

I'm devouring her and it's paradise. Breathing her in and tasting her like this, her flesh under my grip.

115

Her hand flies to the back of my head in protest when I lift it to look at her again. I want to kiss and touch every inch of this woman, but the way she's pushing me back down to latch back onto her pussy tells me I need to wait to do more exploring of her body.

She knows where she wants me, and I'm not about to deny her. I drag my teeth gently. Trace and pierce her opening with my tongue. Pull her clit into my mouth with no sense of restraint. It's a merciless suck and my hands dig into her throat and her thigh at the same time. Soon, her chest is rising and falling more rapidly. She's so wet, so uninhibited, so close.

"I need you to come on my mouth," I demand. "Can you do that for me?"

I keep eye contact with her while my hand releases her throat and moves below my mouth. I push my two middle fingers inside of her, hooking them upward. My mouth is still on her clit, flicking it with my tongue and sucking all at once.

"*Fuuuuck*," she moans. Before, she was writhing underneath me. Now she's still. Eyes slammed shut. Mouth hanging open with short bursts of breath going in and out.

I feel the exact moment she begins to clench and contract around my fingers. I move them faster, hooking again and again against the softest highest spot inside. Trapping every last quiver of her orgasm in my mouth all at once.

I'm so fucking hard just from the taste of her, my shorts are about to rip. Seeing her so blissed out and beautiful when she comes is an image I don't think I'll ever be able to erase from my brain. And I damn sure wouldn't want to even if I could.

Her rigid body suddenly relaxes and collapses into the mattress. It's not easy pulling my fingers out of her as her pussy pulses around them.

Sitting up on my elbows on either side of her stomach, I lick a trail from her hip bone to her right nipple. My hands move up her sides, rubbing and massaging. As I work my way up to be face to face with her, my dick becomes lined up right where it's begging to be let inside.

Patience, buddy. Patience.

"I—" She moves her forearm to rest over her eyes. "That was—"

"Spectacular," she says at the exact same time that I say, "Perfection."

She lets out a breathy soft laugh and the temptation to capture the sound by covering her mouth with mine is entirely too strong. My fight against it isn't going to last. There's no fucking way.

I need to get rid of that stupid ass no kissing rule of hers.

Chapter 19

Blythe

I t's hard work pretending like you didn't just have the best orgasm of your life.

I could win an Academy Award right now because every part of me wants to faint. Scream. Cry. Jump. Faint again. Instead, I run my hands up either side of Gage's strong back. My fingers ripple over the endless muscles and skin.

I'm still working to steel my emotions to be more stoic and calm, but I can't help but pull him down closer. Flexing my hips up to meet his. The groan he lets out is deep and guttural. It's not important to me to play it cool in front of him. It's just that I've never felt such a powerless floating sensation before. I don't know how to process it.

"I was not prepared," he says between grinding down on me and fisting the hair on the side of my scalp, "for how sweet you taste. I'm not going to be able to go longer than a day without having my mouth on you."

"A day?" I giggle. Fucking *giggle*.

"Every." Kiss on my jaw. "Damn." Kiss on my collarbone.

"Day." Kiss on my shoulder.

More orgasms? More distractions from my mess of a life at the moment? Sign me up.

"So this is officially a thing?" It feels more like a statement than a question as I say it out loud.

He stops his relentless kissing and licking of every inch of my skin and props himself up on his hands, hovering over me. The eye contact is unsettling. There's so much hidden darkness yet confident desire there.

"You tell me," he suggests. "Tell me exactly what you want."

We stare at each other for a good minute. No longer losing our minds in exploring each other's bodies, but still feeling the hum of our connection where our hips remain pressed together.

We've already gone over the rules. He isn't looking for anything other than physical, and I made it clear that this was just friends with benefits. I wasn't entirely expecting it to be this good though, for us to be so natural and incredible together. I can already feel myself craving more.

I reach down to hook my thumbs in the waistband of his shorts. When they're pulled below his ass, he takes over and kicks them the rest of the way off. There's nothing between us now and I want nothing more than to know what it feels like to have him inside me. I want to see if he can erase every worry from my mind again. And again.

"This is what I want," I whisper as I take his hard length into my hand and pull it toward my center. The sharp angle to his jaw, delicious muscles, and deep gruff voice wasn't enough? He had to have a big dick too? *God. This man.*

He closes his eyes and drops his head to my chest. My nipples harden even more than they already were, feeling his gusts of breath so close. After a few seconds, he lifts his head and his eyes roam over my body. My face. My hair. My lips. They linger a little too long on the lips and I squirm underneath him. Desperate for friction.

He runs his hand over his face and then quickly kisses the left dimple on my cheek. Dangerously close to my mouth.

I almost full-on whine when he bolts off the bed and jogs into his walk-in closet. He might have only been in there for all of ten seconds, but it felt like a lifetime waiting for him to come back to the bed. When he leaps back on the mattress, it bounces me up and down a few times and I laugh at his enthusiasm to get back on top of me. I realize that he left to put a condom on, and my heart starts to thump with anticipation.

Our eyes meet and he hovers over me not saying anything, just studying me. It's not a nervous pause. It's a silent last-chance invitation for me to say that this is going too far. I appreciate that he's giving me an opportunity to say that I've changed my mind, but I've never felt so sure of anything before in my life.

I almost beg him to fuck me right now or I'll lose my mind, but my body beats me to it. Instinctively, my hips rise and I reach around both of his hips, pulling him closer to where I need him.

He looks down, lines up, and drives straight into me with one swift thrust. It's the edge of pain and heaven. I bite down on his shoulder and scream out while he grips my hip bone, pulls out, and buries himself to the hilt once again.

So hard and slow. So deep. I clench with every thrust, memorizing the intensity. Most everyone wants to experience great sex. It's human nature. I thought I had pretty decent luck in that department until just now. This is entirely different than anything I've felt before. It could be the attraction and the chemistry between us. Or maybe he's just that skilled. Or all of the above. I don't know exactly. But whatever it is, it's amazing.

He picks up a punishing pace after he lifts both of my legs to hook above his shoulders. If I thought I couldn't feel any more full, this new angle proved me wrong.

"*Fuuuuck*," I throw my head back and moan.

I didn't think it was possible for me to feel the edge of another orgasm building in my core so soon, but stars dance in my eyes and my bones start to feel less solid and more like floating ribbons of silk.

"Is this real?" He moans out. I don't know how he's managing to even talk right now, because he hasn't stopped his relentless jolts into me. I rock back into the mattress with every force. Again. And again. Somehow harder and more perfectly placed every single time.

I can't keep my eyes open any longer, losing myself in the rhythmic madness.

"Feel," I pant and grab his hand to put it over my frantic heart. It's so out of control, I can see it beating through my skin. He presses down on my chest and slows for a moment to ground himself in feeling the blood pumping through me at such a rapid pace.

Slowly, his hand slides away from my heart and up to my throat. There's a possessive gleam in his eye and his teeth grind together as I stare into his eyes while he grips his fingers deeper into my flesh.

I'm practically levitating from the combination of my quick breaths and his hand around my throat, but it's a delicious sensation.

He leans down closer over me without pulling out. Our individual pulses turn into one and my walls feel so thin, every minuscule movement is magnified. I'm caged in, with no possibility of escape. And no desire to either. It's an easy thing, giving over control to him. And he's brilliant when he's in charge.

"One more rule," he growls.

My lips part and I hang onto his every word, waiting for the revelation that seemed to hit him after finally being inside of me for the first time.

"I don't share. *Ever.*"

His voice is so low, it's a barely discernible statement. But the words vibrate and rumble through his chest, and they register in my brain as a nonnegotiable command. His thumb runs the length of the vein on the side of my neck and I suck in as much of a breath as I can.

"Only *one* person feels every part of you like this. *Fucks* you until you can't scream anymore. Who?"

"You," I pant.

"Say my name." His face inches closer.

"*Gage,*" I breathe out at the same time that he releases his grip on my throat, moving his hand to press down on my clit instead. He pulls his hips back, then buries himself inside of me in one deep slam.

I'd fight in a world war as a nation of one for the mind-blowing explosion that follows. It's all-consuming. Terrifying. Crushing.

There's no perspective of time or place in the next minute of bliss. It hangs on, refusing to let me breathe or move an inch, wave after wave. He fucks me relentlessly as I float through my orgasm. It's impossibly numbing and yet amplifies every sensitive nerve in my body at the same time.

Only when his roar of release sounds in my ear do I attempt to move. My hands have no feeling in them, but they search for him anyway. I scratch and grip the length of his flexing arms while his face falls to the bed next to mine.

He brings a hand up, smoothing over my cheek, brow, and forehead until it curls into my hair. It's soft and calming.

He's more gentle with every passing second and together, we come down from what I can only describe as the single most astonishing experience of my life.

What.

The.

Fuck.

Was.

That.

And what he whispers in my ear next confirms it. I may never recover.

"Stay with me tonight?"

Chapter 20

Gage

A sound I hadn't heard in ages echoes around my room. The old alarm on my phone is just there for shits and giggles, honestly. But I still have it set every day for those rare times that I get too drunk on the weekends and still need to wake up and take care of some things around the ranch. I get up early every morning like clockwork though, usually.

I shift to push the covers off and stretch my arms out because for some reason they're half asleep. It's only when I open my eyes and look down that I see I'm locked up in a pretzel of bare tan legs and sunshine-colored hair. A satisfied huff of air breathes out of my nose and I smile.

I've never been so happy to not have a fireplace in my room in the winter. She's clinging to every inch of me like a spider monkey. The tip of her nose is cold when I turn to my side and she presses it right to my chest. No matter how numb my right arm is tucked underneath her, I wouldn't move it for anything right now.

The alarm sounds again waking her up a little bit this time, and I groan. It's impossible for her to get any closer to me, but she tries. Hooking her leg tighter around my hip and nuzzling her head a few times to burrow deeper into my chest.

I can't reach my phone from this position to snooze the alarm tone, so it continues to blare.

"Do you need to get up?" Her voice is groggy from what little sleep we got last night. I'd gladly have three hours of shut-eye per night if it meant repeating everything we did. We fucked three times like a couple of insatiable honeymooners that held out before the wedding.

Reluctantly, I free one of my arms from her silky soft skin and fumble around the side table for the phone to silence it. It only takes a second to wind myself back around her and wiggle back down in the sheets like it's our own personal cocoon.

"Five more minutes," I mumble into the crevice between her neck and shoulder.

Her face is pressed against the top of my shoulder and I can feel the corners of her mouth turn up against my skin. My hand is massaging up and down the small of her back when there's a loud bang at my door at my door.

We freeze. My eyes dart to the door and I push Blythe's head down under the covers as the doorknob turns and clicks. I bend one leg in a casual-looking position to cover her body hidden in the bed, and the door swings open.

"I got two cows up being treated for foot rot, a tub delivery, and two angry bastards bitching about not having coffee yet and you're laying your ass in bed?"

Warren.

Motherfucker.

"I'll be out in a minute." Hopefully, that sounded less panicked than it felt.

A hand slithers under the sheets and tickles up the arch of my foot. I jerk away, then raise my eyebrows and lean back on the headboard like nothing happened. It's a silent laugh, but I can feel her shaking with suppressed giggles.

"Are you sick or something?" Warren asks.

I yelp when that same hand sneaks a pinch under my left ass cheek.

"Get the fuck out of my room and make your own damn coffee for once," I demand.

The confused look on Warren's face soon turns to one of amusement and he crosses his arms. He swings one boot over the other, leans against the door frame, pushes his hat to the back of his head, and pulls out his phone to type something.

My phone dings with a new text tone and the grin on his face spreads from ear to ear. He walks out without another word. He makes sure to slam the damn door though.

Instead of a wandering hand, it's lips I feel this time and they kiss their way from my thigh to my stomach. Instinctively, I grab both sides of her head and haul her up to straddle me. She covers her mouth to quiet her laugh.

"Bad girl," I say in a low voice. My hands grip her hips and suddenly I don't give a rat's ass about anything but the breathtaking girl on top of me. My dick gets harder than it already was when I woke up to her naked and pressed against me. In my head, I'm calculating how late I could be without having any of the guys knocking on my door again.

Blythe sits up on her knees and stretches across me, putting her tits right in my face. Now I'm questioning whether or not I actually died yesterday and have been living in some sort of a dreamy afterlife ever since.

She lifts my cowboy hat off the bedpost. It's way too big for her, but she plops it on her head anyway and leans back on her heels.

"You're playing with fire sitting on top of me buck ass naked and wearing my hat," I warn her. My grip tightens on her hip bones and she smirks while grinding back and forth.

"That's it." I take my hat by the crown and place it upside down on the side table. I flip us so I'm on top, but she's on her stomach now.

Leaning down, I pin her arms behind her back and growl in her ear. "Behave. Or I'll lose my job for skipping work to fuck your sore pussy again until you can't walk straight." I kiss her on the cheek, release her hands, and smack her right on the ass.

She laughs and snuggles deeper into the covers like she's comfortable there and has no intention of moving. I don't know what prompted me to swipe my phone and take a picture of her looking so perfect like that. But I do. It's like I never want to forget seeing her here like this.

Red flag.

Red alert.

Get out now.

The voice in my head is a warning. This is a little too perfect. *Stop liking it so much before it's too late. Before she burrows her way under your skin and you're doomed for good.*

But maybe that wouldn't be such a bad thing.

* * *

Coffee drips slowly into the steaming pot on the counter

as I check the ungodly amount of missed text message notifications.

Warren: Gage has some chick in his bed.

Tripp: No fucking way.

Tripp: Picture or it didn't happen.

Warren: Swear! She's probably still in there I didn't see any cars out front when I left

Tripp: Holy shit haha this is a first. I bet it's Hattie

Heston: Hattie Jo Murdoch?

Tripp: Whoops.

Warren: Oh shit.

Warren: It's not Hattie. She wouldn't be caught dead in the bunkhouse

Tripp: True. Maybe it's that stripper that came over for your birthday party last year and put her number in Gage's phone

Warren: Haha hell yes

I roll my eyes and pour black coffee into a Styrofoam to-go cup.

Gage: It ain't a stripper and it's definitely not Hattie. There's no girl in my room.

Gage: I can handle the barns today, y'all are in the sprayers. And all the groundwork needs to be done this week.

Warren: Translation - there's 100% a chick in your bed and you don't want us to know who it is

Tripp: Boooo

Warren: Come on just tell us who it is. And why the fuck you let her stay in your room when I haven't witnessed you do that since the day I started working here.

Gage: Get to work.

128

Tripp: Sir yes sir boss man
Gage: Don't call me that.
Tripp: Defensive much?
Heston: How do you turn off group text notifications?

They can poke and prod all they want, no chance in hell am I admitting that I had a girl in my room last night. Let alone Warren's sister. Nosy motherfuckers.

I know they're just having fun giving me shit, but I think it's deeper than that. When Tripp and I had our conversation the other morning, I know he was trying to get me to open up a little bit. Share some things. It's been so long since we've all started working together and become friends that knowing things about each other seems like a natural progression. I just don't have it in me to stop keeping the secrets that I've locked away.

Not only could it be dangerous for them as my friends, but it's opening a door to a past that I want nothing to do with anymore. Haven't for a while now. I came to Westridge to be a different person. Not the person I was expected to be. The person I *wanted* to be. Living the life that I *chose for myself.*

I had a problem in the past with relationships. I formed connections easily. Daily even. It wasn't real though. Someone always wanted something from me. There was never a time that an ulterior motive wasn't involved. Being friends with me was in some way an advantage to them. As soon as I didn't have anything to offer that would benefit them, they would be gone.

I think my relationship with Blythe, albeit temporary and secret, is one of the most genuine ones I've ever had. In the past, girls never actually wanted *me*. They wanted what I could *do* for them. It was always about lifting their status, impressing someone else, or usually, money.

When I get to my truck, I turn the music up as loud as it can go and peel out of the driveway toward the barn. I need to keep myself busy today and stop overthinking everything. Stay the course. Don't start thinking about why it's shitty of me to be lying to my best friends. Stop wondering if this thing with Blythe could actually be real.

Real would mean telling the truth.

Real would mean never hiding anything from her.

But that's impossible, and it's for her own good. Maybe I'd have an easier time remembering that if I wasn't putting her up on this pedestal in my head.

She's *just* strikingly gorgeous. Lots of girls are.

She's *just* ridiculously sweet and sassy all at the same time. No big deal.

She's *just* the best fucking sex I've ever had. I'll get over it.

She's *just* a girl who swept into town for a short amount of time that I happen to be becoming obsessed with. It's not real. And it never could be.

Chapter 21

Blythe

Sneaking into the loft before Keanna wakes up is a walk in the park. Any time she stayed over at my apartment and didn't have work or school the next day, she slept in until almost noon.

I slip into a pair of shorts, duck into one of the bunk beds, and flop into the sheets. This bed is hard as a rock. Maybe Gage won't mind if I sleep with him again tonight. Maybe his mattress is perfectly firm and soft at the same time. Or maybe the multiple orgasms and big strong arms holding me all night were what made me sleep so good. But *damn* did I sleep good.

It wasn't for long. We didn't drift off until after three in the morning. The little shut-eye that I got was so pleasantly peaceful and serene I could cry just thinking about it.

The afterglow of last night is lingering, because I still feel unbelievably relaxed. I put both of my hands behind my head and smile to myself. I can't believe I actually followed Kee's advice and took some time off from stressing about my career.

I thought it would be hard to do. There's only been a handful of times in the last decade that my head wasn't either worrying about what I needed to be doing, buried in a book, or on high alert in general.

I'm not going to lie and say that it's not a foreign concept to me, but it's been easier than I anticipated.

This feels...good. Better than good. It feels right. A lifetime of seemingly endless shifts in a hospital has never felt right. Neither did being admitted to the hospital as a patient myself because I was focusing so relentlessly on my job prospects that I didn't prioritize drinking water, eating, or sleeping.

The bed next to mine creaks and I lift my head to look over in that direction.

"Hey, sleepy head."

"Morning," Kee mumbles with her eyes still closed. "How are you up right now? You got back so late last night."

"Oh. Yeah, couldn't sleep."

"Is your Mom alright? You barely explained when you texted me yesterday."

"I think so. It's a long story, but she has sleep apnea. Nothing serious, but she needs a routine uvulopalatopharyngoplasty."

"B," she laughs. "I need to hit the books again because I have no idea what that is. How the hell do you remember shit like that?"

I wink and tap my temple twice with my pointer finger.

"Okay, big brains. But you're not as smart as you think," she laughs even more.

"And why not?!" I throw a pillow straight at her face.

"Maybe because *that*," she points at my midsection, "is not your shirt."

My head jerks down to the shirt I'm wearing. *Fuck.*

132

"Must have got mixed up in the load of laundry that I did."

I was so worried about making it up here before she woke up and saw that I hadn't slept in my bed that I forgot I put on Gage's shirt this morning. I couldn't help myself. It felt so soft and smelled just like him. And I didn't have the energy to find the missing sweatshirt I wore the night before.

"I've never met a worse liar than you!"

I face plant into the pillow half-laughing and half-groaning.

"I'll forgive you if you tell me how big his dick was. How bad do you want to pull the collar of that shirt over your nose and inhale it?" Her giggles make me feel more at ease.

I never planned on hiding it from her. But I was worried about bringing it up. Gage made it seem like he didn't want anyone to know about us and I just wanted to respect that. I should have warned him that there was no way in hell Kee would go longer than ten seconds before sniffing it out.

"I'm not describing his dick to you. And I do *not* want to inhale his shirt," I lie.

"Oh shit. So it's big then," her eyes widen to the size of the moon and she hugs her pillow like she needs the support to process this conversation. "Blink twice if it's big!"

"Don't be silly," I roll my eyes. Then I blink twice.

She leaps off the bed in a fit of giggles and I throw even more pillows at her.

"And how many emails have you looked at already this morning?"

"None."

She claps her hands and squeals. "That's what I like to hear! This is amazing. I'm so Team Gage. He's good for you."

"Good for me? You hardly know him," I laugh. "How could you know he's good for me?"

"Oh, I don't know. So far, he's successfully kept you from working yourself into an early grave while you're here. He has a big dick. You're glowing. Take your pick."

"I am not glowing." I touch my hands to my cheeks. They do feel warm. "And that's the most cliché thing I've ever heard."

"It's not cliché if it's true!" She yells as she bounds down the stairs. "Come on, I'm starving!"

I was expecting to see nothing more than beers and steaks in the fridge. That expectation was dead on. "Anything in the pantry?" I ask from my spot in front of the open refrigerator door.

"Yes." She walks toward the island and drops a pile of stuffed Ziploc bags with scribbled labels on them. "Homemade jerky. A lot of it."

"Not the most appetizing breakfast," I scrunch my face up. "Get dressed. We're going to Sofia's."

The smell of green chili breakfast burritos and black coffee comes wafting out onto the patio before we even step foot in the café. I used to dream about the food here when I first moved away. I like bagels, pastries, and muffins as much as the next girl. But there's just something about Sofia's foil-wrapped burritos that makes my eyes close and head roll back.

It's busy in here, practically busting at the seams with customers. The vintage mismatched chairs and little nooks for reading or chatting are just the same as I remember them. It's a comfort being in spaces that remind you of a simpler time in your life.

"Please tell me the food is as good as it smells," Kee says.

"It's better." I smile and make our way closer to the counter. For a second, I consider ordering something for Gage just so I could deliver it to him. I shoot that thought down real quick. He's not my boyfriend, and I sure as hell don't need to be bringing him food just to ogle him. No matter how hot he is.

"49!" a server calls from behind the counter. A middle-aged man in a Carhartt coat shuffles through the crowd to retrieve his order.

Though everything here is familiar to me, it seems a lot more hectic than I remember. Sure, it's always been crawling with locals in the mornings. But it's chaotic and overflowing in here right now.

"Next!" Sofia yells from the register.

"Got any chorizo left?" I ask.

Her head snaps up from her notepad and she grins so big that it makes her eyes disappear. "I was hoping you'd be here, what a treat! Oh!" Tears pool in her eyes and she reaches across the counter for a hug.

"Sofia, this is my friend Keanna." I hold my hand out in Kee's direction to introduce them.

"I love your charming café! Can't wait to try the food," Kee says as Sofia brings her in for a hug.

"This is just wonderful. I'm so happy you could make it for the closing," Sofia says.

"Sorry." I shake my head. "The what?"

"Today. The closing party." She gestures to the crowd behind us.

Closing? I can't imagine this place not existing anymore. It's been so long since I've been here, but the memories feel just as fresh as if I'd been stopping in for a coffee every day for the last decade.

I look around to find the burgundy velvet oversized chair

in the corner by the window. There's a little bookshelf behind it, tattered and worn. I can't even begin to count the times I sat there as a girl studying my life away. Sofia would bring me free refills and usually force me to eat her "leftover" food. I knew it wasn't really leftovers and she just loved feeding me. She took care of me here.

When I turn back to face her, I can't hide the devastation on my face.

"But... why?"

Noticing my shock, Kee wraps a hand around my arm.

"Ah." She waves her hand in front of her. "No sense in fussing over it. Just time to let go is all."

I'm not convinced. This is more than her café; it's her life. It always has been. It's been in her family for years and she's so... talented. This town isn't the same without this cozy little breakfast stop. I can't even picture it.

Of course, my first instinct is to step in and help however I can to save it. It's what I do. I take care of others, especially when it means something to me.

"I see your thoughts spinning," she soothes. "Don't do that, sweet girl. I'll be just fine." She pats me on the hand and offers a sympathetic smile. I can see right through it though. She's hurting.

My fingers grip the reclaimed wood countertop and I force a smile back to her. The last thing she needs is me barging in here and demanding details or making a scene.

So we order one of everything off the menu.

I happen to know a few guys who wouldn't turn down a hot breakfast.

Not before I discreetly quiz everyone I know in the café about why Sofia's is about to be six feet under though.

136

Chapter 22

Gage

I walk into the bunkhouse after a busy day to see Tripp and Warren sprawled out on the couch watching football. In front of them, Keanna is lying on a huge bean bag with a notepad and a textbook in her hands. Heston is standing with his hip leaned against the kitchen counter shoveling chips and dip into his mouth, and Blythe is at the table typing away on a pink laptop covered in stickers.

She's wearing the most adorable glasses I've ever seen. A strand of dark golden hair falls over her eye and she blows it off of her face out of the corner of her mouth.

I kick my boots off and walk over to stand across from where she's sitting. I lean forward on the back of the dining chair, folding my arms over the top of it.

"Whatcha workin' on?"

Her head snaps up and her dimples pop out in full force.

"I've got it all worked out," she says.

"Oh yeah? What's that?" I smirk. There's a sparkle in her eye and she's obviously happy about something. It puts me in a good mood.

"Just a business plan for Sofia. For the café. It's closing down, did you know that?"

"No, I didn't know that," my brow furrows. I heard some rumors about it a while back. I don't make a habit out of asking questions though, so I didn't know whether or not it was true.

I don't drive into town for breakfast most of the time. On the rare occasion that I do though, I always stop in at the café. Her coffee and homemade food are as good as it gets around here. And any interaction however minimal that I've had with Sofia was always warm and welcoming.

"I think it's the profit margin. Look at this," she turns the laptop to face me and I see the detailed spreadsheet. "Her prices are way too low. She hasn't changed them in years, not even to consider inflation. I adjusted the numbers to something more realistic and doable."

I slide the laptop closer toward me and scroll down studying the charts and numbers.

"She could implement these changes don't you think? She could show this plan to potential investors or—"

"You did this?" I look up at her.

"Yes, I worked on it all day after I left there this morning. What do you think?"

I think her intelligence and selflessness make me want to rip my heart straight out of my own chest. I knew she graduated from medical school, and that alone impressed me. But she has business sense too? Is there anything she can't do?

"She's lucky to have someone like you in her corner. You did good," I say.

The satisfied look on her face confirms what I already

suspected. Words of affirmation are everything to her. She doesn't need convincing. She already knows how smart and capable she is. It's the reassurance she wants. A voice of reason that reminds her to keep the doubts in her head from winning.

I decide to make a plate of food and pull out a chair next to her at the table. Before I sit down, I take the oversized cup that she's always carrying around and fill it with some more water for her. When I place it to the side of the laptop and drop to the seat next to her, my left hand finds its way to her thigh underneath the table.

I didn't think about it before I did it. I just wanted to touch her.

Heston takes a spot at the table as well, and Keanna is in the kitchen now just feet away from us. I notice a barely detectable hint of surprise in Blythe's expression, and I test her poker face by inching my hand closer to her waist. Her eyes dart around at first, making sure that any onlookers are none the wiser. I keep a straight face and focus on eating with my other hand like nothing is out of the ordinary.

Then it's my turn to stop breathing because I feel her small and cool palm slide over mine. Her fingers close slowly around my knuckles and I have to try and force myself not to look down at where we're connected.

She scrolls on her computer screen with her opposite hand, and I don't let her go. Not even when I need a drink or drop my napkin. It's comfortable and exhilarating all at once.

Heston eyes me from across the table and I stiffen a little bit. I casually nod in his direction, and he nods back. An entire conversation by his standards.

Blythe reaches over me with her free hand and steals a

tortilla chip from my plate. She scoops it into the bowl of dip in the middle of the table and stops with it halfway to her mouth when Warren asks me a question from his spot on the couch.

"Did you figure out when we can go pick up the new tractor? They keep telling me it's still on backorder every time I call, but it's been months. I swear we need a better dealership to go through."

"Haven't heard from them. I'll give them a call tomorrow and see what I can find out," I answer.

Having a conversation with her unsuspecting brother while I'm secretly holding Blythe's hand under the table? Reckless.

Am I going to stop? No.

I smirk and Blythe rolls her tongue over her lips forming a firm line when I stroke my thumb along the top of hers. I look down and push my food around with my fork, trying to hide my smile when her grip tightens.

Eventually, our hands drift apart when it comes time to clean up the kitchen. Everyone wanders off to their beds and I take a sad shower all by my lonesome. I know Blythe was working on her computer most of the day, and when she showed me her finished project, she was elated but drained. I'm sure she crawled up to the loft and passed clean out.

I shouldn't be disappointed, but I am. I sigh and lay in the middle of the bed on my stomach, head propped up on my arm. All day I thought about how I could convince her to come sleep with me again. I know it's risky when Warren is under the same roof, but fuck it. I respect the hell out of Blythe and we may not have a serious relationship going on, but we're grown adults. He'd get over it if he found out.

I whip the sheets to the side and get up before I change my

mind. Slowly, I pull the door open and wait to see if I hear anything before I tiptoe out. This is stupid considering I don't exactly have a plan.

Get in bed with her? Dumb idea. Keanna is in the same room.

Stand there and watch her sleep? Creepy.

Tap on her shoulder and whisper in her ear that if I don't get to fuck her again tonight I might die? Dramatic. But yeah, let's go with that.

I turn the corner and bump straight into a body covered completely in a fuzzy white blanket.

"Shit," I whisper yell.

Standing there with her hand covering her mouth and wide eyes is Blythe.

I open my mouth to ask her what she's doing out here, but she leaps into my arms instead.

As quietly as I can, I chuckle and catch her as she slams into my chest. Her mouth instantly latches onto the base of my neck. Gripping the backs of her thighs, I lift and haul her over my shoulder. Headed straight for exactly where I want her: my bed.

I would have gone crazy all night knowing she was in the loft right above me. So close but so far away. I needed to feel her.

When I lock the door and throw her on the bed, my arms instantly cage her in and I pin her down with my hips.

With her body under mine, being able to feel and taste her sweet soft skin, another layer to my hard exterior dissolves away. I never thought I'd be relieved just to see her and have her to myself in bed for the night.

But here we are.

"You miss me?" I whisper in her ear.

She arches into me, leaving not an inch of space between us. I tuck my head down in the crook of her neck and inhale her perfect scent. The little moans she makes tell me she did indeed miss me. But I want to hear her say it.

"Hmm?" I hum my question up against her ear again, then nibble on the most sensitive pulse points under her smooth skin.

She lifts her arm and takes my hand in hers, moving them down together ever so slowly over the curves of her breasts and hips. I look down to watch as our intertwined hands dip under the waistband of her pajama shorts. Gliding together through the wet arousal between her legs.

"Does it feel like I missed you?" she whispers.

"*Fuck*," I moan.

She gasps when I press my thumb against her clit and push a finger inside of her at the same time

"I don't want to admit how fucking obsessed I am with your pussy."

"You just did," she breathes out and softly giggles. Her adorable laugh and deep dimples send a rush of blood straight to my cock.

I pull my hand up to my mouth, lips closing around my fingers as I suck on the taste of her until there's none left. Blythe looks up at me, eyes wide as she watches.

I know I'm addicted to how sweet she tastes because I instantly want to slide down and put my mouth on the real thing until I suffocate.

"All day," I groan. "I waited all fucking day to get my mouth on you."

"God. *Yes*."

I should tell her not to let her face get so close to mine. Because the cryptic part of what I just said is that I'm not just talking about her pussy. I want her mouth just as bad. The feel of her breath on my skin makes it unbelievably tempting.

If I die a slow and painful death, it'll be because I never got to kiss Blythe Farrow.

I can't stay in this position, right next to her face. It's too much. So I lift my body away from hers and roll off the side of the bed.

Her disappointed groan makes me chuckle. I don't waste any time pulling her to the edge of the bed so that her head is almost hanging off of it. I smirk while she squeals with surprise. I fucking love taking hold of her and moving her body exactly where I want it.

She's on her back, staring up at me. I look down from where I tower over her. Those mischievous big blue eyes pierce right through me. I place my hands on either side of her and lean down over her body.

"Take off your shirt and your shorts," I demand.

Wasting no time, her shirt is flung across the room. Then she shimmies out of her baby pink silk pajama bottoms. I never expected the slow bend of her knees and sliding of her hands down her legs to be so erotic. Then again, she could be sitting on a beach in a parka with the hood on and I'd think it was sexy because it was her.

She lays back down flat on her back where I put her, peering up at me again.

"Touch me," she begs.

I love when she tells me what she wants.

My left hand smooths down the entire front of her body. I could play with every part of her for hours, but all I can think about is feeling her come on my hand and watching her face while she does it. My free hand shoves my boxers down while the other teases at her opening.

She rolls her head back and moans when I bury my two middle fingers deep inside her. The sound makes my cock twitch and I take it in my hand, taking three slow measured strokes.

"Look at me," I demand.

She opens her eyes and meets my gaze. From my view above her, she's upside down. And every time my fingers move inside of her, she pushes her feet against the mattress, pushing her head to hang farther off the edge of the bed.

It's such a picture-perfect sight, her looking up at me like this that I almost come all over her right then and there. I've never had a problem lasting until now. It's like seeing and feeling her lights a short fuse. And there's nothing I can do to stop it.

I press the heel of my hand against her clit and curl my fingers inside her at the same time. She lifts her hips and gasps but doesn't break eye contact. Such a good girl. I can't read her mind while she looks at me. But her body tells me enough truth. And judging by the way my blood pumps faster and harder just at the sight of her? I'm as helpless as she is.

"Now open your mouth. Stick your tongue out until it touches your chin."

She does exactly as she's told. I bite my bottom lip seeing her mouth so open and ready for me like that.

Gathering as much restraint as I can, I grip myself at the base and slide the head of my cock over the tip of her tongue. Her top row of teeth graze the underside of it, and holy shit I'm going to come so fucking fast. It's too good.

The faster my fingers fuck her, the farther I push into her mouth until I think it's as much as she can take. I suck in a sharp breath when she gags.

"Holy shit, Blythe." I stay deep in her throat but take a few shaky breaths. After a moment, I try to pull back to let her breathe too, but her hands come up on either side of my hips to stop me.

If I wasn't stuffing my cock down her throat, I could ask her if she wants me to keep going. Then again, the death grip she has on my hips says everything I need to know.

"Don't stop."

Finally burying my restraint, I thrust in and out of her mouth. Her hips roll in tandem with my hand while she clenches around my fingers, telling me she's getting close too. I want her to come with me at the same time. I *crave* it.

When I pull out of her mouth completely, she gasps for air. I bend forward to latch onto her pussy with my mouth, and she takes me in her hand, stroking me rougher than I ever thought she would. Dirty girl.

Not dying on the spot or collapsing on top of her when she cups my balls and sucks the head of my dick at the same time is nearly impossible.

I was never much for 69 before this. It's usually a little bit awkward, honestly. But this time? With her? It's nothing short of nirvana.

With one last stroke of my fingers along her g-spot and a long hard suck on her clit, her insides clench and pulse. So tight. I can't hold back another second. I push all the way to the back of her tongue with my cock, shooting my release down her hot wet throat.

My legs about give out when she moans again with her lips

wrapped completely around me. The vibrations of it spread through my whole body. It takes every last bit of my strength not to fall down and crush her in the process.

Somehow, I stay upright. I pull my fingers out and kiss along her hip bone, making her shiver. I must have been a saint in another life. Some spiritual good karma has landed me in the mouth of the girl who won't quit sucking until she has last every drop of me.

I finally pull away from her swollen lips and drop nearly dead on the bed right next to her. Both of our chests are rising rapidly with quick breaths and adrenaline. I roll onto my back, closer to her. My head is near her leg and I turn to rest my cheek against her skin.

I look down when I feel her hand wrap around mine. Her eyes are closed. Mouth slightly open, catching her breath, the flush of her cheeks like a freshly bloomed rose.

"Are you okay?" she pants.

After *that? No.*

"Yes," I breathe out the lie.

I squeeze my hand, tightening my grip on hers.

I'm so fucked.

Chapter 23

Blythe

Most people wake up in the morning and reach for their phones right away. It might be to check the time or their email. Maybe clicking on random notifications, then mindlessly scrolling for as long as they can drag it out before being forced to get up off the mattress. It's a hit of serotonin that their brain craves without fail every day. A habit, an addiction.

In an unexpected turn of events, I've replaced reaching for my phone with reaching for a warm body.

Currently, I'm wrapped around Gage's back. We're always tangled up in each other one way or another in the mornings. Trading places as little spoon and big spoon. I can't decide which one is my favorite, but I might be partial to this one. One of my arms is looped around his waist, his hand covering mine. My cheek rests on his back.

I'm well aware that typical friends-with-benefits don't do this type of thing. They don't sleep over. They rarely cuddle or touch without having sex. And they certainly don't make a habit of never getting up without laying in bed holding each other every day for two weeks.

Every day, he holds me.

I'm choosing to ignore the fact that we melt into each other so easily. When this is over and we go our separate ways, I might even miss it.

Gage spends his days making me breakfast even when I tell him I can get it myself, working tirelessly on the ranch, and pretending it isn't fun sneaking around to keep my brother from finding out about us.

I visit Mom and Dad and spend time with Warren when he's free. Squeeze in a little time to work on the café business plan or weed through my list of residency options. That never lasts long though. Gage usually interrupts with a text asking how much longer I'll be busy and if I can meet him behind the barn.

I bake crazy desserts I find online, annoy the boys with dance music around the bunkhouse, and help with chores. Kee and I talk on the phone every day about Gage and me, and how her internship is going. She's saving all of her exam study binders for me and I could fucking kiss her for that. We don't have the same specialty, but I'll eventually have a surgery rotation and as much as I'm dreading it, I'm glad I have a best friend to help me through it.

For once, I'm not drowning in stress and I don't know that I've ever felt so content.

It's been… incredible actually.

I snuggle in closer to Gage and fight the urge to picture us doing this for longer than I know we can. Sometimes I can envision us walking out of this room smiling and together instead of sneaking around. Sharing details about our hopes and dreams instead of holding those things back to protect ourselves from our emotions.

I smile when his hand over mine moves to soothe up and down my forearm. He tilts his head down to kiss my fingertips before sitting up to rub the sleep out of his eyes.

"Last group of cows need brought in today," he says. His voice is even deeper with more gravel to it in the mornings. I love the little routine we have of telling each other what we're up to that day. You know, normal fuck buddy stuff.

"My mom is having surgery in…" I reach across the bed to find my phone and check the time, "four hours."

"Do you want me to drop you off?"

"The hospital is an hour away," I laugh.

"I know," he deadpans.

Oh. I couldn't let him take that much time out of his day just to drive me to the hospital. And that feels very… I don't know. Serious relationship vibes.

"It's fine. You don't need to do that."

"Maybe I want to."

His jaw clenches and we stare at each other. This is dangerous territory. I know it. He knows it.

I'm reading too far into this and overthinking it. He's just trying to be nice, right? It doesn't mean that he wants to spend time with me outside the confines of this bedroom just because he said he *wanted* to drop me off.

I want to say yes. I'd willingly be locked inside a vehicle with Gage for a road trip to anywhere in the world. That's a little tidbit of information I know I should keep to myself though.

"Warren mentioned I could ride with him," I lie. I'm sure Warren will be happy to have me tag along with him. I just hope he hasn't left yet and assumed I was already there with Mom and Dad.

His eyes narrow slightly and his lips form a tight line.

"Blythe…" he sighs and takes a few steps toward me.

Might as well nip this in the bud right here and now. I cut him off before he says whatever it was he was about to say.

"I should get going," I whip around to gather up my clothes and put them on. Before I bail out the door and run upstairs to take a quick shower, I give him a light punch to the shoulder. "See ya when I see ya, buddy."

I don't wait for him to respond or to see his reaction, but I can feel his eyes on me as I leave the room. They burn a hole in the surface of my skin, searing straight through.

* * *

"I'm going to grab some coffee, want some?" Warren asks from his spot in the chair across from mine in the family area. It's nicer than your average waiting room. Plush couches, soft sage walls, and several windows let daylight filter in. And most importantly, incredible WiFi.

"Definitely. Thanks," I reply.

A doctor has already come to update us once since Mom's surgery began. She said things are going smoothly and that they should be finishing within the next few hours. Even though I'm excited that this procedure is going to help her in the long run, it's still nerve-wracking to be waiting on a loved one who's currently under the knife. No matter how minimal or routine it may seem.

On top of that, the worry of paying for it lingers in the

forefront of my mind too. I've stalked my bank balance several times already today. Since I'm not enrolled for another semester of school after graduating, my first student loan payment was automatically withdrawn from my account, and it wasn't pretty.

You could buy two brand-new luxury SUVs for the price that I'll be paying for the foreseeable future in order to pay for my education. Loans and scholarships were the only option for me though. I didn't have another choice. My parents would have loved to chip in, but they barely get by on their own as it is.

Which is why I need to figure out how I'm going to get her medical bills taken care of. And fast. These hospitals don't waste any time sending notices in the mail as soon as the insurance claim goes out.

I could sell my car and ride the bus or carpool to work for the next few years. And skimp on a cheap apartment with roommates and stained carpets. It wouldn't be so bad. I'm used to a space that isn't exactly aesthetically pleasing or new. I'd be spending 90% of my time at the hospital anyway.

It doesn't help that I won't be raking in as much as I want to for several years and that residents tend to be put through the wringer but paid like they're part-time dog walkers.

I'm pinching the bridge of my nose when I hear a clink on the coffee table in front of me. I look up to see a young man in a black polo with a little floral logo on the right side. He pulls out a tablet and taps and scrolls a few times before looking up at me.

"The family of Gayle Farrow?"

"Yes, I'm her daughter."

"Sign here, please." He holds the tablet screen out in front of me and I scribble my signature on the black line with the tip of my index finger. He turns the screen toward him to check it, then nods his head. "Have a nice day, ma'am."

"Dang," Warren drawls out the word dramatically as he walks back into the room holding three large to-go coffees in a drink carrier. "You got a secret admirer I don't know about?"

I know he's joking around. But I freeze and study his body language anyway. I don't think he'd be upset if he found out Gage and I had a thing going on. He might even be happy, honestly. They get along so well and act like brothers already from what I've seen.

He might not love the fact that he's been railing me from behind while I scream into the pillow across the hall though. Or the fact that we're not exactly a "thing" at all, and have no plans of pursuing an actual relationship.

Brothers can be protective. Warren has always been that in his own way. He's mature and understanding while still looking out for me. I just can't imagine him leaping for joy if he ever found out his friend was secretly using his sister for orgasms behind his back.

These flowers aren't from him, though. I'm sure they're from a family friend or one of my parents' coworkers. I have nothing to worry about.

He casually hands one of the coffees to Dad, who's sitting in one of the complimentary massage chairs facing the floor-to-ceiling windows.

I laugh nervously to brush off his sarcastic comment and pick up the card attached to the tall vase of colorful wildflowers. There are stems of golden wheat and a few cream-colored feathers mixed in. It's a stunning arrangement.

I lift the card from the envelope and hold it out in front of me to read.

Mrs. Farrow,

Don't let your kids convince you that ice cream isn't the superior recovery food. Get well soon.

-Gage

I hold the card still, staring at it for at least another minute. Warren peeks over my shoulder and reads it for himself.

"It's a wonder that dude is single. He's great, don't you think?"

"I... yeah. He's pretty great," I sigh.

He sent my mom a flower arrangement and a card? I shake my head in disbelief.

"Maybe a little sketchy at times though," he says between sips of coffee. He sits down on the couch. I look at the flowers again, admiring them. Then take a seat next to him.

"Sketchy? What do you mean?"

He leans forward and uses his hand animatedly while he explains. "You know. Like, how did he know where Mom's surgery was at today?" He raises his eyebrows and juts his chin out like he's well aware he's presenting good evidence. "I never told him where it was at or what time."

I remain as stoic as I can be. He has no idea that I was the one that spilled that information. While wrapped around his naked body, no less.

"I've worked with him, lived with him, been friends with him for I don't even know how long. Somehow I feel like I know nothing about him at all, yet better than anyone else all at once? I know that doesn't make sense. But you get what I'm saying."

Join the club. I can't even remember him telling me his last name for crying out loud. I never expected Gage to spill his guts to me. In fact, I'm glad that he hasn't. It keeps the barrier between dating and fucking less likely to break like a dam in a flood. I'm fine being in the dark about all the nitty-gritty details.

"I don't know if I'd call that sketchy. He's just a private person is all," I defend him automatically. "Not everyone feels compelled to share their life story."

"Yeah… it's a little weird though right?" He's looking for validation and looks at me like this might actually bother him a little bit.

"Maybe a little," I reassure him. "But Gage is a good guy, just like you said. The rest of the stuff doesn't really matter, does it? You can be a good person and a private one at the same time."

He nods his head and looks out the window, deep in thought.

"He's been there for me. Saved my ass more times than I deserved. I trust him," he says. He thinks for another moment and then meets my gaze again. "Before Tripp and Heston came on to work at the ranch, it was just us. It was a lot smaller of an operation then, and we went through a lot together getting that place to where it is today. He's like a brother to me and I mean it when I say he's my best friend. But I can't help but feel like there's something he's not telling me."

I fiddle with the rings on my fingers and my leg involuntarily bounces.

I take a drink of my now lukewarm coffee to cover up my nerves. I get the feeling that he isn't talking about Gage's secret romantic entanglements though. It's more than that.

I sympathize with Warren more than he realizes. I know

what a good guy Gage is. And I know how closed off he is too.

"I know that he's not very talkative when it comes to details about himself. But he's trustworthy," I agree.

His shoulders shake up and down as he huffs out a few amused laughs.

"What?" I smile and join in on the chuckle fest even though I have no idea what he's grinning about. Just seeing him this way, spending time with him, and talking and laughing makes me happy.

"It's funny... I actually talked about you a whole lot around him while you were still in school," he smiles even bigger and laughs at himself. "I thought maybe you two would hit it off if I ever introduced you."

Oh, we hit it off alright.

I feel a weird sinking feeling in the pit of my stomach hearing that Warren thought enough of Gage that he wanted to talk me up to him. He thought we'd make a good match together. It just proves how highly Warren thinks of him. To the point where he was hoping we might... get along? Date?

I start to feel guilty that he has no idea what we've been doing. What would I tell him though? How would I explain it to Warren when I can hardly explain it to myself?

I desperately needed orgasms and a distraction from the work and stress that was weighing me down like an elephant sitting on my chest so I started having secret sex with Gage within two days of meeting him and we haven't stopped ever since.

That'd be an interesting conversation.

I decide to test the waters a bit.

"You were hoping he'd like me?"

He runs a hand through his long dark sandy hair. "Well, yeah I guess so," he laughs. "I want you to forge your own path, but selfishly I thought it'd be the perfect way to convince you to move back home. You know, if you had a better reason to stay."

Holy gut punch.

"I don't need a better reason to stay. You and Mom and Dad are reason enough. It's just…"

"I know," he shakes his head. "There aren't any good jobs that are close."

He recites the last part like I've been drilling it into his head for years. Because I have. I don't mean to sound so shallow when I attempt to make him understand my reasoning. Family is more important than my career to me. But that's just it. Family is the *most* important thing in my eyes. I'm doing everything in my power to be able to take care of them, even if it means sacrificing a few things like living close to them.

Millions of people across the planet would give anything to have a family like mine. But I'd give anything to know they were safe and comfortable.

If those millions of people *did* have the family that I have, they'd cherish them and spend more quality time with them. They probably wouldn't be living thousands of miles away. Or having to get their arm twisted to visit home.

I just feel like I don't have much of a choice.

The fact that Warren has always felt so strongly about wanting me to move back home is both heartwarming and saddening. I don't know how to respond further. It's a painful topic, but one that I need to face eventually.

"This coffee is disgusting," I wince and laugh, trying to break the tension and change the subject. He smiles and nods, but not very enthusiastically. He's drowning in his thoughts. My lips purse and I tilt my head.

"Are you going back to work tomorrow?"

"No. Gage talked to the boss for me. Told me to take a few days off to help take care of Mom and hang with the fam."

"Perfect! We'll get Mom home, load up on groceries for the house, and then go Christmas shopping. You down?"

"I love you Blythe, but I hate shopping," he throws his head back like he knows I'm going to drag him along anyway no matter how much he protests.

"You'll survive," I smile. "Who's your boss anyway? I've never seen them around or met them."

"Couldn't tell ya. From what I know, they bought the ranch over a decade ago. One of those silent investor situations. They never stop in, so they probably don't live nearby."

I shrug and pick my coffee back up, forgetting how nasty it is.

"Ugh," I groan and cover my mouth after taking a sip.

But it makes Warren burst out in a fit of laughter, and for that, I'd drink ten cups of cold watery coffee.

Chapter 24

Gage

"Ruby," I groan.

I hear a moo from about five feet away but I don't bother to look up. I'm lying down by the campfire: arms folded over my chest, boot-clad feet crossed, and cowboy hat covering my face.

The rest of the guys, with saddles as pillows, are sleeping in various spots around the fire. It's only a low of 48 tonight, but the swift December breeze makes it feel a whole lot more chilly than that. Scratchy horse blankets keep a thick barrier between the cold ground and our bodies and that's about as good as we can do without fussing around with tents.

Another moo. This time a little more desperate sounding.

I lift one hand to the crown of my hat, raising it slightly so I can peer over at her with one eye. The only red cow in the herd.

I saw her at the sale barn one day about three years ago. Her cow had died and the guy that owned them didn't want to have to deal with a bottle calf since she wasn't weaned yet.

She looked pretty sickly at the time, and not a single soul in that building bid on her. Don't ask me why, but I approached the man afterward, offered him cash, and took her home.

I woke up a little earlier every day that spring, making her a bottle and feeding it to her. She tried to follow me around and I eventually got tired of hearing her bawling, so I let her out of the gate from time to time. She'd prance around the ranch like a pet dog, begging for ear scratches and more milk.

She's a grown cow now and despises summertime when we turn them all out to pasture. I thought maybe putting her in the satellite field, the farthest one from the main ranch land, would force her to adjust to the fact that she's not a pet. It didn't work.

My chest rumbles with a laugh when I see her paw the dirt.

"Fine." I put the hat back on the top of my face and cross my arms again. "You can sleep here as long as you stop mooing." I hear the distinct sound of Ruby making herself at home with the rest of us, causing the ground to shake when she grunts and drops her body to lie down.

Spoiled rotten, that one.

I check the time on my phone and see that it's been hours since I first tried to settle in for the night. I've tossed and turned relentlessly, trying to get comfortable and will my brain to shut down and sleep.

We left out to gather this last set of cows for the winter late this morning. It's almost a day's ride, so we always camp out on the prairie instead of trying to make it home in the dark.

I wish it was the hoot owls or lack of a mattress that was keeping me awake. Truth is, those things are fine by me. The sounds of nature are usually comforting. The fresh air and open night sky, grounding and relaxing. Out here, it's a soothing sanctuary from the madness of the world.

If it wasn't for the fact that I've spent every single night in the arms of Blythe Farrow for the last two weeks, I'd be sleeping soundly right now.

I add a few logs to the crackling fire and sparks fly around the camp. Leaning up against my saddle, I rest one elbow on my bent knee and pull up the camera roll on my phone.

I won't admit how many times I've looked at the picture I took of her that first morning. Fucking perfection.

It's hard to believe that it's not a world-class painting that I'm staring at with the early light pouring into the room, the ruffled sheets, and her sheer beauty. I was there. It was real. And I've never seen anything more stunning in my life.

The next morning that she woke up in my bed, it looked like what you'd imagine heaven to be like. The softest smoothest skin surrounded by her favorite cloud-like fuzzy blanket. Tiny freckles on her shoulders and cheeks peeking through strands of wild mussed hair. Her delicate hands rested above her head on the pillow being kissed by the glow of the sunrise. Taking another picture was a no-brainer.

Somehow, that led to pulling out my phone and snapping a pic of her every day. Each one more beautiful than the last.

It's mind-boggling to me that we were complete strangers not long ago. I'm well aware that my addiction to her has come on fast. I could lay here and beat myself up for getting attached too quickly. But I won't, because it'd do me no good. No matter what happens in the approaching future, she's tattooed herself on my skin and the thought of just having these memories instead of the real thing slows my pulse to a comatose rate. So much so that I feel lightheaded if I dwell on it too long.

I continue scrolling through each picture, smirking and smiling at my favorite ones. It started out as just an obsession with her body and how attractive she was to me. But it ended up being a reminder of how she made me feel instead. Like she wanted to be there and kept coming back to crawl under the sheets with me at the start of each night without fail. Like I couldn't believe I really had this smart, ambitious, sassy woman lying in my bed every morning before I left to go to work.

I click on one of the pictures where she was already awake. Her knees are tucked into her chest and she's hugging her legs with her cheek resting on her arms, head turned toward me. A handful of hair hangs in her face but there's no mistaking her expression: content. Happy.

Mine.

I blow out a breath and rub my forehead.

If I had any service out here in the middle of nowhere, I'd Google how to get over a girl you're not even in a serious relationship with.

The same one that called me *buddy* when I offered to give her a ride into the city for her mom's surgery. That nickname made me want to pull my hair out.

By the time the first sliver of sunlight peeks over the horizon, we're saddled up and pushing cows back toward the ranch. I think I finally drifted off just before dawn, getting less than an hour of shut-eye thanks to my borderline obsessive scrolling of my collection of Blythe pictures. I bring my fist to my mouth to cover another yawn when a horse comes up next to mine.

"You good man?"

Tripp doesn't miss a thing.

"Yeah. Just tired," I reply. I drop some slack in the reins and rest the heel of my palm on the horn of the saddle while we ride alongside the herd of cattle.

"How's things going with your side chick?"

My horse whips his head back and forth a few times and huffs dust out of his nose like he knows I'm not about to answer that question. Tripp knows too, but he pushes my buttons anyway. He's the type of guy that loves having conversations like this. I've learned to indulge him enough to satisfy his fishing for information, but never give him enough to encourage him to keep asking about it.

"Side chicks are girls that you have an affair with. I would never do that."

"Well she's a secret, so she qualifies as a side chick," he smirks.

I almost lean over and punch him in the face for referring to Blythe that way. She's a lot of things, a secret being one of them. But not a side chick. That would indicate that I don't care about her. But I'm beginning to realize that I do. Very much.

I can't exactly expose who she is, but he's obviously noticed that it's been an ongoing thing and not just a one-night stand. He lives across the hall for fuck's sake.

It might be a relief to confide in Tripp about my current situation. I know I could trust him to keep it from Warren for now, but I couldn't guarantee that Blythe wouldn't be angry at me for telling him. Not because he knew about us. But because as soon as she found out that I had blabbed to him about it, it'd be obvious that I have feelings for her. And I don't mean the friends-with-benefits kind.

There's a war of back and forth happening in my brain, and

I'm not doing a very good job of hiding that.

"I'm giving you shit, man. Just wanted to see your reaction," he bellows out a laugh. "I know it's Blythe."

My head whips in his direction and I pull back on the reins. Dust flies up around my horse's feet as he skids to a stop and I turn to face Tripp.

"Jesus you're dramatic as hell. I just mentioned her name and you freak out," he laughs. His casual personality is usually a welcomed break from the seriousness of Heston and Warren, but I could throw him on his ass right now for being such shit head. He thinks this is funny.

"What the fuck man? How?"

He shrugs and grins like he can't think of anything more satisfying than figuring me out. This might be the first time one of my secrets has been thrown right in my face and I can't even begin to describe how uncomfortable that makes me. I wasn't careful enough.

"I went to put back your Stetson that I stole, and her pink boots were sticking out from under your bed. I put two and two together pretty quick." His horse circles around, watching the herd go on ahead of us and acting concerned that we've fallen behind.

"So that's where my hat went," I huff.

"I needed it. Mine got bent up in a bar fight a few weeks ago and nothing drops panties like a perfectly shaped black felt."

Can't argue with that.

I look around and take a second to gather my thoughts. I'm good at keeping secrets, but I became a little careless in covering this one up apparently. Maybe subconsciously I wanted someone to find out. I don't hate the idea as much as

I thought I would when we agreed to keep it to ourselves.

Blythe isn't the type of woman that you should hide away. She's the type that you show off. Claim. Beat your barbaric fists against your chest and scream from the rooftops that you're the lucky bastard whose arms she's been sleeping in.

I've imagined being able to hold her hand in front of everyone. Or rub her feet while we're lying on the couch instead of locked up in my room. I could so easily brush the hair off of her neck and kiss her neck while she typed away on her computer at the dining room table.

But that's all it is. My imagination. Deep down, I know better than to think that would ever actually happen. I wouldn't put her in danger like that. And I'd never be able to be open with her enough for her to trust me in a relationship. That's what she deserves. I just can't give it to her.

"It's not that big of a deal, man. Don't look so torn up about it. I won't spill the beans."

I look him straight in the eye, no doubt revealing my mix of disappointment and seriousness. He's reading my thoughts as they spill out of my sunken expression.

It is a big deal. Because I'm realizing just now that I don't give a fuck if you spill the beans. She's more than an inside joke between us or a dirty little secret to me.

"Oh shit. You're in love with her," he deadpans. His jaw about hits the brush-covered ground.

I don't have the heart to deny it.

Chapter 25

Blythe

I hitched a ride into town with Heston this morning. He didn't say a single word to me the entire time, except when he dropped me off. He mumbled it, but I think it was something along the lines of *"See ya."*

There's a quiet strength about him that is equally terrifying as it is calming. He might be as silent as a mouse most of the time, but something in his eyes lets me know that he's a good person. The guys at the ranch all trust him, so that's something. He thinks too hard and can't be bothered with mundane conversation, sure. But I never feel like I have to be someone that I'm not around him and I like that.

I wanted to come into the café for the day. I've been working hard on the business plan for it, and I couldn't hold back from showing Sofia.

Her reaction was emotional, to say the least. The way that she covered her heart with her hand and teared up when I walked her through the plan made it all worth it. Deep down,

I knew it was a long shot in getting the café back up and running. But I think showing her how much I, and others in the community, felt about supporting her and her business means so much more. She agreed to let me help her adjust some things and reach out to investors, but the underlying tone of her voice was laced with already-admitted defeat.

The economy for small business owners is next to impossible right now, especially in a small town with no tourism. She relies on the locals and has been unwilling to up her prices to stay in business, even after the cost of goods has risen so much in the last few years. Her heart is so big. She couldn't bring herself to charge the people of this town more money for her product.

Gently, I tried to reassure her that we could make this work. I care about her success and just want to help in any way that I can. The community would agree with me, no doubt. I know I can't force her to make the changes or reopen her doors to the public, but I wouldn't be able to forgive myself if I didn't try.

It was sweet of her to let me stay and work on my mortifying inbox full of unanswered emails. They still have WiFi up until the end of the month, so I took full advantage when she offered to let me cozy up in my little corner to work.

Opening my inbox to nearly a hundred missed emails was a snap back to reality. Admittedly, I've lost focus of my goals in the midst of rolling in the hay with a certain cowboy. I can't say I regret it though. I've had the time of my life forgetting the rest of the world and leaning into the way he makes me feel.

Alive.

Special.

Wanted.

I just hope I haven't ruined my chances of matching with one of my top-ranked programs. I've been procrastinating getting back to them all because, to be honest, I don't know where I want to go. If work was my top priority right now, I'd be doing mock interviews on Zoom, or visiting programs around the country that have invited me to come.

I take a second to sip one of my many emotional support drinks, close my eyes, and pinch the bridge of my nose.

Remember why you are doing this. You need this career to take care of your family. To feel accomplished. Successful. You can't quit now just because you're feeling rusty and unmotivated.

This is exactly why I stayed away from distractions throughout medical school. I never wanted to miss a single opportunity or slip even an inch below greatness. I blow out a breath and shake my head back and forth. Cracking my knuckles and tilting my head from side to side, I dig deep for the mental clarity that used to come easily to me.

Hours later, my head is starting to feel light and my eyes are doing that droopy thing that happens when you stare at a screen for too long. I fumble through my bag to find my phone and sigh when I realize it's almost four o'clock and I've been here since seven this morning. My brain is going to turn to mush if I don't pack up and head back to the bunkhouse.

Getting back to the ranch is overwhelmingly exciting to me. *Much* more so than working on my computer and having to stare at the screen for the rest of the night like I normally would. But we'll ignore that little fact for now.

Lately, if I needed to be picked up, Warren is my obvious go-to text. He said he was going to be pretty busy with something this afternoon though, so I suppose I could just ask Heston or Tripp. Since it's Friday, I'm sure they're almost done with work and coming into town for one thing or another anyway.

But I can't help but shoot Gage a text instead. I haven't seen him in almost four days. Between helping my mom with recovery and him being so busy on the ranch, our paths have barely crossed.

I wiggle in my seat and can't wipe the smile off of my face when I click on his contact in my phone. Now would be a great time for another self-pep talk. One that includes *"you're pathetic"* and *"rein it in a little for goodness sake."* But I can't bring myself to care. I like feeling a little giddy over something for once. Even if it's as simple as texting Gage.

Me: Can you pick me up from the café?

It takes a minute for the text to be read. I smile when I see that he's opened the text. He suggested we turn on our read receipts the day after my Mom had surgery and I didn't reply to his text all afternoon.

"How am I supposed to know if you're not hurt or something when I don't even know if you opened the text?" he said.

He doesn't know the real reason that I didn't reply is that when I saw that he texted me, I was over the moon excited. I'm talking buying-new-sparkly-boots excited. It worried me. I hated the feeling because I never wanted to like him as much as I do. I didn't reply just to punish myself for getting in too deep with my feelings.

It didn't go over well. Let's just say he has an overprotective side and that's the understatement of the century. It's cute that he worries about me and I won't admit what it did to my lady parts when he scolded me about needing to know if I was safe. Throbbing, I tell you.

I was slightly annoyed at the time, but now I realize that's his way of showing that he cares without actually coming out and saying it. He didn't have to check in to see if my mom was doing alright or if we needed anything. But he did. And he wanted very much for me to reply.

Gage: Look outside

Pulling into the parking spot under the shade of an oak tree is Gage's old blue single-cab truck. The thin strip of chrome along the side gleams in the sunlight as he comes to a stop. The rumbling of its engine matches the one inside my chest at the sight.

I lunge for my bag to stuff all of my things inside, silently cursing myself for always feeling compelled to bring along the world's largest variety of pens, sticky notes, and notebooks. But what if for some reason I needed the neon pink highlighter instead of the pastel one?!

Finally sliding my laptop into the front pocket, I race to the door. Before I open it, I realize I don't want to make a fool out of myself and trip over nothing just trying to get to the truck faster than lightning.

I blow my bangs out of my face and smooth down the ends of my hair. Willing myself to fake indifference. Calmly, I open the door and waltz out in the most casual manner possible. He won't suspect a thing.

When I'm about ten feet away, he gets out and opens the passenger door for me. He leans against the side of the truck, crosses one booted ankle over the other, and smiles.

"Hi."

"You're here," I breathe out. *Pull it together Captain Obvious.*

"Thought I could wait until later, but I couldn't," he speaks low and slow.

"Wait? For what?"

"To see you."

A flaming hot red creeps up my neck. I open my mouth to say something, but words escape me. There's no easy way to say *"I wanted to see you too, so bad, and you look so hot in your faded jeans and white t-shirt and smelling all manly. Can I please jump your bones now?"*

Rather than blurting that out, I smile. A full, bright, happy smile. Suddenly, the stress of everything else in my life doesn't seem so bad. Because getting to hear that he couldn't wait to see me? It's a shot of liquid heat straight into my bloodstream bringing me back to life.

I tuck one side of my hair behind my ear and rest my hand on his arm while I slide into the passenger seat. As soon as I sink back into the seat cushion, a long exhale escapes me. Between barely sleeping the last few days and how long I worked today, I could use a nap. Preferably a naked one with this guy right next to me.

"Long day?" Gage asks as he shuts his door and turns the key to start the engine.

I kick off my Chucks and bring my feet up on the seat.

"So long," I sigh. "Lack of sleep, taking care of my Mom, and staring at a computer all day don't mix."

He laughs and backs the truck up, then pulls onto Main Street headed back in the direction of the ranch.

"Something funny?" I cross my arms and shoot him a teasing glare.

In the next second, my feet are swept off of the seat as he pulls them onto his lap. His thumb rubs a circle on the arch of my right foot and I nearly moan from the sensation. He applies pressure with the rest of his fingers on the top of my ankle and drags his hand down all the way to my toes. His touch is always intense and electrifying to me, but this feels less sensual and more caring. I lean my head sideways to rest on the seat as the tension leaves my feet and another wall around my heart comes crashing down.

"Can't sleep without me, babe?" That devilish grin is all too satisfied.

"Don't flatter yourself. For all you know, I've been shacked up with someone else and that's what's been keeping me up all night," I quip back.

It's subtle, but I catch the way his jaw grinds and his grip on the steering wheel tightens.

I giggle. I was hoping he'd hate that possibility. He looks at me, furrows his brow, then rolls his eyes and gives my leg a little pinch.

"Kidding." I tap his abdomen with the side of my foot and grin wildly.

"You're a pain in my ass," he grumbles. But he does a terrible job at hiding his amusement.

"Uh-huh. Keep telling yourself that while you pick me up, tell me you couldn't wait to see me, then rub my feet on the way home."

"Got me there," he admits.

His window is down and the air swirls around us. There's no music playing. Just the sound of the truck and my heartbeat that won't quiet down. I pull the plaid blanket he keeps on the seat into my lap and snuggle in. Imagine getting this every day after work. One can dream.

"How were things on the ranch today?"

He looks between me and the road and his hand curls around my calf instead of massaging my foot for a minute.

"Not bad," he clears his throat

Just say you missed me. I promise I won't squeal.

There's an unabridged version of us in some alternate existence that I wish I could see. One where we aren't holding anything back. I'd tell him how much I've thought about him while we've been so busy and away from each other. And he'd kiss me and tease that he missed me more.

Occupying space together outside of his room feels edgy and new. I like riding around with him, feeling his hands on me in a different way, and throwing caution to the wind. The list of rules that we made flashes in my mind, but I shove it back to the little dark corner that it's been hiding in.

For a minute, I pretend that our secret arrangement doesn't exist. What would I say to him right now if it didn't? Maybe the time it takes to get from where we are now to the ranch could be a little bubble of suspended rules and time.

"Where did you live before you came to Westridge? Do you miss it?"

His hand slides down the side of the steering wheel to flip up the blinker before we take the next turn. The steady and continuous clicking is the only audible sound for a minute and I assume he's going to pretend I didn't just ask him a prying personal question. But he surprises me.

"Not anywhere around here, that's for sure. And no. I don't miss it."

His tone is less conversational and more coarse now. There's a loathing to his admission that's clearly been bubbling under the surface for quite some time.

"What made you want to live here instead?"

I don't ask why he left wherever it is that he came from on purpose. That'd be going straight overboard with no lifesaver. Keeping the focus on the here and now might work a little bit better in getting to know him instead.

He rubs at the scruff on his jawline and again lets silence fill the cab of the truck before answering my question.

He's so uncommonly handsome. I study his profile while he thinks.

"I've never felt uncomfortable here."

It's a simple answer, but I know exactly what he means. Sometimes you can't put your finger on a reason why you feel like you're in the right place. It's less a reason and more a feeling.

"Living in a concrete box that I never chose for myself wasn't survivable for me. The wide open spaces here suit me a whole lot better," he continues. "Easier to keep people at arm's length and my hands busier than my mind that way."

It's one of the most honest and unbridled things he's ever told me. I'm like a dry sponge soaking up every drop of his words. I want to know more. I want to know why.

Interrupting my curious interrogation, his phone lights up and vibrates several times on the dash. He cranes his neck to read the caller ID but doesn't bother picking it up.

We pass the last of the quaint little houses on the edge of town, finally reaching the dirt road. The miles of fences, cattle, tumbleweeds, trees, and burnt orange bluffs are beginning to give a whole new meaning to the word beautiful. I took for granted how much I love the peaceful simplicity of life here. Driving by what I consider to be my real "home" never gets old. I'm appreciating it a lot more these days.

I'm leaning against the door, thinking of how to respond to what he said, when Gage's phone starts vibrating once more. Again, he looks but doesn't pick it up.

"It's okay if you need to take a call."

"It's not important."

"Well, I really don't mind—" I start to say, but he cuts me off.

"Stay in the truck." The seriousness of his demanding tone has me sitting straight up in my seat. We're approaching the front gate to the ranch, but parked in front of it is a large SUV with blacked-out windows. A man with sunglasses on leans against the front bumper. Waiting.

"Who is that?" I ask as we pull to a stop not far from the SUV. He leaves the truck running and starts to get out. I turn toward my own door and grab the handle to open it.

His large hand grabs my elbow and pulls me back.

"I said stay in the truck."

I've never seen him like this. Sure, I'm used to him being a little bit grumpy all the time. He's not afraid to tell me what to do when we're naked and alone, but never like this. Like my life depended on it. I look back and forth between his eyes and the man outside.

"Blythe, do you understand me?"

I take a deep breath in and out of my nose and nod.

Gage releases my arm and steps out of the truck. Before closing the door and approaching the man, he turns back toward the seat and lifts it until a compartment underneath is uncovered. With one push on a latch button, a drawer snaps out toward the gas pedal.

There's a knife and several boxes of ammunition, but he doesn't take those. My eyes widen and my lips part on the verge of blurting out a million questions. In one swift and entirely too practiced motion, he checks that the gun is loaded and stuffs it in the back of the waistband of his jeans. He doesn't meet my bewildered gaze before he slams the driver's door shut.

Judging by his swift and precise strides toward the SUV, either he's overly protective when it comes to strangers on the ranch, or he knows this man and believes he's bad news. I'm betting it's the latter.

As slow and quiet as I can, I roll down the window. *Just* a crack. I know he said to stay put, and I trust him enough to listen. I'm not trying to escape, but that doesn't mean I can't eavesdrop.

Gage says something, but I can't make out the words. His voice is as deep and low as I think I've ever heard it, a snarl almost. Based on his wide stance and tense shoulders, he wasn't extending a pleasantry.

I scoot closer to the window hoping to catch more of the conversation.

The man takes his sunglasses off and smirks.

"Long time no see, brother."

Chapter 26

Gage

"Skip the brother bullshit and cut to the chase," I spit.

"The devil works hard, but your security team works harder. I finally find you, and this is how you greet me?"

"Bash," I snarl.

"It's Sebastian to you, motherfucker."

He's got a toothpick in the corner of his mouth and the same dark eyes I remember. My eyes. Our father's eyes.

I scan behind him, across the road, and back at my truck. I don't know for sure that he's here alone, and I can't take the risk of waiting to find out the hard way.

"Relax. It's a solo intervention. For now."

I scoff at his use of the word 'intervention.' Bash and the rest of the men involved with our father's business tried for a short period of time to get me to come back after I left. It didn't take them long to realize that I was never going to do that. They gave up pretty quickly. Until now apparently.

He takes his toothpick between his thumb and forefinger,

rolling it back and forth. His eyes are narrowed, studying me. I can't even remember the last time we saw each other in person. No doubt, I had a full suit and clean shoes on at that time.

I know he thinks of himself as an alpha. Always on top, always in charge of the conversation. He's eyeing me just waiting for me to crack. It's a power chase. Knowing he has full control over any given situation is everything to him.

But I'm just as stubborn as he is, if not more so.

So I remain silent while he stares me down, flicking my gaze back to the truck periodically.

This is why I never allowed myself to get close to anyone, let alone a girl. At this moment I'm not thinking of anything but her safety. The guilt of putting her in danger by letting this go too far is already starting to eat away at me. I'm not naive enough to think that Bash showing up here is a show of good faith or a friendly visit.

Somehow, they've finally found me after all these years and it just so happens to be when I absolutely cannot afford for my secrets to come out. I've worked too hard to keep them.

He nods in the direction of the gate, and a questioning brow quirks up to the middle of his forehead.

I shake my head slow and confident. He's not getting through those gates even if I have to shoot his ass.

He sucks in through his teeth and nods like he knows what'll happen if he tries to force his way in. Pursing his lips, he leans to the side to get a better view of what's behind me. His long and drawn-out whistle fills the tense air between us followed by an amused laugh.

I can only hope Blythe was keeping her head down and out of sight, but I know better. If I had to guess, she may have even smiled and waved at him. Good fucking grief.

"I've seen all I needed to see now," he says.

I lash my hand out, grab him by the collar, and shove him back against the hood of his car. He grunts at the impact, and I hope it leaves a bruise the size of Texas.

When he wipes at his jaw with the back of his hand and plasters a devilish smirk on his face, I realize my mistake. Throwing him on his ass just for looking at Blythe probably wasn't the best way to hide the fact that she's someone I care about. And to the people in my family? That'd be considered something to use against me.

My weakness. And their smoking gun.

There's nothing they can do to me to force me back. To her on the other hand? I'd swim through muddy water and lick the slimy bottom of a gator-infested swamp to keep them away from her.

"Who's the girl?"

"None of your business," I snarl.

He huffs and puts his hands on his hips like it exhausts him just trying to get me riled up.

"I didn't come here to fight," he says.

"I don't give a fuck *why* you're here Bash. I just know that you shouldn't be."

"You're not even the least bit curious?"

"No."

"Well, too bad because we need to talk."

I can't help the condescending laugh that escapes me. The fucking nerve of this guy. Standing in front of me saying we need to *talk*. After what I've been through to cut ties with not only him but the rest of my family, the last thing I'd like to do is *talk*.

"Not interested."

"Yeah, well, you don't have much of a choice," he says, his voice growing more impatient.

"And how's that? You going to hold a gun to my head and force me to listen? Cut a few fingers off? Lock me up in a basement?"

"Don't threaten me with a good time," he sneers.

"Fuck off, Bash. I'm serious." I've already given him more of my time than I planned.

"I have a meeting in the morning that I need to get back for."

"Have at it." I throw my arm out toward the road inviting him to be on his merry way.

But at the same time, a tiny voice in my head fights with my common sense. I know I'm being hard on him. But I swore not to go down this road ever again. Unfortunately, I'm not a completely cold-hearted bastard. Because deep down I want to hear him out.

Just not here. Not now. Not while Blythe sits there and watches and will likely relay every exhilarating detail to everyone at the bunkhouse.

It hits me that as soon as he's gone, I'll have an even bigger issue to deal with. He obviously knows where I am now, and the others likely do too. No part of me wants to pack up and leave. It's not a matter of just loading up my shit and throwing a dart on the map for a new hidey hole. I have a lot more invested in this place than anyone here realizes, especially after what I did today.

Bash opens his car door and I think he's finally given up and decided to leave. But, he fishes something out of the center console and turns back toward me. He's grown up a lot since the last time I saw him in person. I've seen his pictures in magazines and newspapers from time to time, but in the flesh, it's shocking how much taller and more filled out he is compared to his sixteen-year-old self. Sadly, he was already messed up in the shit my father considers *business* at that age.

He holds out his hand toward me, offering a small black flip phone. A burner, no doubt. I lift the hat off of my head and run a hand through my hair.

"You've got to be kidding me," I say.

"Take it. Get rid of the chick, then call me. My number's already in there."

"No," I deadpan. "I want nothing to do with whatever the hell's going on."

His cool demeanor slips for a moment. He tries to hide it, but there's desperation seeping into his expression. He tilts his head slightly and plants me with a look that says more than he'd be willing to admit with words.

I'm your brother.

I'm in trouble.

I need you.

I kick the dirt under my boot back and forth, then turn my head around to see the outline of Blythe's figure in the truck. By now, the sun's about to set and it's just a warm glow of orange lighting up the lowest parts of the sky, so I can't read her expression.

I look up to the clouds, blow out a heavy breath, and try to fight the inevitable. Reluctantly, I grab the burner phone and shove it in my back pocket.

"Stay away from this ranch. And stay away from her." I subtly nod towards Blythe. I don't know that I've ever been more serious in my life than growling those words. My warning tone is firm and final. If he chooses not to listen, there'll be hell to pay and he knows it.

He nods once with his jaw clamped down and his hands in tight fists at his sides.

I'm not happy about this, and that's putting it lightly. But there's a lingering spark of obligation to my brother that never fully burned out. I could have *forced* him to come with me when I left. Taken him under my wing and got him out. I tried, but not hard enough.

Now, seeing him here in front of me with that fucking look on his face? It's the only reason I walk back to the truck knowing I'll be calling him to get to the bottom of this within minutes of dropping off Blythe.

I buried my old life long ago.

Now I'm about to pick up the shovel and dig the grave right back up.

I brace for the barrage of questions from Blythe as soon as I close the door to the truck and watch as Bash pulls away in the SUV.

The questions don't come. Her hand delicately wraps around mine. I pull her across the bench seat and still without saying anything, she lets me tuck her under my arm.

When all I can see on the road is the glow of his disappearing tail lights, I push the button on my visor that opens the front gate. I know Blythe is waiting for me to offer up whatever information I'm willing to give. I'm just not sure what that is yet.

I do know once I tell her, there's a good chance I'll lose whatever small part of her that was ever mine.

I park on the side of the bunkhouse where I usually do, on the far left side of Tripp, Heston, and Warren's trucks. We used to make fun of Tripp for always being the first one done for the day. Warren wanders in a bit later. Then, Heston and finally me once the sun goes down. Our trucks end up parked in the same spot in the same order at the end of the day. You can say a lot of things about our wild bunch, but at least we're predictable.

They're going to lose their shit when they hear about this too, not just Blythe.

It's possible that I won't have to tell them anything at all, and this whole ordeal with Bash is a lot less serious than it seems. That'd be ideal. But the likelihood of that is pretty low. He wouldn't be here if it wasn't bad.

At that moment, I decide to control the fire instead of completely putting it out.

"Gage?"

"Yeah?" My hold on her tightens and I rest my chin on the top of her head.

She melts further into my side and I squeeze. We've been parked for at least a few minutes, but haven't made a move to get out of the truck yet. If this is the last time I get to hold her, I'm not moving a fucking inch until she does.

Looking up at me, she whispers. "Is everything alright?"

I bring my hand up behind her head and fuck if I don't want to lean down and kiss her like it's my last chance.

"We're going to be just fine."

Going to be.

It's a cryptic promise to her. No, everything is not alright. Judging by her tone, I think she already knows that. I take a deep breath and let go of her head before I change my mind about going to meet with Bash and just put this thing in reverse. Maybe I should. Run away from here. With her.

I've been doing that very thing my whole adult life though,

and I don't think there's much left in me that wants to keep running.

"I need you to do something for me," I say.

She sits up a little bit and eagerly awaits what I'm about to say.

"I have something to take care of. Don't tell anyone what you just saw, okay? I am going to come back as soon as I can and I'll explain everything."

"You're leaving me here," she huffs, unimpressed.

"Do you trust me?" I take her face in both of my hands and stroke her jaw with my thumb. I search her eyes for the answer that I so desperately need to hear. It doesn't take more than a few seconds for her to reply.

"Yes. I trust you."

I nod and press my forehead to hers. We share several breaths. Holding her gaze so close like this has me questioning once again how bad things would get if I threw her over my shoulder and left with her. God, I want to kiss her more than I ever have. I need that comfort.

I don't dwell on that temptation. She's not mine to keep. I have to start facing things straight on instead of running if I ever want her to be.

"There's a safe in the back of my closet. Behind a few boxes, under the floorboards."

"Gage what the fuck is—"

"You trust me," I cut her off in a more stern voice. It's not a question, but a reminder of her own words. I need her to know that I'm serious and that if she doesn't follow my directions, she'll be in even more danger than she realizes.

"I trust you," she repeats.

"Alright then. The code is 41165. Type that into your notes

app so that you don't forget it."

She pulls her phone out and quickly types out the sequence of numbers. Opening her bag, she stuffs the phone back inside. Then she turns back to face me and I take her hand.

"There's a loaded gun in there. Do *not* use it if you don't have to."

That sends a flash of fear into her expression. She swallows and blinks rapidly a few times but gives a determined nod.

"Leave the safety on. Put it on the bedside table where it's easy to reach. Just wait for me okay?"

"I really want you to explain what's going on right now."

"I know. I will," I promise.

"I'm not scared, just confused. You can tell me, Gage."

My brave girl.

I look down at her hand that I'm holding and squeeze. She squeezes back and it feels like it's my heart she's wrapped around and not my hand. I hate leaving her in the dark, but I don't know what I'm dealing with yet. There's no way for me to move forward if I don't talk with Bash first.

I'd like to live in this little fantasy world a little while longer. The one where my best friends are inside probably serving up steaks and shooting pool. They don't hate me yet. The one where I can pretend Blythe belongs to me and nothing is about to change on this ranch. She hasn't left me yet.

I thought I should walk her inside, but it might be best to send her in without me. There's plenty that I remember about the way things worked in my old life. And the first thing is that in situations like this, time is not your friend. I can't afford to waste any more of it right now.

I lift her hand and kiss the back of it. She leans in and wraps her other one around my neck just under my jaw.

"Close your eyes and pretend you're dreaming," she whispers.

"Go inside, Blythe." I flex my jaw. She's so close.

"Not yet."

With one hand still holding mine in her lap, and one pulling and squeezing at the back of my neck, I look down at her mouth. That perfect set of full lips.

I shift my focus back to her twinkling eyes. If I don't stop looking at her mouth, I'll lose my mind knowing what I want to do next. My body responds to her grip on me, and I lean in closer toward her. I'm selfish. Because at this moment, the consequences no longer have a single shred of influence on me.

I grind down on my molars. I can't take the torture of pretending I'm not desperate for her anymore. *Fuck it.*

"Are we done playing by the rules?" I ask.

"The rules?" Her voice is shaky and her hand at the back of my neck trembles.

"We're past them at this point, don't you think?"

Please say yes. *Please.*

She lets out a breath that borders on a sigh. Her lips part and her face inches closer.

"I want to say hell with the damn rules, Blythe." My hand holds hers tighter in a pleading squeeze.

Fog covers the windows inside the cab of the truck. I hold my breath, and her beat of silence is only a moment of hesitation, but it feels endless.

"Kiss me," she whispers. "Kiss me like my mouth and every other part of me belongs to you."

Before she changes her mind or my chest explodes, I pull her in.

185

Her eyes slam shut and she sucks in a breath through her nose when we close the distance between us completely. Mine stay open, watching her intently. I can't look away. Our mouths mold together firm and unyielding. It's a lightning bolt. A sweet surge of electricity that strikes right through us both.

Eyes still open, I see her brows rise as she pulls away and gasps for air. A sweet flush of pink covers her cheeks, and she touches a fingertip to her cupid's bow like she's trying to make sure it's still there despite the numbness.

The undertone of tenderness from our first kiss soon disappears. I want more. *Need* more.

In a flash, I grip her right leg and pull it over my lap so that she's straddling me. She takes either side of my face in her hands before I can even take another breath, bringing her lips to mine in a rush of desperation.

If I could freeze a feeling, it'd be this one. I'm such a fool. A stupid, dumb, cowardly fool for waiting this long to kiss her. It's better than I dreamed it would be.

As it turns out though, we were right to avoid it for so long. Because now that we've kissed, I know for an absolute fact that there will never be anyone else who could send my heart into overdrive like this. It's not possible.

I coax her lips open with my tongue, begging her to give in to me even more. She opens them, tilting her head to the side and surrendering every defense.

She arches her back and grinds down on me hard enough to make me lean back and bring my hips up to meet hers in a match of force. My hands smooth under her thighs, trying and failing to lift her closer. There's not an inch of space between us and still, I want her pressed further onto me. The only way that'd happen is if we ripped off our pants and I sunk into her.

"Stop thinking about sticking your dick inside of me unless you're going to do it," she pulls away and pants. It's not enough that she's got a hold on me stronger than an industrial magnet. She can read my mind too.

"I wish I had time to do that right now. You have no idea," I say as I smooth back her hair and hold my palm over the shell of her ear. It's less about the urge to fuck her, and more about the need to be closer to her. To hold on to her.

I'd like to kiss her until our lips fall off, but the buzz of my phone reminds me that there are other things to take care of.

"Blythe…"

"I know," she says as she presses her forehead to mine. I press my lips to hers for what I hope isn't the last time.

She gathers her things and steps out of the truck, letting her hand linger in mine.

"Hurry back," she orders.

And with that, she slips through the front door. It closes behind her, and all that's left to look at is the red cranberry wreath that she hung there because she thought the bunkhouse needed a little more holiday cheer. She's left her mark on me and every bit of this place since she arrived.

And I need to make sure that whatever Bash is up in arms about will do nothing to ruin that.

Chapter 27

Blythe

D*on't tell anyone what you just saw.*
I'm a lot of things, but a good liar isn't one of them. I need to act casual. Gage asked this of me, and the urge to not let him down is too strong. I have to make this work.

Things have been so easy with him up until now. I should've known it was too good to be true. He has a lot of explaining to do when he gets back. I'm not taking *"Do you trust me"* as a good enough cover-up again either.

I inhale and push out a cleansing breath. Smoothing down the ends of my hair with one hand, and opening the door with the other, I step inside with a forced smile on my face.

"Hey B! Grab some food and come play the winner," Tripp yells from across the open space. He's bent over the pool table, one eye closed, planning his next move.

There's music playing from the jukebox, something old and classic. I wonder how that thing hasn't kicked the bucket yet. It's hardly ever not playing. Warren makes his way over to

me, smacking Heston on the back of the head as he walks by
him.

"Motherfucker," he mumbles and rubs at the spot.

"That's what you get for ditching me this morning."

Heston scowls.

"Not his fault Hattie Jo showed up. He's terrified of her,"
Tripp laughs.

I make an attempt to smile, but it's no use. My lips don't
even twitch with amusement. These boys and their constant
bickering and joking have never failed to cheer me up. Right
now, all I can think about is if Gage is alright. The unmovable
weight of worry drops to the pit of my stomach.

I'm no stranger to worrying about others, but this feels
different. Less like a constant dull ache and more like an
urgent throbbing. A *need* to take action and make sure nothing
else goes wrong.

I right my face which undoubtedly reveals my distress at
the moment. With a sweet tight-lipped smile, I sidestep
Warren, grab a water bottle from the fridge, and head down
the hallway.

"B, wait," Warren calls out.

"I'm just going to jump in the shower! Be out in a bit!" I
sing-song in my most convincing gleeful voice. I had already
made it halfway through the door I'd been going in and out
of every morning and night for the last three weeks when
Warren chose the worst moment of all time to decide to pay
close attention.

"Uh, shower in Gage's room?"

I stop in my tracks and turn around slowly, making sure
to wipe the guilt from my eyes. Tripp's lips twitch like he's
fighting a smile. It's not his usual shit-stirring look. More

smug like he's shoving down the urge to blurt something. Does he know? I narrow my eyes at him and he stuffs his hands in his pockets and looks at the ceiling like there's a stray bird hiding somewhere in the rafters.

Heston pays no mind at all. I can't imagine he gave one single thought to what room I was or wasn't walking into.

But Warren looks firmly confused as his left eyebrow rises higher and higher waiting for an explanation.

I stand tall and roll my shoulders back. "I thought there might be some clean towels in there. I threw mine into the washer earlier today and forgot to switch them to the dryer," I wave my hand and let out a laugh to really sell it. "Silly me."

"Right." He looks behind him to the front door and then back at me. "Speaking of Gage, where is he?"

Heston clears his throat. "He asked where Blythe was earlier. I told him she was at the café, and then he said he was gonna go pick her up."

All three of them look at me. I shift my weight from one foot to the other. This is why I figured being a doctor was my best chance at a successful career. I wouldn't make it past a day as a lawyer.

"Did he pick you up?" Warren asks.

"Yes, but," I hesitate and wring my fingers together in front of my waist, "there was something that he had to go check on. I'm not sure what it was, but he said he'd be right back." Not *entirely* untrue.

Warren shrugs his shoulders. "Alright. But hey, can we talk for a sec?"

"Sure thing," I say entirely too quickly. I rush into Gage's bathroom and grab the closest folded towel that I can find in the bathroom. "I'll be done in a jiff!" I shuffle into the guest bathroom, shut the door, and lock it.

I'd rather avoid my brother than risk having to tell him that Gage is actually meeting with a scary-looking dude driving a blacked-out SUV that I've never seen before or that he may or may not have acted like something was wrong when he sent me inside the bunkhouse.

I lean against the door and rest the back of my head on it. Closing my eyes, I breathe and pretend that I have nothing to be worried about and that Gage can handle whatever it is that needs handling. There's no reason for me to freak out. I can just go about my night and wait for him to get back like he said.

Still, I pull my phone out of my bag and check the screen. There's a missed call and a voicemail icon that has my heart skipping a beat, but it soon sinks when I see it's not from Gage. The caller ID reads *Dr. Mullen* and I click on it to listen to her message.

"Blythe, this is Dr. Mullen from the Medical Honor Society. Just wanted to check in, make sure you got my letters of recommendation, and see how interviews were going. I haven't heard back from you, but I'd love to sit down and discuss your plans for the future. Hope all is well!"

I pull the phone away from my ear and stare at the screen, waiting for that jump-for-joy feeling. Finishing top of my class, I knew that I had caught the eye of the honor society director. She's contacted me several times since graduation to discuss my plans and has always praised my publications and accolades. It feels incredible when you're recognized and celebrated. When it's something that you're passionate about, that is.

I love helping people. But I don't love the hospital or the

academic setting. I have the brains and the work ethic to be a successful doctor. But judging by my reaction to Dr. Mullen's voicemail, I'm just not sure that I'd make a happy one.

I turn on the shower, letting it get warm as I kick off my shoes and shed my clothes. Maybe it's from the adrenaline coursing through my veins at the thought of Gage having a potentially dangerous conversation with that man right now, but my cheeks are flushed. I look more alive and vibrant than I think I ever have. I touch my under eye with the soft tip of my middle finger where dark bags used to be. The red splotches and little blemishes that used to be sprinkled across my forehead and cheeks from time to time have vanished. All that remains in their spot is a clear healthy glow.

I guess good sleep, a few orgasms, and time away from stress will do that to a girl.

I test the water to make sure it's not too hot or cold, then step in. The white noise of the spray against the shower floor and the soothing beat of water on my skin clear my thoughts. I'm glad for the blissful few minutes of inner peace.

There's a disgustingly sweet-smelling watermelon shampoo on the shower shelf, no doubt left here by one of Tripp's 'buckle bunnies' as Heston calls them. I laugh as I pour it into my hands and lather it up. Surely, she won't mind me using it.

By the time I'm finished and in my comfiest sweats and hoodie, Warren is waiting on the couch. I bring my brush with me, sit next to him, and start running it through the tangles in my hair.

"What did you want to talk to me about?"

"It's about Mom."

I pause my brushing and widen my eyes. "I just stopped by

yesterday and she was doing great. Is she okay?"

"She's fine. Nothing like that."

I blow out a breath of relief. I could not handle more bad news about her right now. I want so badly for her to be comfortable and healthy. She told me just this morning over the phone that she slept wonderfully last night, and I can't even begin to explain how incredible it is to know that the surgery is already helping her.

"I dropped off some cheese to her this morning. Said she needed it for her homemade potato soup or something. I stayed and talked with her in the kitchen for a little bit, and noticed some mail from the hospital on the counter."

"Bills?" I ask quietly. The thought of having to pay off the cost of her procedure triggers me in the most painful way. It's going to take a lot of saving to make those payments on top of getting them out of their trailer house as soon as possible.

Warren shakes his head and forms a tight line with his lips. He leans forward to put his elbows on his knees. "It wasn't a bill. It was a receipt. When she was fumbling through the pantry, I picked it up and scanned the whole page as fast as I could. At the bottom, it said there was a zero balance. How'd you pay it so fast?"

"I—I didn't." Shocked doesn't even begin to cover it. I know for a fact there's no way Mom and Dad had over ten grand just laying around to cover the entirety of the bill. Mom said herself before I told her to make the appointment for the surgery that she was waiting because they were having to save up to be able to afford it.

"I've dumped every dime that I've earned into my business, so it sure as hell wasn't me."

"What business?" My head jerks back and I try not to look

193

too surprised. But I am because this is the first I've heard about it.

"I've already got the land to build on. I had an investor reach out recently, and he's helped me get things going. It won't be until summer that it'll be ready, but I'm opening my own farm and ranch equipment dealership. Sales and full services," he smiles.

"Warren," I put my hand on his knee and genuine contentment sweeps over me. He sounds so confident in this. And excited. "That's amazing! Is this something that you really want to do?"

"It is," he admits. "I'm always fixing equipment around here. Pretty much daily, so I know that side of things like the back of my hand. And I've always wanted to own my own business. Don't get me wrong, I love working on the ranch. But it's never what I wanted to do for the rest of my life."

"You are going to be a great business owner," I assure him, and I mean it. "I'm proud of you." Tears well in my eyes. This is all I've ever wanted for him—to do what he loves and to be happy.

"Thanks, sis. I appreciate the vote of confidence," he chuckles. "We'll see how it goes."

"So the paid hospital bill… it's got to be some sort of mistake," I suggest. "Right? I mean, I just can't think of how that's possible."

"We should ask Mom and Dad about it I guess. But I'm betting they assumed you took care of it and then didn't think twice about getting the paid-in-full notice."

"Yeah." I twist a strand of wet hair through my fingers to help me think. "We can have Mom call the hospital. They should be able to clear it up." I bring my thumb up to my mouth and chew on the side of my thumbnail.

"You seem a little off tonight. You feeling alright?"

"I've been thinking a lot is all."

"You think way too much, that's your problem," he says.

I shake my head and smile, knowing that he's right.

"I know. I've just realized a few things while being here is all," I confess.

He perks up at that statement. "Oh yeah? Like what?"

"You really want to know?"

"Of course, I really want to know, B."

I look at him and I'm met with worlds of hope in his eyes. I know he'd love for me to say that I've fallen back in love with life here and have every intention of staying close to family from now on, trading the big city fast-paced lifestyle for the comfort of home.

It's not the idea of a slower life that scares me. In truth, I've never wanted anything more than that. I enjoy the simple things. Bright orange sunrises over the bluffs on the prairie, clean open sky, familiar faces everywhere I go… and *family.*

What scares me is that I made the wrong choice leaving in the first place. I'm lost now as to where to go from here. I still plan to take care of my family the best I can. I'm not a quitter, and I can't just abandon the plan I've had in place.

But why have I stressed so much about taking care of my family? They have roofs over their heads and smiles on their faces. Mom and Dad aren't materialistic people, and I don't think they've ever spent a day wishing they had more stuff or fancier things.

Maybe I've been wrong all along. My family *is* rich. Not with money, but with love and compassion and heart.

I see that right now in the way Warren is excited about his

new business. And how he scoots to the edge of his seat, no doubt wishing for me to admit that I feel safe and connected here. Down to earth, loved, surrounded by support and the things that matter. Not the amount of money in your bank account at the end of the day or how spectacular your car or house is.

I see it in the way Mom and Dad hold hands for no reason. How Dad sets out her coffee mug each morning before he leaves the house. How she laughs at his ridiculous Dad jokes, despite them not being the least bit funny.

I see it in the way Gage has shown me that letting other people take care of you doesn't make you weak. It makes you human. Feeling human is something most people take for granted, myself included. When you're working your life away, you feel more like a robot. Not a living, breathing, *feeling* human.

"The truth is that I think I've put too much pressure on myself to take care of our family. I don't have any regrets. But I'm starting to wonder if I'm not where I belong." Water fills in around the edges of my eyes, blurring my vision.

He takes my hand in his and lovingly rubs his thumb across the top of my wrist.

"I support you, no matter what you want to do. Or wherever it is that you want to be. I just want you to do that for *yourself*. Make a few decisions based on what's best for *you*. Not everyone else."

I nod. I know that what he's saying is sound advice. I've been ignoring it for years, but I think I'm finally beginning to see how much it's going to negatively impact my life if I continue to pursue a career that I'm not in love with. Or live in a place that I have no real connection to. Truly loving both my home and my job means more to me than I ever thought. It's obvious to me now, seeing how happy and relaxed I've been lately.

I know that Gage has a lot to do with that. I may not know all of the nitty-gritty details of his life because he hasn't felt comfortable enough to share those with me yet, but I also feel a strong pull to him. Like walking away would be nearly impossible. Saying goodbye would gut me.

Spending a few nights away from him this week was unexpectedly hard. I can't imagine how tough it would be for months at a time.

Thinking of Gage reminds me...

"Also, please don't overreact, but there's something else I should probably tell you because I feel weird keeping it from you."

He tilts his head and he narrows his eyes suspiciously. "You found my stash of stroopwafels and ate them all didn't you." He crosses his arms.

"No. Well, yes," I admit.

He scoffs and rolls his eyes but I see the corner of his lips tip up like he's fighting a small smile. He could never be mad at me for too long. At least I hope not.

"But that's not what I'm talking about. It's not a big deal it's just... well, Gage and I—"

"No fucking way," he cuts me off.

My mouth hangs open, waiting for my brain to send a signal as to what I should say. But I just stare at him like a deer in the headlights. Is he just shocked or mad? Happy?

"Damn I'm good," he claps his hands together once in front of him. "I knew you guys were perfect for each other."

"Oh. Well, it's not really like that, I don't think it's too serious."

Not serious for him, anyway.

"I'll keep that in mind when I give my best man speech at your wedding."

"Not happening," I laugh. "He's… closed off. And up until recently, I planned to stay out of relationships in favor of focusing on my career. I'll be honest though. I don't know what my plan is now."

"No matter what you decide, we can figure it out together. And you know I always have your back."

"I know," I whisper as I lean in and give him a great big bear hug.

"Now sit through an old Western with me as punishment for sneaking around with my best friend behind my back."

I slap him on the arm and scoop up the closest blanket to wrap around my legs.

He winks, smiles, and folds his hands behind his head while sinking into the couch cushions to relax.

"That's not a punishment, I'll gladly watch. I have a thing for cowboys," I tease.

Predictably, he picks the same old favorite that I know for a fact he's already seen a million times. The introduction music alone sends me into a tailspin of nostalgia. We had a slew of movies on VHS just like this growing up. We'd ride around on our stick horses playing sheriff and the bandit. Our cowboy hats were too big, they'd wobble and fall off, and we'd have to start the whole scene over.

The comfort from the fireplace, the quiet simplicity of the low hum of the classic movie playing, and having my brother right here in the flesh spending time with me is almost too much. I've missed this feeling more than words can describe.

Warren laughs as the deputy shoots a drink out of a man's hand at the saloon and a fight breaks out. As the movie goes on and the glow of the TV starts to lull me to sleep, my phone buzzes.

Hoping it's Gage, I rip it from under the blanket. It's just an email, unfortunately. The subject line reads '*Looking forward to your visit soon*.'

My stomach sinks. Not only from the reminder that I'll be on my way out of here after the New Year but also because I notice the time at the top of my screen. Gage has been gone for hours.

Chapter 28

Gage

I walk into the hotel lobby and immediately wrinkle my nose from the pungent smell. This place is a dump. The old wallpaper is stained from smoke, dust hangs heavy in the air, and the floors creak beneath the floral carpet that looks like it used to be green, but is now brown. The front desk attendant doesn't bother making eye contact with me, but I pull the brim of my hat farther down my forehead as I pass her just the same.

The burner phone buzzes in my pocket and I pull it out to see a text.

Unknown: 209

I'm sure his security team alerted Bash to the fact that I'd finally walked inside. I noticed them within seconds of pulling into the parking lot a few hours ago. I watched them intently, knowing full well they were watching me as well. I don't trust my brother any more than I trust a hungry pack of howling coyotes in the middle of the night. Scanning the area and making a plan for how I could get out fast if needed was a priority.

There's no elevator, so I trudge down the hall to find the staircase. Coming as a shock to absolutely no one who grew up scoping out meet-ups like I did, there are several guards along the way. They're noticeably trying to be inconspicuous and blend in around here with what they're wearing, but they aren't as slick as they think. The bottom of their jeans are too tight and skinny around their boots. Their hats are straw in the dead of winter. City slickers.

I know both sides of that coin. I may have grown up in the city, but I've lived in Texas on the ranch for over twelve years. You wouldn't catch me dead in that getup.

One of them eyes me a little too long and spits on the ground as I round the corner of the second floor. In my younger days, I'd have decked him right between his eyes. But I ignore him and keep my right arm close to my body. Ready for a quick draw at all times.

The door is cracked, so I walk in without knocking. Bash is seated in the corner at a pathetic excuse of a desk. It's old and battered, covered in scratches and stains. His legs are long enough that he can't scoot all the way under the desk, so he's leaned back and at least a few feet away from it. No way to conceal a gun or weapon. Exposed.

The fact that he's sitting at all is a good sign in the first place, and I scan the rest of the room to see who else will be joining us for this little conversation. There's only one other man in the room, bald with a silver and black goatee.

Not for long though. Bash looks at him and jerks his head toward the hallway. The man nods and walks out, closing the door behind him. I don't have a perfect view of the bathroom or closet without opening their doors, so I can't be completely certain that there isn't someone in either of those two places. So, I remain standing with my back to the wall opposite Bash.

"Will you fucking relax? Damn," he says.

I cross my arms and pin him with a look that says I have no intention of relaxing.

"Thought this was a solo intervention," I say jerking my head in the direction his minion went and where the rest of his men are.

"I lied. Have a seat," he gestures with his hand around the small room, but there's no other furniture. "On the bed or something."

"I'm good."

"Suit yourself." He takes a sip of his amber-filled tumbler and pulls a black folder from the bag next to his chair. It makes a loud slap on the table in front of him. When I don't immediately grab for it, he leans forward and pushes it toward me with his index finger. It swishes across the wood surface and I reluctantly pick it up.

I was not prepared for what I was about to see when I opened the folder. Inside is a full-page photo printout of Blythe walking down the center aisle of the horse barn. It's slightly grainy like it was taken from a far distance and zoomed in for the shot. My breaths pick up speed and I clench my jaw.

I flip to the next one. Blythe is petting Heston's dog, Lucky, on the patio. Then another of her, this time next to the campfire where she's straddling me while I sit leaned back in my chair. I recognize immediately what night it was. The rest of the boys were out at the bar, and the weather was so nice, I dragged her out to the fire pit. My hand is up her shirt and she's smiling into my neck.

I slam the folder shut and draw my gun, making a point to turn off the safety and step closer to Bash.

"Is this some sort of threat? Because if it is, I'll save us all the time of you explaining your demands that I won't meet and just kill you right here and now."

He holds his hands up like it'll somehow prove his innocence and laughs. *Laughs.*

"They're not my pictures. I didn't take them, I acquired them," he says.

"Explain," I snarl and move the barrel of the gun an inch closer to his forehead.

"It's a long story."

"Start talking then. I don't have all night," I bark.

"You got that right. You're lucky I'm even here. I'm risking a lot showing you those photos, you know?" He scoffs and shakes his head. "Dad's messed up in some shit."

"Shocker," I deadpan.

"It's a lot worse than you think."

"I already hate him. No need to drag it out. What the fuck does this have to do with him?"

"I bet you didn't hate him when you cashed in that trust to buy some fucking ranch and your idea of a new life," he spits.

I grind down hard on my jaw and the hand at my side forms a tight fist. I've never not hated my father. I saw firsthand the type of horrible people that he had no problem representing and keeping out of prison. On the rare occasion that things didn't go exactly according to plan, there were always dangers lurking around every corner for me and the rest of our family. He put us all in that position countless times whether he meant to or not.

"Fuck him and fuck you too," I seethe.

Bash points to the folder of pictures as if to remind me that we're not the only ones involved here.

I narrow my eyes and add a few seconds to my patience to hear him out.

"What I came here to do was to warn you. A man by the name of Eddie Reynolds tried to get Dad to represent him a while ago. Dad refused." He pulls another picture out of his bag, this time of a man. "This is him."

I study the picture. Memorizing every detail down to his stature and complexion. The most obvious identifiers are his stark white hair and full-neck tattoos.

"He's involved in human trafficking and shit," Bash goes on and I raise my eyebrows as I listen. "Dad's not all straight and narrow, but he's not that crooked. So Dad refused to defend him in court. Reynolds started picking off our guys one by one and told Dad that if he didn't get him off with no prison time, he'd kill his whole family."

I lower my gun and twist my face. I don't ever remember my father turning down a potential client, no matter how heinous their crimes were. He's a big-shot lawyer. His typical clientele is criminals, those with mafia ties, or just rich enough for my Dad's exorbitant fees.

His moral compass has always been a little more gray than black and white. All for the money. And I hated him for it. He'd represent anyone if it meant a big payday, and made an absolute fortune in the process. But human trafficking must be the line he wasn't willing to cross.

"This is exactly why I left New York City," I sigh.

"Yeah, well, Reynolds got hold of Dad's old bank records. Your name is on the trust."

"I emptied that trust the day I turned eighteen. That was

over twelve years ago, and it's a sealed document."

"These are criminals we're talking about," Bash reminds me.

"Right." I rub my jaw and pace back and forth. "But why the fuck does he have pictures of Blythe? And how did you get them?"

"He's here. He's been here," he says. "Gathering intel on you."

I drop the folder of photos on the table and cover my eyes with my palm, willing them to stop burning.

"I got a guy on the inside the day I got a whiff of this whole thing going sideways. He found these pictures on a flash drive and sent them to me. I had no idea who the girl was, but then I saw that you were in some of the pictures with her. Figured you'd got married and started a family down here or some shit." A subtle cringe flashes across his face. "We tracked a few of Reynolds' guys to a house." He scrolls on his phone to pull up a dot on a map and points the screen toward me so that I can see. "I saw it with my own two eyes this morning. They're holed up about 60 miles from here."

"You've got to be fucking kidding me. You have surveillance on it?"

"No. Couldn't risk them knowing we had their location," he answers.

I put my hands on my hips and blow out a breath.

"My point is, they have every intention of taking down this whole family and it's not an empty threat. They've turned over every stone. When I saw these pictures they had, I prepared myself for the possibility that you and your little girlfriend might already be dead by the time I got here. You need to leave. And fast."

"And go where?" I scoff. "Let me guess, New York? So I

can put my ass on the line to help save yours? That's the real reason you're here right?" It's harsh, but I don't exactly have the extra time for beating around the bush.

"I don't expect you to drop everything to help. You may have abandoned us, but I still thought you might want to step in if someone was trying to kill your family. My bad," his words are laced with anger now.

A disbelieving evil laugh erupts from my chest. "Abandoned you? You mean like how Dad abandoned my mother and lied to me about her being dead?"

I was young enough to believe the story my father fed me.

I received a letter from a man when I turned eighteen saying that my mother had just passed away and left behind a few things in my name. I was shocked because I was told that she'd already been dead for years after a car accident when I was a child. In truth, my father had forced her away when she couldn't get on board with the constant danger he put her in, and I'll never forgive him for that. I came down to Texas after getting that letter to find a horse, an old truck, and a little piece of land that she had lived on. All passed down to me, along with a file of notes she'd written detailing the devastating nature of her absence from my life.

I was accustomed to lavish mansions and brand-new sports cars. Prep school uniforms and rooftop parties that were held for no reason other than to show off how much money you could spend. I hated every second of it. Even as a young man, I was well aware that my father made his fortune from crooks paying him out the ass to keep them out of jail. It never impressed me, and the posh lifestyle didn't suit me one bit either.

I hated the way I never knew if a girl was dating me for

my money or because she genuinely liked me. Or if a friend was using me for status instead of actually wanting to hang out. I knew if I ever got out of the rich and famous circle, I'd prevent myself from ever having to feel like that again.

"She gave Dad an ultimatum and ran when he wouldn't clean up his act," Bash scoffs like it's a well-known fact.

Wrong. She was scared, and he forced her out when she refused to support him. Swallowing hard, I stare him down.

"You don't know shit about what happened," I growl.

"Maybe not," he shrugs. "But I know we're brothers. And unless you got a death wish, we're going to have to shove the Mommy and Daddy issue baggage into the closet and focus on not getting killed."

I hate that he has a point. I nod reluctantly.

"Look, I know we have a piece of shit Dad. And I get why you left and made a whole new life. But if we argue about the past until our noses bleed, we won't survive long enough to see next week. We need a plan," he says.

Thoughts of Blythe and my friends being in danger remind me why I took this meeting with Bash in the first place. He's right.

"How many men do they have and how many of yours did you bring?"

"Not sure how many they've got to be honest. Ten at least from what we saw around the house where they're at. I have eight. You have a lot of manpower at the ranch don't you?"

"Not really. I have several employees, but there are only four of us at the ranch full-time right now. And about that…" I trail off.

"What?"

"They might be a little surprised." *Understatement.* "They

207

don't exactly know who I am. I mean, they know who I am they just…" I struggle to explain the situation. "I wanted to leave my previous life behind. Start fresh. They think I just work at the ranch. I've never told them much of anything that has to do with Dad or what I used to be involved in or… money."

And rightfully so. Because look what my past has dragged them into now.

At this point, there's no way around not telling them. Not when continuing to lie puts them in danger like this. I just hope they understand and don't immediately get pissed and never talk to me again. My three best friends and the only girl I've ever really cared about may no longer be a part of my life by the time this day is through, but I'll risk that possibility to make sure they have a life to live at all.

"Oh shit," he howls. His fist covers his mouth and he coughs from cackling so hard. He leans back in his chair and beams. "So they just think you're some poor motherfucker living off canned beanie weenies and roping cows for a living?"

"More or less," I admit.

"That is rich. Richer than you," he laughs even harder. "Your girl know?"

"No. And she's not technically *my* girl."

Not yet.

I'll have a short ride back to the ranch to figure out how to tell her all of this and convince her not only to forgive me for not being totally upfront with her but that we should drop the act of friends with benefits. The protectiveness I felt over her when I saw Bash at the gate earlier was a clear sign to me. Whether or not she or I realized it, she's mine to protect. To love and the be with. I'm done with the fun and games.

This is a fucking *mess*.

I couldn't even fit all of the ways this could go wrong on one sheet of paper.

"Damn," he wipes the tears from laughter from the corners of his eyes and takes a cleansing breath to steady his voice. "I have so many questions."

"Save them. How much time do we have?"

He walks over to the window, pulls the curtain aside barely an inch, and then looks at the time on his watch.

"Not much," his voice has grown lower and more serious. "What's it going to be?"

Blythe's face flashes in my mind. It's always the same image that I picture. When she tests my will in the mornings by snuggling her face closer to mine. Looking up at me so sleepy and goddamned gorgeous. Her sweet dimples, fluttering lashes, and contented sigh.

"You're sitting ducks here. Load your shit up and meet me at the pin I'll drop to you," I demand and pick his drink up off the table, finishing it in one shot. Wiping the corner of my mouth, I turn to walk out of the room.

I leave him with one last reminder because I know we won't see eye to eye every step of the way, and I can't have that. Not with Blythe and my friend's lives on the line. "We do this on my terms."

Chapter 29

Gage

There's a burst of light yellow cascading through the bunkhouse windows onto the hardwood floor. The edge of the sunrise creeps further into the room with each minute that passes. Each minute that I procrastinate the inevitable.

I could lean back in this chair, chin rested on my fist, legs spread and eyes staring at Blythe sleeping on the sectional until I rot in place. But she startles awake when Heston opens and then slams closed the fridge door. She blinks slowly and it takes her a second to realize that she fell asleep on the couch last night. When I walked in a few hours ago and saw her there, I wondered if she'd been waiting up for me.

I stand, brush the hair out of her sleepy eyes, and kiss her on her cheekbone. She takes a sharp breath and I don't linger on the fact that she looked relieved and happy to see me before I walk into the kitchen to get her a coffee.

There's your trouble.

I'm so hung up on her every reaction.

She pads down the hallway, and I busy myself at the coffee pot. Out of the corner of my eye, I see a honey bear sitting on the counter. I know that she likes coffee and drinks it often, but I think she prefers hot tea.

I don't have a kettle, but I warm up some water in a mug in the microwave, then search through the rest of the things in the kitchen to find her stash of Earl Grey that I've seen her use. I dip a tea bag into the mug with a spoonful of honey. By the time I'm done making it and sit back down, she's walking out of the bathroom. She searches my face, asking questions with her eyes that I'm still not ready to answer. But I no longer have a choice.

I gesture for her to sit back down on the couch, and hand her the steaming mug. She takes it, but not without sliding her fingers across my hand. After blowing on it to cool it down and taking a sip, her eyes close and she sinks into the cushions.

"Thank you," she sighs.

I just offer a close-mouthed smile in return.

Heston is standing not far behind me in the kitchen, but I text in the group chat anyway.

Gage: Meeting in the living room. 10 minutes.

I hear the ding of Heston's phone and he looks up at me after reading the text. I clench my jaw. At least I can rely on him not to flood me with questions before I have the chance to let them in on the current situation.

Warren: For what? I'm at the barn.

Tripp: If this is about the hay trailer it wasn't me I swear.

Heston: It's important.

Heston doesn't say much, but when he does, we all listen. I think he recognized right away the energy I was putting off.

Like I wasn't fucking around.

I twirl the phone around in my left hand several times, needing to fidget with something to help me focus on not fucking up the conversation that I'm about to have. It hits me all of a sudden that I probably shouldn't be blindsiding Blythe with all of this at the same time as the rest of the group. I should have planned this out better. I should have pulled her aside first. That'd be the right thing to do. Time just hasn't been on my side.

"Blythe," I say just above a whisper.

She tucks her feet underneath her blanket and looks toward me.

I look to the side to see Heston walking down the hall. Dude can read a room like a road map.

"There are some things that I have to tell you," I say turning my head back toward her.

"Okay. I'm listening."

"There's a lot that you don't know about me. I need you to believe that the reason I haven't been totally straightforward was to protect you."

Her eyes search mine, but she lets me continue.

"I haven't been honest about who I am. It was selfish of me to start this thing with you. You weren't completely aware of what you were stepping into. And now…" I shake my head and run a hand roughly through my hair. I know that she's in danger, but I can't bring myself to say it out loud at the moment. It makes it real. And I don't want it to be real. "This is all my fault and I want you to know how sorry I am. I fucked up."

"Gage," she reaches across the space between us and takes my hand, "I knew exactly what I was getting into. What on earth are you talking about?"

"No, you didn't," I shake my head even harder and can't bear to look her in the eye, so I focus on our joined hands. Her soft tan skin collides with my callused fingers as I rub my thumb back and forth on her palm and squeeze like it's the last time I'll get to.

"Whatever it is that you didn't tell me at first, you can tell me now. I never expected you to reveal every little thing about your life to me. This, us," she squeezes my hand back until I look up at her, "It's not what it was three weeks ago. It's more. And if there are things you wish you had said, say them now. Because I want to know, Gage. I care about you."

"You care about me," I repeat her words just so I can hear them out loud again. My rib cage feels like it's collapsing in on itself.

"Yes," she breathes out. She stands, keeping my hand in hers and pulling me up with her. Her arms circle around my waist and time stops still when she places her cheek on my chest. I rest my chin on the top of her head and hold her.

Thank God.

She tilts her head up to look at me and I lean down and kiss her on the lips. It's tense, given the current situation. But her body melts against me and I breathe her in with everything that I have. I'm trying to say so much more with this kiss than I ever have. I don't want it to end, but I pull away from her lips.

"I more than care about you, Blythe."

She smiles and leans her head back on my chest. Hugging me tighter. I bring a hand up to the back of her head to keep it in place. I can't let her move away from me.

I hate how perfect this feels. My heart beats steady and calm

213

like it can finally function properly with her in my arms. Now that she's not staring straight through me, it's easier to blurt it all out in one soft breath.

"There's a group of men, enemies of my father, that plan to kill me to get back at him. I had nothing to do with the reason that they're at war, but they're after me to bend him to their will. They're ruthless and have no hesitation when it comes to hurting people to get what they want. They have pictures of you and me together. You're not safe with me."

The last part comes out like slow-flowing lava. A burning truth that nothing can stop. My confession makes her go completely still, and I can feel every part of her harden like a statue.

"I think I misheard you. I thought you said kill," she whispers.

"I know it's a shock. I—"

She lifts her head abruptly and looks up at me. "Wait. You're serious?"

I press my lips together and nod.

"My father is not a good person. My family... they're greedy and dangerous and it's why I left New York City to buy this ranch and get away from all of that. It's not who I wanted to be."

Her eyes slam shut and her cringe is so visceral that her nose wrinkles up and the color drains from her face. I move my hand to cup her jaw, but she doesn't lean into it. "Buy... this ranch? You don't work here? You... you..." she's stuttering and shaking her head in disbelief when my time of getting to explain this all to her in private is cut short.

The front door opens as Warren and Tripp walk in, brushing their dirty boots back and forth on the rug before walking into the living room. I try conjuring up an excuse as to why I'm holding his sister like we're not just friends, but Warren doesn't look surprised in the least. He strolls right past us and sits on the couch like there's nothing out of the ordinary. I lift my head slowly, studying his expression.

"I told him about us," Blythe reveals. And then she does the worst thing in the world and pulls away from me without even giving me a glance or a response to what I just admitted to her.

I pride myself on being able to easily read people, but she's not giving anything away at the moment. She sits between Warren and Tripp, crosses her legs, and looks up at me with no obvious emotion.

Tripp lets out a low-pitched whistle. "The fuck is going on here? Somebody die or what?"

Blythe covers her mouth and the dam finally breaks. She tries to close her eyes, but the tears beat her to it and find their way to the apples of her cheeks, spilling down over the rest of her face. She's full-on sobbing within seconds, and Warren wraps an arm around her while shooting me an accusing *"what'd you do?"* look.

"Hey," he soothes her in a hushed voice. "You okay?"

"Obviously not," Tripp scoffs.

Heston smacks him on the back of the head as he rounds the couch. He doesn't sit down though. Just places his feet wide apart, crosses his arms, and looks at me.

"Out with it," he says.

Chapter 30

Blythe

We're all silent as Gage repeats to the guys what he just told me.

"So you're, like, rich then?" Tripp asks enthusiastically. As if that's the most important detail out of everything Gage just said.

"You could say that," Gage admits.

"And you still drive around that old truck," Tripp laughs. "I never would have guessed."

"I'm sorry for lying to you. I never considered you my employees, I think of you as my best friends. Money got in the way of that for me in the past. I didn't want it to affect things for me anymore. I didn't want you to treat me any differently."

I'm not mad at him. But I could knee him right in the junk for keeping this all from me. From everyone here. There's a genuine and sincere regret behind his words. He's not sugarcoating it or begging us to believe that it wasn't his fault that this all happened. He's owning up to the fact that he lied by omission.

I don't know if he thought I'd sprint out the door and block his number if I found out about what he's been hiding, but that's not the case. I just wish he would have told me sooner. I'm shocked is all. It's a shit ton of new information that my brain is trying to take in all at once. I need a minute to process this.

And he said that someone is trying to kill him?

I don't even know how to react to that, so I just cry.

I wipe my nose and the tears sliding down my chin with my sleeve. Maybe if I don't look at him, I'll forget that someone is out there plotting his death.

"I shouldn't have, but I hid the fact that I was the owner of this ranch and came from money because it doesn't define who I am. I wanted a life based on other things. *Real* things that matter, not dollar signs. I understand if you no longer respect me, and maybe I deserve that. But I am sorry.

"Above all else though, I was trying to protect you all. I left a dangerous life. I didn't want any of you to be caught up in that. I guess that didn't really work out."

"Can I get a raise?" Tripp blurts out.

"Dumb ass," Heston mumbles and rubs his temple like this much new information is causing him a headache.

Gage ignores them and takes a few steps toward me. "Blythe…"

Warren stands abruptly and holds his hand up. "Don't."

Just yesterday I was telling Warren how much I cared about Gage. I'm sure he's confused as to why I'm bawling my eyes out. He probably thinks I'm furious with him.

My eyes meet Gage's.

"This can't be the end of us," his say.

"It's not. I won't let it be," mine say back.

He doesn't break our eye contact even when Tripp stands to pat him twice on the shoulder.

"I forgive you, man. Water under the bridge."

Gage's phone ringing is what finally pulls his gaze away. He reaches into his pocket and looks at the screen, but furrows his brow. A realization crosses his face and he sets that phone down and pulls out the little black flip phone from his other pocket instead. I recognize it as the one the man at the gate gave to him before he left.

"Yeah," he barks into the phone after opening it.

One hand moves to his hip, and he gives a pensive stare down at his boots as he listens to the person on the other end of the line. Heston and Warren look at each other, then at me as I try to suppress the worry on my face. Not a minute later, Gage hangs up and pockets the phone back into his jeans.

It's been an emotional morning so far, but suddenly his voice is confident and even.

"I need you all to be saddled up and ready to go in the next ten minutes," he demands.

"Now wait just a fucking second. What makes you think we're going anywhere with you? How can we trust anything you say?" Warren bites back.

"If you'd like to stay, be my guest. But I'm taking Blythe and she's staying with me until I can be sure that she's safe. Eddie Reynolds is not going to rest until he gets what he wants, and he's here to kill not only me but most likely her as well. My intel says he intends to *take care* of me and my family, and he thinks Blythe and I are together."

"You're *not* together?" Tripp asks with a disbelieving tone.

The room falls silent.

218

Gage and I look at each other. After this shit storm of a morning, I know he's gutted right now. I can see the regret on his face. Maybe even a glimmer of fear. I might be shocked, and still a little confused with the news he dumped on us all, but not about this.

Without breaking eye contact with him, I throw it out there without hesitation. "We are actually." I wait with a lump in my throat for his reaction.

Warren turns toward me in a flash of disbelief, but Gage's face turns from dread to pure delight.

"Hang on," Warren interjects. "You're not pissed at him for lying about all of this?"

"Maybe a little bit," I admit. "But I understand where he's coming from. He didn't want anyone to get hurt. I'm just as scared right now as you are Warren, but he was just trying to protect us. We heard him out and now we're going to stand by him until this is all over." The last part is more of a strong statement than it is an explanation for Warren.

If you care about someone, defend them out loud. It means more than empty words or promises. It's proof.

Warren softens his expression and takes a minute to think. I know he's not furious with Gage, not really. This is just his way of hiding his fear. Fear that his best friends, his sister, and even himself are in actual danger.

His shoulders fall and he nods. I smile softly at him and loop my arm in his to remind him that we're all in this together.

"Well, I'm not leaving my sister," he says.

"This is some fucked up shit, but I'm in. I'm a better shot than any of you anyway," Tripp laughs.

The thought of *anyone* shooting at the moment sends prickles down the back of my neck.

Heston walks past us and pulls his shotgun off the rack on the wall. "Kinda seems like we don't have a whole lot of time to waste chit-chatting. If y'all are done crying and bitching and moaning, let's get this shit taken care of. Where we going?"

My jaw drops. We all stare at him in disbelief. That's the most I've ever heard him talk by a long shot. His tone of determination was intercepted loud and clear though as we all jump into action.

There's so much on my mind at the moment, it's unbelievably overwhelming. But I'm changing into jeans and throwing my hair into a messy bun anyway. There's a switch that I flipped inside my brain years ago that prevented me from feeling too much. Instead of crying myself to sleep over all of the things in my life that were going wrong, I decided to take charge and do something about it. I need to channel that again right now.

I sink the heels of my feet into a pair of shoes and pull the strings tighter on the neck of my light lavender hoodie. Something about it makes me feel more secure. Like when I have it on, it creates an illusion of protection and the people around me can't see the way that I'm feeling on the inside no matter how tumultuous it feels.

"Jesus. If a spy movie and old Western had a lovechild, it would look like this," I say as I make my way down the steps from the loft. They're all huddled around the kitchen island looking at something on a computer screen. At first, I can barely make him out through the sea of denim jackets and cowboy hats, but Gage stands slightly taller and darker than the rest.

Everyone else is looking down at whatever is on the computer while he looks right at me. I walk up to him and slide my hand into one of the back pockets of his jeans.

Tripp squints and points toward the laptop. "So, this is your property line?"

"No, that's the county line. I own everything up to this line here," Gage scrolls down several times and points at the very bottom of the screen.

"What's the black area?" Tripp asks another question. I'm so thankful he's here. He never takes anything too seriously. If I was stuck going through this with just Gage, Heston, and Warren tonight, there'd be an hour of silent brooding and glaring followed by a ceremonious fistfight.

Gage's face twists like he doesn't want to answer the question, but we make eye contact again and I think it jolts him back to his new reality of transparency. He leans toward the screen and points. "This part is a warehouse. And this is a house…" He pauses to think for a moment and looks at me again and clears his throat. "It's my house. That's where we're going."

"There's no road," Heston says as he looks confused at the map.

"There is. It's just hidden. Not accessible from a map or public road. You know the far south field we planted Sorghum on last spring?"

They all nod.

"The ditch road that runs along that field has a gate at the end of it. It looks like there's nothing but trees beyond it, but there's a narrow clearing. Maybe a mile or so long. It leads up to the house."

Warren blows out a stressed breath and suddenly closes the laptop, tucking it under his arm. He turns toward me and places his hand on the middle of my back. "You good?"

221

I shrug and give a tight smile.

His mouth forms a thin line, but he nods.

We all follow him out the door, Gage being the last one. He locks the bunkhouse door and when he turns, I see he has my favorite blanket tucked underneath his arm. It's a comfort to me and he knows that from our many nights spent together. The fact that he thought to grab it sends a flare of longing straight through the center of my chest.

He catches up to me in a jog and threads his fingers through mine.

"I'm sorry, Blythe."

I don't reply right away.

"I disappointed you."

I nod, tears in my eyes.

"I never meant for…" he reaches for words that aren't coming to him.

"I know," I say and squeeze his hand at the same time.

As we make our way to the horses, I notice the rifle that Gage is strapping onto the side of his saddle. The knife he tucks into the saddle bag. The pistol he clips into the holster laced under his jacket.

We're not going down without a fight.

Chapter 31

Blythe

The thundering of hooves sounds against the dry prairie earth as we ride toward this mysterious house that I've never seen, let alone heard of. My curiosity grows more and more the closer that we get.

Sure enough, as Gage said, there's a barely visible path past the gate at the end of the field. The thick leather reins in my hands threaten to snap from my death grip on them while we navigate as far down the road as possible. As if breathing for me, the sharp whip of the wind forces air into my lungs. I suck in the oxygen and will the looming fear inside of me to exhale.

We cross a shallow creek and on the other side of it, a large log cabin comes into view. It's almost completely surrounded by gigantic shade trees, and the sun filters through them, leaving rays of gold light streaming onto the porch.

It's huge. At least two stories above ground and spanning so far into the woods that I can't see the back of it. We ride off to the right where there's a barn. After dismounting, I check that the horses have water inside the corral while the guys untack.

It feels entirely secluded here. It's silent apart from the sounds of nature, and the house and barn blend into the landscape. No manicuring or bulldozing for a view or a pool or decorations. It's been left in as natural of a state as possible. I head toward the house, the heavy footfalls of several pairs of boots close behind me.

As I climb the half-log steps, I fight the urge to grab my blanket out of Gage's hands and curl up on the bed swing in the far corner of the porch. It sways ever so slightly in the breeze and is covered in light gray pillows. Between the birds chirping and the rustling of the leaves all around, I can imagine myself napping or reading there for hours on end. It's the picture of peace.

The exact opposite of how this day has gone so far.

Gage hustles ahead of me to reach the door first. He types several numbers into a keypad and scans his thumbprint into a screen. When a green light flashes, the lock dislodges from the door with a heavy click. Shoving the door open, he ushers us all inside.

I was expecting something more rustic and cozy, but the inside of the house is almost completely bare. The hum of computer monitors echoes in the space. Turning to my left, I see a large room, flanked by French doors, that is most likely supposed to be a family or living area. But instead, it's filled with screens showing security feed from around the ranch. One of the screens shows a recognizable view of the bunkhouse's main space.

I'll ignore that disturbing little discovery for now.

I have to crane my neck all the way back to look up at the

tall cathedral ceiling draped with natural wood beams. We make our way into the kitchen, which seems to be the most habitable room. Just as I pull a bar chair from the island to sit, an alarm blares through the entire house. I cover my ears and duck my head down, feeling two arms wrap around me and pulling me toward the wall. Most likely Warren's since he was standing closest to me a second ago. My heart races from the jarring noise and I relive the shock of Gage's words: *"You're not safe with me."*

"Sorry," Gage yells over the insistent beeping. I look up to see him typing furiously on his phone until the alarm stops. He shuffles into the security screen area that we just passed, and returns just a moment later. "They're here."

"Who's they?" Always Tripp with the questions.

"My brother and his men. I gave them this location and asked them to meet us here."

"I thought you said your family was dangerous," I say in a worried tone.

"They are. But he's as much of a target as I am. And we're a stronger defense if we work with him instead of against him. He knows more about Reynolds' operation than I do, and I want them taken care of. I don't have much of a choice."

Taken care of.

His words are cold and calculated like he's on a mission. Nothing at all like the warmth they usually exude when he speaks to me.

He looks down at his phone again, scrolls a few times, and tilts the screen sideways for a better view of whatever he's looking at. Then, he marches over to the door and unlocks several deadbolts just in time for it to swing open and just about hit him right in the face.

"Party's here, boys." The man I recognize right away from the gate throws an arm out and struts in like he owns the place without so much as a verbal invitation from Gage to step inside.

Jet black hair falls in thick locks around his forehead, but the bottom and sides of his head are shaved close. There's a darkness to his almond-shaped blue eyes, the color that I imagine the ocean to be just before you're so deep that the water turns pitch black. He's got a black leather jacket on now instead of a suit, and an enormous black gun in one hand that's resting on his left shoulder and pointing toward the ceiling.

"Sebastian Sterling," he salutes with a grin. At least one of us is smiling and having a good time. He must be deranged to act so amused amid of a threat on our lives.

"This is Heston," Gage points. "Tripp. And Warren."

He and Gage are the same towering height and have an identical tone to their olive skin. Although Gage's hair is more of a dark chocolate brown, there's no mistaking that this is unmistakably his brother. They both have a tense temperament, one that only comes from surviving in the wake of wreckage and pain.

I knew from the moment that I met Gage that he was a good person. I felt comfortable around him instantly, and that's not something that you can fake. But I also suspected that he was closed off because he was jaded. Sadly, there was more truth to that hunch than I realized at the time. Trauma has settled into his DNA and it sparks a deep sympathy in me.

There's no loving exchange of a hug or handshake, but Gage sharply nods his head in greeting. "Bash."

"Brother."

226

"There's a gun safe and other supplies downstairs just through the first door in the hallway there," Gage points toward a white door just off the kitchen. Sebastian looks behind to his squad of equally scary-looking men and juts his head toward where Gage is pointing. They all peer around on alert but disappear through the door and down the stairs.

"Nice place you got here," Bash says. He tilts his head from side to side like he's checking out the space. "A lot better than that shitty old commune barn you've been shacking up in. What a dump," he laughs.

Heston crosses his arms and Tripp narrows his eyes. Warren's jaw hardens and he looks like he wants to say something, but Gage holds his hand up before he gets the chance.

"Let's just get this over with so you can clean your shoes and skip your pretty little ass back to your fancy penthouse. Wouldn't want you to collect too much dust."

"My thoughts exactly," Bash agrees like Gage wasn't being entirely sarcastic. When his gaze finally lands on me, I do my best not to squirm. He slides the toothpick in his mouth from side to side while smirking at the same time. "Nice to see *you* again." His eyes travel from my face to my feet and back again.

Real subtle.

Gage all but growls, Tripp holds Warren back from charging him, and I roll my eyes.

"Wish I could say the same," I say. Gage wasn't happy to see his brother last night and so far hasn't had a single nice word to say about anyone in his family. I may not know Bash, but by proxy, I hate him.

"Is that any way to talk to your future brother-in-law?" His tone is teasing and I know he's just trying to rile me up. He seems like the type to get bored if there isn't some sort of altercation happening.

It still brings bright pink to my cheeks. It's hard to miss the corner of Gage's lip turn up. Either he thinks it's a funny joke, or he likes the idea of it.

"Kidding. Kind of," he winks. "So! Did we get past the Gage-being-a-millionaire-with-a-criminal-record part yet?"

Gage blows out a long breath and looks up to the ceiling like there's something up there that will help him stay calm.

"Criminal record?" I stutter in disbelief. I don't think my eyebrows could get any closer to the hairline above my forehead. I'm starting to get whiplash from the amount of surprises and shock I've experienced in the last few hours alone.

"Great!" Bash sets his gun down on the entry table and claps his hands together with one loud smack. "Now that that's over with, you got anything to eat around here? I hate killing on an empty stomach."

Other than Gage and Bash, our faces all turn stark white. This is too much.

"No easing into it, huh? *Fuck,*" Warren says.

"I didn't think ahead to providing a pre-ambush feast. I'm never here, so there's not really anything to eat or drink. Sorry," Gage says. "And I *don't* have a criminal record."

"Right, because Dad scrubbed it." Bash howls with laughter.

"Whatever. I did what I had to do whenever his junkie or bloodthirsty clients came knocking on our door," Gage fires back. Shadowed circles ring his eyes and his voice is hoarse. It's obvious that the old part of his life bothers him, and that he would have preferred to keep it packed away. I'm not familiar with the world that he came from, but judging by Bash's cold indifference, it was dark.

CHAPTER 31

For a moment, he hangs his head. What we don't need is him feeling defeated and guilty all day. That'd be a good way to get killed. I walk over to him and place a hand on his bicep. He lifts his gaze to look at me, and I do my best to explain that we need him to be strong right now with just my expression.

It seems to perk him up enough to lead us all back into the kitchen where he opens the laptop. The guys all huddle around and spit jargon about position, ammo, and signals. I'd rather not hear the gory details. At this moment, I wish I was the type of girl to jump in on the action, but I just don't have the energy. I find the blanket that Gage brought, wrapping it around myself.

"So here's the house they're at," Gage points to a spot on the screen. "It's a mostly straight shot from the ranch on this road here."

"We staked out until daylight. There was no movement on their end," I hear Bash say.

"Maybe we should send a team back over there. Make sure they haven't moved," Warren suggests.

"No. That's what they'd want us to do," Heston counters.

"Do they even know Bash and his guys are here?" Tripp asks.

While they argue over protocol and bark opinions at each other, I slip out the front door and snuggle up on the bed swing I noticed when we walked in. It sways lazily from the momentum of my weight. I lay on my back, staring up at the hazy late morning sky scattered with thin wispy white clouds.

The sounds of nature and the gentle rocking lull my eyes closed, and I soak in the floating feeling that I know won't last as soon as Gage or Warren find that I'm no longer inside the house.

A branch snaps not far away, and my eyes shoot open. It could be an animal. Or maybe not. Another branch breaks and I start to sit up, a little spooked.

I don't even make it to a full sitting position before a white-hot pain sears through me. The liquid heat starts at the base of my neck and immediately bleeds to the rest of my body. It feels like I drank a boiling cup of water and it's burning down my throat, making its way to my stomach.

My hand goes instinctively to the source of the feverish pain, and I feel a small metal tube sticking out from above my collarbone. I gasp in a breath and open my mouth to scream.

But no sound comes out before my limbs turn to water and the world around me fades to black.

Chapter 32

Gage

"The longer we wait, the more likely it becomes that they realize we're on to them," Warren says. "I say we ambush their little safe house before they know what's coming."

"We don't know what we'd be walking into, though. At least here we have security cameras," Tripp argues.

"*Fuck* no. Blythe is here. The last thing we'll be doing is letting them know exactly where we are and bringing them right to her," I bark.

Warren cocks an eyebrow but tilts his head like I made a good point. There's an undertone of reverence between us. I know he's not happy with what's come to light today. Or rather, not happy with how I lied to him about it all for years. But we're on the same page trying to make sure that Blythe is safe.

I hope he knows that nothing else matters to me at the moment. It's a punch to the gut to realize that my carelessness has put her right in the middle of this dumpster fire.

If what Bash is saying is accurate—that they're hell-bent on picking off our entire family until our father gives in to their demands—then by default, Blythe is looped in on it. They have the pictures to prove it. And there's no better way to hit your target than to hurt someone that he loves. If they were smart, they'd use her against me. I'd do anything they asked if it meant keeping her out of harm's way. Including forcing my father to help a dirty crook like Eddie Reynolds stay out of prison.

I look around to check and make sure that Blythe is doing alright. I know this has all been a shock to her, and if we weren't pressed to make a quick game plan, I'd be talking through it with her right now. Begging her to forgive me. On my knees asking her to let me explain the best that I could. Every detail. Every motivation. Every reason. Every regret.

When she stood up for me at the bunkhouse, I swear my heart soared right out of my chest. She deserves every bit of my insistent apologies, no matter how much she thinks she doesn't need them. She chose to not only believe what I was saying but to stand by my side after I said it. And I'll keep trying to prove to her that she's worth a million years of groveling.

But I don't see her in the kitchen or the living room. There are several rooms upstairs, but there's nothing in them. Other than a few boxes, they're completely empty. And I would have heard her climb the steps to get there.

"Where the fuck is Blythe?" I growl.

"She was right there a minute ago," Bash says.

I lock eyes with Warren, and he takes off in a sprint down the hallway. The vein in the middle of my forehead starts to throb as we all begin tearing through every room in the house.

The pantry. Under the table. Behind doors and in closets.

She's not here.

Tripp comes bounding up the stairs out of breath. "She's not in the basement."

Mirroring the rapid beat of my heart, the alarm sounds again in the house. The one that only turns on if the perimeter boundary has been set off. I rip my phone from my back pocket and click on the security app, but it's taking too long to load.

With a frustrated roar, I storm into the room of security monitors and start clicking through each and every angle in and outside of the house. The others follow me, and we search the screens for what I hope is all a misunderstanding. Maybe she just went for a walk.

"There," Heston steps forward and takes control of the remote that was in my hands. He clicks on a specific monitor and then rewinds.

Sure enough, a blurry black figure slips through the treeline just next to the fence. There's a flash of gold as he turns to step around a log, and I stumble back when I realize what it is. It's hair hanging down his back, but it isn't his. It's attached to a body thrown over his shoulder.

The room is silent. No one is sure what to make of the situation yet without more proof. I snatch the remote back out of Heston's hands and switch its control to the monitor showing the back of the house. Nothing out of the ordinary there. I scroll through more feed from the side of the house and there's still nothing, but I finally decide to look at the feed from the front porch.

As I rewind it a few minutes, it shows Blythe sneaking out the front door and creeping over to the bed swing. I hold my breath. I saw her eyeing the swing when we first got to the house. When she gave me shit about not having more patio furniture or a place to relax and enjoy being outside around the bunkhouse, I installed the porch swing here.

I never thought she'd be able to see it or appreciate it, but I put it there anyway. It would have been the perfect place for me to sulk once she inevitably left. Right now, I'd like to spend ten minutes chopping it to bits and using it as firewood.

Seeing the look of pain and shock on Blythe's face has me shaking. She falls to her back like a dead weight, and a person covered from head to toe in black hauls her over their shoulder. In a split second, they're gone and I turn away from the screen.

"I've never killed anyone. But today might be the day," Warren snarls.

My body's first instinct is to panic and hyperventilate, but I fight it.

"Yeah and then you'll go to jail," Tripp directs to Warren after his morbid threat.

"You want the good news or the bad news?" Bash says as he pulls a cigarette out and begins to light it. Heston flicks it out of his mouth and he takes a few steps away, pulling out another one.

"Good news? What could possibly be good news right now?" Warrens seethes.

"Dear old Dad is the best lawyer in NYC." Bash tilts his head to think, and then smirks like none of what is happening at the moment concerns him in the slightest. "Probably in the entire country actually. None of us are going to jail, no matter how much blood is shed. Bad news is, that's exactly what's going to happen. Bloodshed. And their little compound isn't going to be easy to get into. Assuming they haven't already started to leave town with her."

Tripp swallows and Warren narrows his eyes. Heston unbuttons the cuffs of his shirt and rolls them over his forearms.

I throw the nearest item to me, which happens to be a lamp, against the wall and it shatters. Broken glass covers the floor. The release of anger does nothing to calm me down, unfortunately.

I turn toward the group with my eyes dark and stance wide. "I don't care how hard it'll be to get in. We're going to that house. Be ready in two minutes."

The floorboards groan as I stalk out of the room and back into the kitchen. Now that my money isn't a secret, maybe I could order a helicopter to air-drop a case of whiskey right now. For the right price, it'd be here fast and I could use a stiff fucking drink.

My eyes widen slightly and my mouth drops open. I don't know why I didn't think of it immediately. It's faster than moving in on ground. Perfect visibility too. We'll air raid their asses.

I whip my phone out from my back pocket and scroll to my contacts. Hitting one of the few numbers I keep on speed dial in case of an emergency, I put a hand on my hip, tap my foot, and impatiently wait while the dial tone rings.

Finally, a click sounds on the line.

"Dax."

In a low and serious voice, I snarl into the phone. He's a three-hour drive away, but can fly here in less than half that time.

"I need a chopper. Now."

Chapter 33

Blythe

Something old? *My dusty pink boots that have carried me through the happiest times in my life. The prairie rose necklace from my Mom and Dad would be my something new.*

I'd steal the little black bottle of perfume from Kee's collection for my something borrowed.

And the something blue would be his eyes.

I know it's a drug-induced dream that I'm having. I've already woken up twice, just long enough to look down at the blood dripping from the cuffs around my wrists and then drift back into the abyss.

The person who said the memories of your life flash before your eyes on the verge of death lied. It's the future you'll never have that invades your every thought. Made-up fairy tales swirl around behind your eyes reminding you of what could have been, but never will be.

Gage stands tall and strong as I walk toward him in a long flowing cream gown covered in vintage lace, just like I always wanted. The sweetness in the air from champagne and flowers almost feels real.

He takes my hand when I'm within his reach, pulling me in closer and faster than I expected. I slam into his chest, placing a hand on his arm for balance. We laugh. I smile all the way to my eyes. He doesn't let go. Just keeps me right up against him.

It feels like more than an embrace. It's him holding every part of me. Keeping me. Just the way that I am.

Disturbing my fantasy of a dream, a door slams across the room. My eyes would normally spring open, but they blink lazily instead, trying desperately to clear the blurred vision. Muffled sounds that I think are a pair of footsteps filter into my ears, but even my hearing is distorted at the moment. My head lobs to the side at the contact when a hand slaps me on the cheek.

"Time to wake up, princess."

I attempt to sit up, but with my arms bound in front of me, I can't use my arms to prop up my upper body. Shouldn't have skipped all those crunches I guess. Suddenly, the grogginess from the drugs and the inability to think straight or even use my limbs seems silly. I cough out a defeated laugh and a thick metallic taste coats my lips.

"Help her up. We're not done with her yet, we need videos and pictures."

"This is a waste of time. Just shoot her. The others will come looking and walk right into a rain of bullets."

That sobers me, lifting the outermost layers of fog. I only get a few good tugs on my hands to try and break the cuffs before I'm dragged by one leg across the floor to the middle of the room.

An involuntary whimper escapes my lips and I resent it.

237

The last thing I want is for them to think that I'm scared.

"Don't fucking touch me," I manage to mumble even though my whole face feels numb.

A bright white light is turned on above me, making me squint. I bring my arms up to shield them from the glare, but they're grabbed and shoved back down to my lap.

"Shut up, bitch," a voice roars. "Now say cheese."

The audacity of men.

I roll my eyes into another dimension. I've never not kicked a man in the balls for calling me a bitch, and I'm not about to start now.

Wading through the blinding light, I open my eyes to see him standing above me, one foot on either side of my legs. He's got a phone in his hand and it's pointed down at me. Most girls would be telling themselves to use their heads right now. And I tend to take that mantra more literally than most.

In a flash, I rear back and bring my hands up above my head. With the last bit of strength that I can muster up, I slam my arms forward as hard as I can. Crotch? Meet elbows.

"Ahh!" he screams out, instantly dropping the phone and buckling at the knees. He's bent over and at eye level with me now. My mouth forms a tight determined line and I head butt him with enough force to knock him all the way down. Adrenaline helps me to my knees, and I stand one leg at a time.

The throb in my skull is killing me after that, but it was worth it to hit him where it hurts.

"Wimp," I mutter and spit on his pathetic crumpled-up body on the ground.

A slow clap coming from behind me echoes around the room.

I turn to see a sinister smirk on a man much different looking than the one I just sack-whacked. He's taller, stronger, and has hair the color of snow. There's an air of confidence around him that's unmistakable. I get the feeling he's running the show.

I huff out a breath, unable to hide my exertion. He looks me up and down, lingering on my rapidly rising chest like a certified creep. The way he licks his lips about makes me dry heave.

"You're sure nice to look at. I could make a pretty penny off of that body. Too bad I have to kill you now."

"Yes. What a shame," I reply with a tone dripping in sarcasm. I try to keep my voice casual for the next part. My strategy? Keep him talking, and he won't have time to kill me. "You might want to reconsider offing me. Wouldn't you lose your leverage if you got rid of your bargaining chip?" I point to myself.

"I don't negotiate. No matter what else happens, you're meant to die and that's a decision I've already set in stone." He ogles my chest again like he can't even give me the common courtesy of eye contact.

"Hmm. Dumb idea. Seems to me like you could get what you want a whole lot easier by using me to get them to agree to your demands. What are you, amateurs?"

"No one asked you!" he yells and his neck strains like he's about to pop a vein.

"Maybe if you apologize we'll kill you fast," the guy lying on the ground groans. He tries to kick me from his spot on the floor, but I don't have to move more than a few inches to sidestep him. I roll my eyes and rub the side of my head on the top of my shoulder. These two are fucking idiots.

239

"You want me to apologize? Fine. Sorry for having great tits and an opinion."

The man across the room laughs and pulls a gun out from the waistband of his pants. There's a sharp click when he slides the top of the gun back and loads the chamber.

I widen my stance and lift my chin. If I'm going to die, I refuse to lie down and cry.

At least I went down swinging.

A radio beeps from where it's sitting on a small side table against the wall, and a crackly voice comes through the speaker. "We've got company."

The man with the gun keeps it trained on me while he walks to the radio and picks it up. "How many?" He releases the button on the side to let the other man's reply through.

"Five. All armed. They didn't come through the front gate like we expected them to."

I don't want to give away any hint of fear or hope, so I force myself to keep a calm expression on my face. Internally, I want to scream. It has to be Bash, Gage, and the boys that they're talking about.

"Where are they?" The tatted man snarls into the radio.

"I—I'm not sure," the other voice trembles. "They picked off several of our guys already and made their way toward the house pretty fucking fast. Should we follow them in?"

He thinks for a minute, tapping the antenna of the radio on the cleft of his chin. At first, he wears an angry expression. He was hoping to have them shot upon arrival I'm sure. The thought makes my skin crawl. Slowly, the corners of his lips tip up and a cruel gleam darkens his eyes.

"Two of you follow them at a distance until I give you the signal to shoot. Tell the rest of the group to load up and meet us at the airport. I don't need any more of my men dead." He pauses to lick the top row of his teeth and narrow his eyes at me, then continues his orders to the man on the other end of the radio. "It'll be more fun this way. Getting to see them drop to their knees at the sight of her lifeless body before we kill them one by one."

No.

No!

As much as I try to push it back down, the fear spills out of me in the form of slow and silent tears. I close my eyes and attempt to wipe the worst-case scenario from playing over and over in my head.

I've taken time for granted and wasted so much of it doing things I never truly wanted to do in my life. Time I should have spent really living, in every way that I desired, not in the way of false obligation.

Living.

Something I'd very much like to get another shot at.

In slow motion, the man takes a step forward. His index finger wraps around the trigger and I swear I can make out the clench of the muscles in his hand as his finger curls.

A shot rings out in unison with a deafening blast at the door behind him.

I duck down.

But not in time.

Chapter 34

Gage

"We don't have the luxury of surprise, so this has to be quick and dirty," I say into the headset.

The thrumming beat of the chopper blades is almost deafening, even with our ears covered. The trees and ground below us shake as we whir above them. There's no way they won't see us coming.

Bash flashes a sparkling grin as he loops a belt of bullets around his neck and over his shoulder. He's always gotten off on danger. Sick bastard.

I look to the side at the guys I also consider brothers. They don't seem sick to their stomachs or uneasy about the idea of us jumping out of this thing and facing whatever team of men are on the ground waiting for us. They're ready to do whatever it takes to get Blythe back and end this.

What happens after that? I wish I knew. But that's a problem for future me. Right now, I have to get my girl.

A hint of worry must cross my face because Heston fist bumps me. The most obvious gesture of encouragement

I think I've ever received from him. Warren nods in my direction, gun in hand. It's solemn and reluctant. But there's a sliver of respect still lingering there between us. He has every right to be more angry with me than anyone.

I didn't just leave out the details of my life or owning the ranch. I put his sister in danger. And I think that's the real reason he's been the slowest to come around.

He hasn't tried to punch me yet, though. I guess that's a good sign.

"Shouldn't we be blasting some hard rock music to set the mood or something? Feels like a missed opportunity," Tripp asks. He's dead serious.

"Sure! Is Hells Bells good with you?" Dax sarcastically answers from the pilot's seat, then shakes his head with derision. "*No* dipshit. This ain't karaoke night and we're already here." He points out the windshield.

Warren stifles a laugh and Tripp purses his lips, clearly disappointed.

"And you are?" Heston questions skeptically from next to me.

"Sorry, I guess I didn't introduce you," I say. "This is Dax Jordan." I nod in Dax's direction. "An old friend."

"He keeps his jet at my hangar," Dax casually explains like we all have pilot buddies that own airstrips and store our private planes for us.

"Nice," Tripp grins and nods his head enthusiastically, no doubt counting the ways he can convince me to let us use my plane for a trip to Vegas in the future.

I feel the chopper slow slightly as if we're about to descend. Grabbing the handle above my head, I lean over and look down to see the house not far ahead.

"Check out the fence line," Warren says into the headset microphone, and we all lean toward his side to see. The air in the chopper suddenly turns more tense.

Shit. There's a fence around the entire property and from a bird's eye view, it's not hard to see what their plan was. There are too many men to count who are all facing away from the house, aiming their weapons toward the surrounding woods on all sides. There's no way we would have been able to get past that on the ground.

The closer we get, several of the men down below look up and point. Some pull radios from their belt, some run for cover, and most of them aim their guns right toward us in the sky.

Tripp and Bash are closest to the group of men down below. From their side of the chopper, they both drop to one knee and fire off a relentless chain of bullets. Several of the men on the ground fall to the ground and the rest scatter.

Dax dips the open-sided aircraft at breakneck speed, just in time to dodge most of the rain of fire coming back up at us while we tighten our grips and crouch at the ready. His voice bellows through the radio communication system. "Drop in three."

One by one we ditch our headsets and bail off the side, grabbing the landing gear bar as we go. The burn from sliding down the paracord rope doesn't last long because Dax got us pretty close to the ground.

As our feet meet the dirt, more shots are fired and we sprint behind the building nearest the house. All except for Bash. He creeps along, bent at the knees, gun aimed.

He's calculated and quick, firing off two pops. A man who was charging toward us crumples to the ground, and another closer who was coming from behind the shed we're using as a base point falls face forward into the dirt. Bash steps over him, makes his way to us, and leans his back against the tin-sided building.

"Stay behind me next time. And how about some fucking backup? Shoot a motherfucker!" He whisper shouts. "They're not fucking around. Keep close and let's get in and out of there fast."

"Two o'clock," I say.

Bash lifts and aims, sending a shot straight through the ear of a man in a beanie thinking he could still run into the house from the trees. A second later, another man charges from the brush, and Heston wastes no time sending him to the ground with a shot to the chest.

Heston doesn't lower his gun, still scanning the tree line. His breaths are as even and steady as ever, but his eyes tell a different story. I feel guilty for putting him in this position. But I'm proud that no matter how fucked up this is, my brothers are willing to do anything to save Blythe and each other. Bash holds his hand out toward the man that Heston shot and looks at the rest of us as if to say *"Now that's a good shot."*

Warren taps on my shoulder and I look to see him pointing at a window above us. I push on it and it swings open.

"Through here," I grunt as I grip the edge of it and swing a leg up. Someone boosts me up to get through all the way. The rest of the guys follow me over the window sill, and we reach over to pull Tripp in as the last one. A few bullets hit the side of the building in the process, but he makes it through and slams the window shut.

We walk through piles of old parts and tools until we're on

the side of what we now realize is a garage. It's not technically attached to the house, but there's barely a few feet separating the two.

I open the dust-covered side door just a crack to make sure that there's no one on the other side.

Engines start outside, and I crane my neck to look. Several men jump into the bed of two trucks and peel out of the driveway. Guess Bash's sharp shooting scared them off. Either that or their job here is done. They were meant to lure us in.

"Our welcome party is scattering," I say.

"I'll text my men to cut them off at the end of the road," Bash furiously types on his phone relaying the message to his guys that are hiding down the road for backup. Or in this case, to make sure none of these fuckers make it out unscathed.

I didn't see Blythe or Reynolds among the guys that rolled out, but they could have been in the cab of one of the trucks. *Dammit.* We'll have to search the house to make sure.

I realize we're in a bad situation just sitting here waiting. They could blow this garage to smithereens any second with us all inside.

"Let's go," I open the door wider, letting Bash go through first.

We file out behind him, looking in every direction to avoid any unexpected fire. He turns the knob of the door to the house with no resistance and slips inside. It wasn't locked, and that feels like a bad sign. If we made it past the men outside, he *wanted* us to come in the house.

It's eerily quiet and empty inside as we sneak through the hall and into the main living area. Still nothing. No lights on, no men, and no sign of Blythe.

"The fuck?" Heston whispers.

Bash nudges the butt of his gun into my arm and points to the staircase around the corner. I nod sharply. On the outside, I'm focused and calculated. On the inside, I'm terrified that we're not moving fast enough. Or that we might even be too late.

At the top of the stairs, there's a closed door with a light shining through the bottom. Bash presses his ear against it, widens his eyes, and jerks his head in the direction of the inside of the room.

I listen intently, but there are only muffled sounds—until the distinctive click of a gun loading rings through the air. I open my mouth to yell, but Warren covers it with his hand from next to me. Bash waves us back, and Warren has to pull me to get me away from the door.

I scramble to break free of his grasp when I see Bash try and fail at opening the locked door. More muffled sounds come from the other side, this time more heated and loud.

Bash holds one hand up in my direction and pulls a small hand grenade out of his vest with the other. Before any of us have time to protest, he rips the clip out with his teeth, places it at the bottom of the door, and leaps back toward the top of the stairs where we're standing.

We barely have enough time to duck and take cover.

The door blasts open and flames instantly surround the frame. Smoke billows in and out of the room, and I move to charge toward it with no hesitation. If there's screaming or crying coming from inside, I can't hear it because the deafening explosion has my ears ringing with full force.

Before I make it all the way in, Warren yells "Behind!"

I whip around and crouch down as two men bound up the stairs. I shoot one of them in the neck and he falls back, tumbling down the steps with loud thuds. The other man sprints to jump on Tripp, but Heston anticipates his move. Before he gets his arm completely around Tripp's neck, he sends a bullet through his arm.

It's not enough to kill him, but Tripp is able to shove him off and to the ground. Bash steps over the man, pulls out a knife, and plunges it between his ribs. When he pulls it out, he wipes the blood from the blade on his thigh.

"Make sure there aren't any more coming. Guard the stairs," I bark. I stand and turn back to go into the room with a cloud of dark gray smog billowing out of it.

A few feet in, two men lay in a heap on the floor, surrounded by blood. Both clearly dead. I recognize one of them from the picture Bash showed me. Eddie Reynolds.

I bring the front of my shirt up to cover my mouth, trying to protect it from the smoke, but it's no use. I cough and step over them in search of her. My eyes dart to every corner of the room until I see her.

How her freckles seem to shine through the black soot on her face, I don't know. But it's the flicker of her eyelids that causes me to sink to my knees in front of her. I feel for her pulse. It's weak, but it's there.

Before I scoop her into my arms, I yell for Warren. He's by her side in an instant and spots what I missed. A whole lot of blood coming from her leg. He rips his shirt off to wrap it around her upper thigh, and I swing her over my shoulder.

Hopefully, the rest of Reynolds' men are long gone. Because I'm running straight out of this house with her in my arms and into the nearest vehicle. And I'm not stopping.

Chapter 35

Gage

"Thanks, man. I owe you one," I say quietly into the phone.

"Anytime," Dax answers. His voice is deep and monotone like this was just another day on the job for him. "I took a sweep over the house after y'all got out. Cleared it all out."

Dax is a former ace in the Air Force and I met him when I first moved to Texas. He needed money for his charter pilot business, and I needed a place to keep my plane. Not to mention someone who wouldn't question me or have a problem keeping a few secrets. Being pretty secretive himself, we made a good partnership. I hope he cashes in on my IOU one day because if it wasn't for him, I don't know that we'd have been able to get to Blythe without getting killed first.

I nod my head. "Appreciate it. You make it back alright?"

"Yeah, I'm home. Any more trouble stirs up, just let me know. Happy to help," he says and ends the call.

Bash and I are standing in the hallway while nurses and

doctors whiz past us. Thankfully, the police haven't shown up to question us about the nature of Blythe's injury. I have Bash to thank for that.

"You gonna call him?" he asks.

"Who, Dad?"

"Yeah."

I sniff in a sharp inhale through my nose and look off to the side. "No. But do me a favor and have him pull some strings to keep this out of the news if you can. And try to keep him from getting a price put on any of our heads again for fuck's sake."

He nods, understanding.

"She gonna be alright?" He gestures to the room behind me where Blythe is.

"I hope so," I breathe out.

His hand starts to twitch and I can tell he's about to bolt out of here.

"Stay out of trouble," I tell him.

He pulls a toothpick out of the pocket of his black leather jacket and sticks it between his teeth. He turns to walk away, but not before winking and a final word. "Never."

When I moved away from New York City and my family, I thought it would solve all of my problems. If I kept a low enough profile and didn't let anyone know the details of my previous life, I could start a whole new one.

In a way, I did. Living in a new place, new friends with no preconceived notions about you or where you come from, completely different job and daily lifestyle. One that I enjoyed and most importantly one that I *chose* for myself. I was proud of the fact that I could run the ranch. I like the quietness and the endless hard and laborious days. It suits me.

I just wish that my secrets would have done their job and kept the people I loved from getting hurt. Guess that's not how it works.

I walk into the hospital room. She's sleeping soundly, so I slump down in a chair.

Not much shakes me, but seeing Blythe in a hospital bed all because of me has done it. Gripping the arms of the uncomfortable plasticky fake leather chair, I watch every single one of her slow breaths. Never looking away just to make sure that the next one always comes. Feeling sick with guilt, I know for certain now that I don't deserve her and I never have.

That realization still doesn't stop me from wanting to hold her hand in both of mine and never let go.

The curtain just in front of the door to the room swishes to the side and Blythe's father walks in. Instantly I stand, wanting to give him some privacy. I swore I wouldn't leave her side, but since he's here, I could use a drink or something quick to eat. It's been since last night that I've had either of those things.

"Please. Sit," Wade insists in a hushed voice so as not to rouse Blythe.

There's a chair identical to the one that I'm sitting in just across from a side table, and he takes a seat in it. There's a decent-sized window behind us, but I pulled the shades closed first thing this morning to make sure that the brightness wasn't too harsh. We're facing the side of the room where she lays, and for at least a few minutes, we don't talk. I decide to break the silence first.

"I never meant for this to happen," I say.

"We know that, son."

"I can't stand to see her hurt. I would never do that intentionally, you have to know that."

He chuckles and shakes his head. "We know that, too."

"She means everything to me." My voice is lower this time.

His head turns toward me slowly and he takes in my expression. I know he's probably searching for a sign that I'm exaggerating or lying but he won't find it. I'm as serious as I've ever been.

"When Blythe was young, we moved into a new house in town. Right by the school and not far from the park with the duck pond over on Rhode Street."

I know the area he's talking about. It's one of the nicer parts of town for sure. My eyes widen and I listen intently.

"Gayle and I had saved and saved for it. It never bothered us living in a home that's not a fancy mansion, but we did what we could to make the kids' lives better than what we both had growing up."

I clear my throat and swallow hard.

"Not long after we moved in, there was a fire. Insurance fought us tooth and nail. The investigation said the fire, although unintentional, was the fault of the resident and they barely covered much of the damage. Blythe had left a candle burning right next to the curtains in her room," he solemnly admits. "I'm glad we have a wonderful fire department in this town. They were able to pull her out. She kept going back in to grab her mamma's things that had been passed down through the family generations. Irreplaceable things. She's got a pretty sick burn scar on her arm from it."

I remember how I traced the outline of that scar on her arm. At the time, I didn't know what had happened or how it got there.

"Anyway, long story short, we weren't able to repair and keep the place. We moved back to the trailer," he lets out a long sigh. "Her mom and I, we're happy there. We were just glad that our kids were safe. We don't need the best house in town. Our neighbors are our best friends, and we love sitting out on the porch. You don't get that kind of view in the middle of town." He shakes his finger.

"You're saying that she felt guilty and hasn't ever let it go," I suggest.

"Bingo. She's always been the smartest one in the room. But after that, it was like something changed in her. She cut herself off from a lot of the things that she used to enjoy. It all became about her career from then on."

Nodding, I place my elbows on my knees and fold my hands. He goes on after we both look in her direction again.

"She means everything to you, you said?" he questions me.

I know Warren filled him in on the shitstorm yesterday. But I realize he probably has no idea that Blythe and I have been seeing each other behind closed doors or spending so much time together since she's been home.

"Yes sir," I say. "Everything."

He purses his lips and ponders over what that means.

"She deserves better than me," I say and I mean it.

"No shit. And if you put her in danger like that again I'll bury you in my backyard," he sounds like a prison warden now and sweat starts to bead on my forehead.

How do you tell the man sitting across from you that you love his daughter and you're sorry that you almost got her killed without getting punched in the face? I'd take the punch at this point, honestly.

I take a deep breath.

"I love her," I confess. He raises his eyebrows and crosses his arms. Blythe stirs in the bed but doesn't fully wake up, so I go on. "If she gives me that chance, I'll protect her. And I can promise you that no matter how messed up my past is, there's no future that I see without her in it and I'll fight for it. Even if that means convincing you and everybody else how much I mean that."

The corners of his eyes soften slightly, but he squints and studies me.

"I'll take her word for it, not yours. She's smarter than you," he says.

I chuckle. "That's for damn sure." I look over at her, then back at Wade but he holds his hand up.

"Save the corny lovey dovey crap," he says. "I get it. She's incredible. It's no surprise you're in love with her." He smiles now that he's talking about her, and my shoulders drop at least three inches. "Look. I hope she gives you hell for this. And then follows her heart. Nothing I say is going to change her mind. Just promise me you'll take care of her from now on."

I sit up taller in my chair and nod. "Yes, sir. I will, I promise."

A silence falls between us, and thankfully the feeling that he might murder me starts to disappear. I don't blame him, of course. And I'm sure I'll have to win him over. But he's right: if anyone is going to put their foot down and say I need to kick rocks, it's not going to be him. It's her.

Having her family on board is important to me though.

"You think she could be happy here?" I ask.

"I do. If she lets herself. If she opens up to the fact that changing direction or changing your mind about where you want to be and what you want to do with your life isn't failure."

He rubs the spot between his nose and upper lip with the side of his index finger. "She hates change. But I think staying somewhere that she doesn't belong could dull her light."

My stomach feels like it dropped to my feet. There's so much I haven't allowed myself to think about the last few days, and what Blythe is going to do after her temporary stay in Westridge is over is one of them.

A nurse walks in briskly and flips on several lights. The brightness of her smile matches the now lit-up room. I'd hate her for coming in here every few hours to disturb Blythe, but I know she's just doing her job.

We both stand and as I turn to go to Blythe, Wade catches my elbow and stops me.

"Don't fuck it up," he tells me.

He soothes the side of his daughter's arm and kisses her on the cheek before he walks out of the room. I step closer to her once he's gone and take her hand in mine.

"How's she doing?"

"We've been over this, Mr. Sterling. I'm not supposed to be talking to you about her medical status and you're not even supposed to be in here," she whispers as she scans Blythe's wristband and then types into the computer. "You're not technically family."

"Come on," I roll my head back and tilt it to the side. "Please."

The hand I'm holding squeezes back lightly and I look down in a rush. I sit on the edge of the hospital bed to get closer to her and I search her eyes as they sleepily blink open and shut.

I'm glad to see that she's awake, but I'm also terrified. I hate that there's a possibility that this has all been too much for her and that she'll leave as soon as she possibly can.

I'll beg her to let me love her if I have to.

255

I'll beg on my knees.
"Gage—"
"Yeah, baby?"

Chapter 36

Blythe

"How long have I been sleeping?"

"Since late afternoon yesterday. It's eleven in the morning now."

I shift my shoulders back and forth to get more comfortable, and when I do, a sting lances through my thigh. It's not a crippling pain though. The soreness on the back of my head from falling backward is almost worse.

"Can I see my chart?" I croak out.

The nurse laughs and waves me off. I know that doctors make the worst patients, but she hands me the tablet anyway. Gage leans over to read while I do, but I doubt he understands any of it.

He realizes pretty quickly that the numbers and abbreviations don't make sense to him, so he leans closer and kisses my collarbone that's sticking out of my too-big hospital gown. It's not aggressive, his lips barely touch my skin. The ripple of shivers it sends electrifies my tired and weary body. I perk up and turn toward him.

257

He doesn't hold my gaze. Instead, his forehead falls to my shoulder and I wrap my hand around the back of his neck.

"Vitals look good," the nurse reminds us of her presence. "I'll be back in a few." She winks at me and shuffles out of the room, closing the curtain on her way out.

The latch of the door echoes in the small space around us and Gage lifts his head. He starts fumbling with my gown as delicately as he can to inspect the injury.

"Stop fussing. I'm fine, it barely even grazed me," I assure him. But my head feels like it's floating above my body at the same time. "Just tired."

His lips form a firm line and his brows furrow.

"I'll go get some food ordered and then you can sleep as long as you want."

"We should talk." I hold onto him firmly not wanting him to skip out of here just yet.

He turns back to me. I can see in his expression and his body language that that was the very last thing he was hoping to hear out of my mouth.

"What, you just thought we could go on like everything's fine and never speak about it?"

"Yes?" His shoulders do a cute shrug and the look on his face says he's at least halfway joking.

Despite the pain in my leg and my head, and the heavy weight of our complicated situation, I laugh. How is it that he can make me smile even when I feel like melting into the ground?

"We don't have to talk about it right now," he says.

"But—" I start, but I wince from the headache, and Gage cuts me off before I finish my sentence.

"You should be resting."

"I'm fine," I remind him softly.

He shakes his head and clamps down on his jaw. His muscles tense and he looks away.

I lay my head back down and tighten my grip on his hand.

"Okay. Just listen to me then," he gives in. "I've never been so scared in my life than when I couldn't find you at the house. I knew in my gut that something was wrong and I was right. You were gone and I—" he clears his throat and chokes back his emotion, "I was dying inside, Blythe. I knew right then and there that if I ever got you back, I'd never let you go."

A tear slips out of the inner corner of my eye and works its way down my face, trailing over my smile.

He leans down and kisses me like I might break. So I bring a hand up to cup his cheek and pull him in closer. The fact that we're both safe and in each other's arms right now is sweeter than relief. It's *happiness*, which seems like such a simple word. But now that I'm feeling it in its truest form, it's anything but that. It's everything.

Gage's touch is delicate and careful, but he grips either side of my face with such surety, that it's more comforting than anything I've ever felt. I pull away slightly to check him over for any injuries, but he proceeds to plant soft peppered kisses all over my face. It sends me into a fit of giggles, and I clutch the front of his shirt to keep him close.

"Tell me you meant it when you said we were together," he whispers. "I've never felt like jumping for joy before," he laughs, "but I came real close to doing it when I heard those words come out of your mouth."

My fingertips trace the line of his jaw. "I meant it," I say.

He huffs out a breath and the corner of his mouth turns up in a satisfied grin. My heart feels like it's in my throat just seeing how happy it makes him that I wasn't just throwing out those words in the heat of the moment.

"I have no business staking my claim on a girl like you. You'd fall back asleep if I started listing all the ways that you amaze me," he chuckles but hardens his expression a moment later. "I know we haven't known each other for very long, but I can't bring myself to waste time pretending like there's any doubt in my mind that you're mine."

Those words sound so right rolling off of his lips. I smile up at him until I hear the vibrating of my phone coming from the side table.

Gage reaches for it and hands it to me. Keanna's name and a picture of us at our favorite restaurant light up the screen.

"Hey," I say as I answer her call, voice slightly hoarse.

"You're awake! I just landed, I'm coming to the hospital right fucking now. I left as soon as Warren told me what happened. Are you feeling alright? I mean, all things considered?"

"Take a breath and calm down, Kee. I'm perfectly fine, just a few bumps and bruises. Nothing serious, I promise."

She sniffles and blows out a harsh breath. "Don't scare me like that again. I'm going to kill Gage."

"It wasn't his fault, Kee."

Gage cocks a brow as he listens in on the conversation.

"We have so much to talk about," she says.

I lift my gaze to take over the handsome man next to me.

"Yes. We do," I agree and smile.

* * *

"It's hot as balls in here," Warren complains as he hangs his hat by the door and walks through the main living area of the bunkhouse.

I'm on the couch surrounded by one too many pillows that Gage insisted I needed. He carried me to this spot after washing my hair in the shower and demanding I not move. If it wasn't for the Christmas Eve party, I'd probably still be in bed on his orders.

"I wanted to keep the fire going. Make sure it was comfortable in here," Gage says. He runs a hand through his damp hair and kisses me on the cheek.

I whip the blanket off of my body and sit straight up. "For the love of biscuits and gravy, I am not on my deathbed," I laugh. I stand and touch Gage on the shoulder. "I am *fine*. Even the doctor said I am good to go as long as I change my bandage every day and get some rest. I've done both of those things, and I enjoy you spoiling me, but can I help with the side dishes or something? I'm bored just laying around!"

Gage wraps his arms around my legs and pulls me to him. I'm standing in front of him while he sits on the edge of the couch. He looks up at me and I don't miss the lingering concern in his expression. My hands run through the stubble on the side of his face, and then the hair behind his ears. I've found that kissing him is the best distraction from his overprotective tendencies, so I plant one right on his lips. Per his usual reaction, he groans and his hands move from my thighs to my ass.

"I get you're her boyfriend now, but can you not?" Warren cringes.

Gage laughs and gives me one loud slap on the ass, then stands to grab my hand and lead me into the kitchen where everyone else is cooking for the party. His grip is tighter than your average handhold. And he checks on me out of the corner of his eye every ten seconds.

He's worried that this has all been too much for me, and that I'll bolt at any second. But I'm not afraid. He can worry all he wants about keeping me safe, I'm not going anywhere. Metaphorically speaking, anyway. I *am* going somewhere.

Fate may have brought me here and introduced me to this amazing man, but I'm not about to up and quit my entire career to be with him. It's a sore subject between my head and my heart at the moment.

"Ta-da!" Kee sing-songs from her spot next to the Christmas tree. Her arms are held out wide, and she wears a proud grin. I smile and clap, pulling out my phone to take a picture. Sending Heston to the store for the largest tree they had in stock and an enormous amount of lights and ornaments was the most brilliant idea she'd ever had. It's gorgeous.

A knock at the door sounds, and I move to go answer it, but Gage stops me. He pushes my water bottle in front of me and pulls out a chair at the kitchen island bar. My eyes roll, but I laugh and reluctantly sit. I don't need the extra attention despite my injury, but having someone dote on me so attentively anyway spreads warmth in my chest.

Gage opens the door, and on the other side are Mom and Dad, grinning from ear to ear. Their arms are full of baked goods and wrapped gifts. Gage removes his hat and reaches to take the things out of my Mom's hands while ushering them inside.

"Wow!" Mom gasps, sniffing the air and admiring the festive decorations. "The food smells amazing and the tree?! Just lovely dear," she pats Warren on the cheek and shuffles toward me.

"Good to see you, sweetheart." She snuggles into me and I hug her back with a tight squeeze. The part of my body that is actually starting to hurt is my face because I haven't stopped smiling since we got back from the hospital.

Gage, my friends old and new, and my family are all here in one place... home. Gage and I make eye contact while he moves around the kitchen. I've always thought the gesture to be a little cheesy, but when he winks at me, I almost fall out of my chair. It should be illegal for him to look so sexy doing that.

"Mrs. Farrow," Gage says, "I hope you like soup. I'm no chef, but I think it turned out pretty good." His hopeful shrug is too cute.

Water pools in my eyes as I watch my Mom hug him, taste-test the soup, and give him an approving nod. She's been avoiding solids since her surgery, despite her recovery going extremely well so far. The fact that he thought to make soup for her makes me wonder if Warren was right about it being too hot here. Because I feel like melting on the spot.

The table is set, the boys serve up prime rib and an assortment of sides, and soft music plays from the jukebox. The lights in the room start to blur as I take in the scene of everyone eating, laughing, hugging, and sharing time with one another.

I take a sip of the champagne that Kee poured for everyone to have with dessert, and feel a strong hand glide across my back. Without turning to look behind me, I know it's Gage. I lean back, settling into his chest, and he tips his head down to rest on my shoulder.

"I saw the letter that you left on the dresser in my room," he

263

says.

The smile on my face falls and is replaced with a stab of sadness. I have no intention of breaking up with Gage. Not when this beautiful thing between is just getting started. But I don't know what the future holds for us.

The letter that I received was from the residency program that I had always hoped I would match with. They sent the letter to formally welcome me for my upcoming interview and tour.

I won't find out where I'll officially be going until March, but it's not hard to discern which programs are showing the most interest in you. If I receive good feedback from them, I might even look at apartments in Tucson while I'm there to visit.

"Does it make you angry?" I ask.

"Does what make me angry?" He cocks his head and looks at me in shock.

"That I won't be living here. That this would be," I look down at his arm that is wrapped around my waist. "I don't know. Long distance?"

The drink in my hand is suddenly taken from me and set down on the nearby table. Gage takes each of my elbows in his hands and turns me to face him. His eyes are fierce when I look up at him.

"I'd rather know you're mine even from a thousand miles away, than not have you at all," he says. "If your goal is to go and start your career there, then I'm going to annoy you with constant weekend trips and FaceTime calls. I'm going to support it, not ask you to push it all aside."

The way I care about this man is immeasurable. In such a short time, he's shown me more support and love than I've ever experienced from a man other than those in my own family. It feels strange, being so confident in something. But nothing has ever felt so right to me, trusting him with my heart. I lean my head forward to rest on his chest, and his hands move to my back, pulling me into him.

"I knew there was a reason I liked you," I smile into his shirt.

I can't lie and say that I'm not worried about trying to start a relationship with someone long distance. My gut tells me it'll be worth it, though. We can make this work.

"Do you want your gift now or later?" I ask

His eyebrows wiggle and I laugh.

"Come on. It's in here," I say as I take his hand and lead him down the hallway to his room.

* * *

Gage

I close the door to my bedroom behind us. Blythe reaches up to the top shelf of the closet and pulls out the gift, handing it to me with a smirk.

The box isn't heavy, but it's fairly large and flat. I rip the top of it open, trying to be careful not to damage whatever is inside. My hand dips in and I latch onto a thin cardboard sleeve. As I pull it up and out of the box, a grin spreads wide across my face. I can't help but laugh out loud and my shoulders shake with amusement.

It's a vinyl record with 'special edition' written in silver lettering in the bottom right corner. On the cover is the Man in Black. He's holding his guitar off to the side, biting his lip, leaning in toward the camera, and flipping it off. At the top left, it says 'Johnny Cash at San Quentin'. It's fucking perfect.

I toss the box onto my bed and walk over to where I keep the other records that I've collected over the years. I'm going to need to get a display shelf for this one and move all of this stuff to my house eventually. But for now, I place it right on top of the stack.

I back up and place my hands on my hips, admiring how it looks. I swallow hard and blink away the emotion threatening to drip out of my eyes. Instinctively, my hand covers my face. A bubble of air gets stuck in my throat and my eyes feel like they're burning.

"Hey," Blythe says as she walks up behind me and slides a hand over my shoulder blade. "Do you hate it?"

I shake my head and turn to pull her in for a hug. My chin rests on the top of her head where it fits just right.

"It's perfect. You're perfect. You're still here… and I already miss you."

"I saw it at the flea market last weekend and I thought you'd love it," she says.

It's a more personal gift than I've ever received, other than the custom leather belt Warren got me for my birthday a few years back. This is more special though. She never asked me what I might want for Christmas, she just knew what I'd like. Old records used to be my favorite thing to collect. I have a feeling that's changing because now all that I want to collect are as many memories as possible just like this one.

I hope she likes the new laptop I got for her. The one she uses now never has as much storage as she needs, and it looks like a woodpecker mistook it for a tree. I had to overnight a pink one with some new stickers to go on it. Something told me she'd be secretly sad if it was a boring silver.

Chapter 37

Gage

The packed suitcase across the room taunts me from where I lay in bed. It sits next to the door, just waiting to be taken to the airport. I stare at it with a mix of disdain and pride. I'm unbelievably proud of Blythe for going for her dreams. I never would have fallen for a girl who wasn't as driven and determined as she is.

It's not my place to beg her to stay or find something closer. I don't want to fuck this up, and I don't want her to make decisions about her career based on a new relationship.

She's it for me, and I know that with every fiber of my being. But that's beside the point. I can't expect her to feel that strongly about us yet.

The selfish part of me is on the verge of tears. From our conversations about what a residency entails, I know good and well I won't be seeing as much of her as I'd like. For *years*. I'm stuck between coming up with ways to get her to reconsider leaving and figuring out the logistics of flying to Tucson every day just to sleep next to her.

I'm next to her now, so I push away the negative thoughts and snuggle closer to her.

"Mmm," she moans as she arches her back against me. You'd think I was floating by the way her ass pushing back on my cock makes me feel. Weightless. Out of this world. I kiss her hair and smooth my palm over the flat of her stomach.

"Gage," she whispers.

"Yeah, baby?"

"I need—"

My hand travels farther south, slipping under the waistband of her shorts and pressing down on her clit. She throws her head back and I take the opportunity to move aside, letting her turn completely on her back. As I pull down her shorts and hover over her, it's my mouth that takes over this time.

If you ever catch yourself smiling while eating a girl out at the same time, you're a goner dude.

And that's exactly what I'm doing. Fucking happy as a clam just to taste her. I'm right where I need to be. Her hands digging into my skull and my tongue on her. She pulls at my hair, telling me to come up for air. I'm not having it.

"Gage, *please*. I want to feel you inside me when I come," she begs.

My chin only lifts for a second. "I'll fuck you when I'm good and ready," I growl before pulling her clit back into my mouth with one long suck.

I plan to devour her until my face falls off before she leaves today, even if my cock straining against the mattress under me agrees with her and would rather me stop and fuck her as soon as possible. I'm too busy savoring her to do that yet.

Only minutes later, when the insides of her thighs are red from my beard, and I feel her insides clench and tighten around my fingers, do I crawl up her body. I leave kisses and licks over every surface of her skin as I go, not leaving a single spot untouched. I want to memorize every part of her.

When I make it up to her mouth, I suck on her bottom lip. She brings a hand to the back of my head and lifts her hips up to meet mine. We speak our own wordless language with the next kiss.

I'll be back soon, she says.

You can go wherever you want. As long as you come back to me, I say back.

Without breaking the kiss, I pull my hips back and then push into her. One, two, three, deep and claiming thrusts.

"I'm not going to last, you feel too good. I need to get a condom," I grunt.

"I'm on birth control," she whispers between scratches on my back and another kiss.

I pull back to look at her. I'm waiting for the punchline, but her eyes tell me she isn't joking. She's mentioned she's on the shot before, but never in the heat of the moment. When we're both about to come apart.

"Don't stop," she says. "Keeping fucking me with nothing between us until you own me, Gage. I need it."

Goddamn. Say less.

I grab the side of her hair and pull her head back, latching onto her neck. Madness takes over and I plunge into her fast and hard enough to knock the headboard against the wall. Her mouth gapes open in shock and her eyes are slammed shut.

No one ever tells you the best part about being with a doctor.

They'll be able to revive you after you give yourself a heart attack from fucking them so hard.

"Mine," I snarl against her ear and move a hand down to her clit.

"Yes. Oh fuck. *Yes*," she cries out.

It's the sound of her voice and the way she suddenly pulses and clenches around my cock that does me in. I can't hold back any longer, and I explode right along with her.

I fist her hair in my hand, holding on for dear life, because the blast of this orgasm is powerful. It takes over every cell in my body, leaving me shaking and panting above her.

"Sorry," I say. I'm practically crushing her with my full-body collapse. She just wraps her legs and arms around me instead of pushing me off.

"Crush me. I don't care," she laughs breathlessly.

We stay that way for what seems like a lifetime, and yet for me, it's not long enough.

"I should probably get up and get ready," she whispers.

I shake my head and bury my face into her neck. "Five more minutes."

Chapter 38

Gage

"Why is there a damn llama in the front pasture?" I bark as I step inside the kitchen after another long ass day.

"I'm good how are you?" Tripp jokes.

I huff out a breath and go straight to the fridge for a beer without even bothering to kick off my boots or hang up my hat. I won't be staying here tonight anyway, just like I haven't for the last week. It's pathetic, but I don't like sleeping in my bed here without her. I barely get any sleep with her gone, even less in that particular bed.

She's been in Arizona for almost a week, interviewing and touring the facilities and the city. That part made me excited for her. The part that wrecked me was when she mentioned that she had a good feeling about the possibility of her matching there. And she proceeded to look at apartments with a fellow potential resident.

I've been nothing but supportive, but it feels like a cruel punishment to find the girl I want to be with just in time for her to leave.

I could lean into my inner caveman and tell her how sad I am about it, but I won't. I'm still a grumpy motherfucker at the moment, though.

"You told me to do something about the coyotes. So I got a llama. They keep them away apparently," Warren smiles and shrugs from his spot on a stool at the kitchen island. He's got his hat pulled down low and is staring at something on his phone.

Tripp laughs. "Who'd have thought we'd have a llama boys?"

It's the same type of easy conversation that we've always had. After the wild experience that was taking down the Reynolds ring together, I feel we're bonded even more than we were before. I normally avoid serious conversations, but I tried to sit down and talk to each of them about everything that had happened.

Heston waved me off within the first few sentences that came out of my mouth. He told me he didn't give a fuck about the past and, "I'm not leaving the ranch. We're good." For him? That's the equivalent of *"I love you, bro, let's move on."*

Tripp's conversation was predictable. He launched into a ten-minute rant about how he knew I was keeping shit from him and that I need to be more open with my friends. Oh... and to buy him a new fucking truck. Not happening, but we settled on a new silver belly Resistol.

Warren's was by far the hardest to comprehend. We've been best friends for so long that I was worried everything about the ranch and my past and then his sister would throw a wrench in it all. He wasn't necessarily happy about the whole situation, but he seemed fine with it all after a few minutes of talking. Even though he didn't yell or curse at me, he still seemed disappointed when his sister was brought up. That confused me until I realized that it was just because he missed her.

Same.

"You still pouting?" Warren asks.

"Maybe," I say. He lifts an eyebrow and crosses his arms. "Yes." I slump down in a chair at the kitchen island bar.

"You're starting to make Tripp depressed and trust me that's hard to fucking do," he says. "Are you really that hung up on her or are you just being dramatic?"

That catches my attention, and I straighten up to face him, looking him right in the eye.

"I know it seems crazy with what little time has passed, but I'm in love with your sister."

Heston chokes mid-drink and spits water in front of him. "Shit," he coughs, "full send."

I nod. Tripp smiles, and Warren stares at me. I don't break eye contact. He seems to think for a moment, but then puts both of his hands on the counter and leans toward me.

"Then get off your ass and stop sulking for fuck's sake," he lectures. "We all miss her, most of all you, apparently. Figure out a way to convince her to come back for good."

Maybe he's right. But my gut tells me he's not.

"She has to make that decision for herself," I sigh.

Chapter 39

Blythe

My rule of thumb has always been to follow your dreams, not a man. And I stand by that to this day. But the redacted truth in that cynical philosophy is that with the right partner, you shouldn't have to choose between the two.

So I'm not choosing. I want both.

Problem solved! Unicorns and rainbows!

Wrong.

It's a lot harder than it sounds.

That realization is why I'm standing beneath the spray of a lukewarm shower in the hotel room with my hands braced on the wall and my head hanging low. Have I ever really understood that stupid little organ in my chest?

It beats slow and sad, protesting the distance between itself and Westridge. Not just because Gage is there, but because it got a taste of close proximity to my family and my hometown. And it wants to go back.

Right there with you, heart.

As a part of the resident tour, I sat in the gallery to observe a routine surgery this morning and felt nothing. I waited for the burst of passion or a rush of adrenaline, but those sensations never came. My heart didn't sing the way it did when the fresh air sweeping off the fields of the ranch touched my lungs.

I lather face wash into my hands and scrub at my tear-stained face, begging for the soap to wash away more than just the makeup. I miss home. I miss him.

What am I doing here?

* * *

"That's wonderful news! I'm so happy for you Mom."

"We haven't worked the details out yet, but I'm thrilled about it."

She called me first thing this morning, as she always does, but this time with a surprise. She's been offered a job as the head baker at Sofia's newly renovated café. It's a huge pay upgrade, and she has adored baking for as long as I can remember. Sometimes I dream about the bread she used to wake up early to make for us.

Hearing her looking forward to her new job, a lightness enters my chest. I'm proud and beyond happy for her. I pick up my pace as I look both ways and cross the busy street before the stop light turns green.

"I'm here at the hospital for a meeting. Send me pictures of all the yummy bread you make for the café tomorrow okay?"

"Of course, sweetheart." She pauses on the line for a moment while I continue my walk. "How are things there?"

The dreaded question. She, Dad, and Warren quit asking

me so frequently a few days ago when I begged them to stop. But they still try to squeeze it into our daily talks like this morning. Am I loving the prospect of moving here? Hardly. Does it matter? No. It's a means to an end.

"Don't worry about me, Mama."

"Can I tell you something?"

I sit down on a nearby bench to tie my shoe while holding the phone up to my ear with my shoulder.

"Of course."

"Your father and I... we've never been in a better place in our lives."

I stop what I'm doing and grab the phone with my hand again. Sitting up straighter, I wait for her to continue.

"We love where we live and work, we love our little community, and we have a routine together that is just right for us. We are doing just fine, sweetie."

"Mom, that's great. I love hearing that, but why are you telling me this?"

"You've assumed for so long that we're struggling and that it's your responsibility to remedy that. Maybe we've had some hard times in the past, I won't deny that. But that's what made us stronger. We're so proud of you and Warren. There isn't a thing I'd change about our wonderful little life and I want you to stop worrying about ours and start living yours. I want that for you more than anything."

I see where she's going with this. She thinks I'll hate my job and that I'd be happier living in Westridge. She'd be absolutely correct. Pride keeps me from confessing it out loud to her though.

I fiddle with the hem of my shirt, looking for the ounce of truth in what I'm about to say, but I can't. I say it anyway

277

because reassuring her no matter how miserable I am is a habit that's hard to break.

"I am living my life. I'm totally *fine*."

My voice cracks on the last word and a slideshow of my family, my hometown, the ranch, and Gage flashes through my mind.

"I love you, Mom. I've gotta go now."

"Love you. So much."

"Bye."

I hang up the phone and tuck it into my bag. Stifling a yawn, I mentally chastise myself for not stopping for coffee before this. When I step through the automatic sliding doors, the woman I scheduled a meeting with waves me down right away.

"Dr. Farrow!"

I don't know how she jogs in those heels that she's got on, but she approaches me quickly and with a big smile on her face. "I'm Mrs. Heron, the head recruiting coordinator. I'm so glad you called."

We shake hands and trade friendly smiles.

"Nice to meet you in person," I say.

"Do you see all of your needs being met here?"

I freeze. Okay, then. She's a straight-to-the-point kind of gal. It's a simple question, one that should be easily answerable. I could say no, but then I'd have to explain myself and I don't think she wants an emotional rundown of how I'm questioning taking this job should it be offered to me.

"Ah. The pause. It's okay. I get it all the time. It's more common than you think for potential hires to second guess their new position."

"It—it is?"

"Most definitely. Why don't you come to my office? I can help you sort it all out," she pats my arm in a supportive way. "I don't work for the hospital you know? I'm just freelance. I can find tons of options for you if you're interested in trying to match somewhere else?"

I stare at her like a deer caught in the headlights. For the first time, I'm seriously considering other options. What is best for *me*? What do I *really* want to do? I know whatever I set my mind to, I can be successful.

Mom's phone call was a reality check this morning. Maybe I've been going about this the wrong way all along. How many women out there are pursuing a lifestyle based on what's best for everyone around them but themselves? I don't want to add to that statistic anymore.

She gives me a knowing look and holds her hand out in the direction of the elevator. I blow out a breath that's been sitting at the bottom of my lungs since I was in high school.

I'm about to make a change and the euphoria of finally taking that risk is overwhelming.

Here goes nothing.

Chapter 40

Gage

"Y ou're sure these are going to last on the drive over there if I keep them in water? It's a long trip," I say with a worried expression.

"Hell if I know," Warren shrugs.

"They look a little mangey," Heston says. Hearing him give his opinion of the bouquet of wildflowers that I picked this morning cracks me up. He's supportive in his own way. I definitely couldn't have got the house ready without him these last few days.

"She likes them. Trust me," I argue.

The first thing I did after getting that phone call from Blythe on Friday was make the house I've left empty for so long exactly like I thought she'd want it. I filled the extra office with books and blankets and a new electric fireplace. I moved a new bed in the primary suite and put shelves in the closet for her. I rounded up all of the vintage teacups, decorations, and rugs I could find. Put in a new sound system so that she could dance in the living room while I cook her dinner.

I envisioned her in every spot of that house while I tried to fill it with things that would make her feel like it was ours to share. Tripp talked me out of asking her to move in right away once I convince her to come back to Westridge. The last thing I want to do is scare her off. But at the same time, I want her to know that I'm serious about us. And that there's nowhere else that I'd rather be than at home with her every single night.

Especially when there's a brand-new security system around every inch of land that I own. More intelligent video surveillance, more sensitive motion sensors, biometric keypads at the gates, you name it. Hopefully, Blythe is fine with bulletproof windows too.

It's a little overboard, I'll admit. But I once told her that she wasn't safe with me. At the time, I knew it was true and it wrecked me. I have to prove to her that that's changed.

She might be mad at me for overstepping with this one - but I also bought the trailer house that her parents live in and signed the deed in their name. I sent over a crew of guys to help fix anything that needed it there. I even hired her Mom as the new baker at the café, a job that I knew she would enjoy and would be good at.

I invested in reopening the café within a day of seeing her business plan. I could feel how much that place meant to her. Maybe I can find out what other types of tea she likes and have Sofia put them on the breakfast menu.

I didn't buy her parents' house and give it to them or pay their medical bills or even invest in the café to impress her. I did it because I know those things are important to her, so they're important to me too. And I take care of what's important to me. To us.

I fixed up the loft at the bunkhouse to have comfier beds in case she wasn't keen on officially living with me yet. I stocked the pantries and fridges with her favorite foods and drinks. I even had some plants brought in to liven up the place a bit. I know it wasn't much to look at from the outside. But she loves flowers and landscaping, so I think she'll fall in love with how it looks now.

I painted fences. Restored old gates and windmills. Made everything look the best it possibly could. I know that's not important to her, but it's important to me. I need her to love it.

The next thing I did was probably the dumbest of all, most would say. I don't care how risky it was or the painful daily reminder I'll have to put up with if she doesn't agree to move back. But I don't regret it, even after signing the papers. If she doesn't understand how much I want her in my life after seeing the front gate when I finally get her back here, I don't know what else to do but get on my knees and beg. And I'll do that too if I have to.

After packing for a few nights just in case and driving through the night without stopping, I finally pass the highway sign that says *Welcome to Tucson*. Warren got me the details of where she might be, and I called ahead last night to plead my case to the nurse over the phone and convince her to tell me if she would be there or not.

She said the tours and interviews were over, and that Blythe wouldn't be there. I panicked. I shuddered at the thought of her deciding to bolt for some reason without me knowing. She was so upset the other day, I wasn't sure what exactly was running through her mind at the moment.

The phone call that convinced me to drive up here was not a

fun one. Blythe cried buckets of tears over how confused she was. I tried to console her, reminding her of how intelligent and capable she is, and made sure to let her know that I'd have her back no matter where she ended up. But it didn't seem to calm her down. She went on and on about how much she missed her family and her hometown. And me. My heart melted into a pool of liquid hearing that.

It killed me to hear her so upset. I listened to the millions of reasons why she was unhappy, but none of them included being with me. That filled me with a burst of pride, and I knew that the only way to make sure she was okay was to come here as soon as I could.

I'll admit that I came here to tell her that I'm in love with her and to bring her home too.

The same nurse that I initially contacted ended up calling me back last night. "I found out some information for you," she'd said. "She mentioned to one of the staff here that she wanted to see the sunrise tomorrow at Saguaro National Park. I don't know exactly where in the park, but I think she'll be there."

Sure, I could have called or texted Blythe. But deep down, I was scared to have the conversation of asking her to come back over the phone. It didn't seem right.

I made a mental note to send that nurse a huge vase of flowers and a thank you card.

I pull into a parking spot at the head of a trail at the eastern park. There are two parks on either side of the city. I gambled guessing which one she might be at. After stepping out and smoothing my shirt, I grab my hat from the front passenger seat. Looking in the rearview mirror, I run my thumb and forefinger along the brim checking that it doesn't need a quick

283

shape-up.

I'm covering all the bases and not above using a little cowboy charm to break the ice.

Hopefully while walking around this place until I see her, I can write up a speech in my head. You'd think driving across two states last night would have given me enough time to come up with something better than *please come back I fucking miss you.*

The sky is glowing with a smoky blend of pink, orange, and early morning baby blue. I'm surrounded by larger-than-life cacti. I didn't realize how big they were in person.

I pass a few groups of people that are hiking the trail. After about twenty minutes, I start to wonder if I should start over in another spot. Then I see it.

The breeze picks up about a hundred yards away, sending endless strands of golden hair flying into the air. My feet slow down in awe, but my heart picks up speed. I pull at the collar of my shirt, re-tuck the back of it, and head toward her.

I almost walk face-first into a few tall prickly succulents as I watch her smiling while she snaps a few pictures. She looks more incredible than I have ever seen her. I didn't even think that was possible, but she's somehow more vibrant. Soft. Relaxed. Free.

That confuses me for a second because of how down she'd been just a few days ago.

I do nothing to hide the sound of my approach and it doesn't take long for her to turn in my direction.

When our eyes meet, I stop in my tracks. Her lips part in a silent gasp and she holds a large breath in her chest. Then she just stands there staring at me.

Fuck.

Maybe I shouldn't have shown up unannounced like a creepy stalker who can't leave her alone any longer.

As the sun rises higher, its light catches on a single tear running down her cheek. The glisten of it guts me to my core and I start to go over the options in my head of how I can apologize to her for barging in on her morning hike like this. I can't help but do that with her. Something has always drawn me to invade her space, from the very first time I stepped into that shower. I was a goner then and I'm a goner now.

I take my hat off and hold it over my stomach.

Not the time to be nervous, Gage.

It only takes a second for me to realize that she's grinning from ear to ear while running toward me.

I don't know why I start laughing. Nothing's funny, really, but I can't help it. It's like a dam of emotion that I've been keeping blocked off inside of me is finally broken. She's really *running*. Fast.

With a few feet to go, she leaps into the air and I catch her. The sheer force of her momentum knocks me back, and as hard as I try, I can't stay upright. Halfway to the ground, her lips find mine. I squeeze her so tight and press my lips so hard against her, that I'm afraid she'll burst out of her skin when we land on the ground.

But she doesn't. And we don't break contact as we crash into the brush. Dust flies up all around us and she bears her full weight on top of me. We narrowly avoided a cactus. If I rolled even a foot to the left, we'd have smashed into it.

Time stands still as I keep my hat from falling to the ground and hold her head under her hair at the same time. Every second that ticked by since the day she walked onto the soil of my ranch has been wasted not begging her to stay. I coax her mouth to open, and she lets me right in. My tongue dances with hers between moans and she arches into me enough to make me wish I could never leave this very spot ever again.

A minute goes by… or maybe twenty. But when we finally come up for air, she rests her forehead against mine. We pant in unison and search each other's eyes. Waiting for the other to say something. Anything.

"Hi," she whispers.

"Hi, baby."

Chapter 41

Blythe

"For the last time, I don't want your private plane to come pick us up. I was already planning on driving home this weekend. Before you showed up I might add," I point my finger. "Although I'm glad I have an official ride in your truck now. I sold my car and was going to rent one," I laugh.

"You sold your car?"

"Yep!" I smile even though I know he can't see my face right now. It was a hunk of junk anyway. It made a nice hefty payment on my student loans. Although when I went to submit the payment, it kept saying there was an error and that there was no payment due. I need to look into that when we get back to Texas.

I was over the moon to see Gage. *Obviously.*

But I had already made the decision to come home permanently on my own terms. I changed my preference list before the deadline. My top choice is now the program nearest Westridge. It's a little bit of a commute, but it's worth it to be by my family and in the town that I love so much. I realized that no job, salary, or number in a bank account would ever be worth as much as those things are to me.

Mrs. Heron was a tremendous help and inspiration for me. After hours of dissecting, she helped me realize what was missing from my career and future. At first, I thought I didn't want to be a doctor anymore. I knew for sure that working in a hospital for the rest of my life just wasn't for me. It felt crowded and impersonal. And I never really wanted to teach or do anything at a prestigious university far from home either like Dr. Mullen had wanted me to do. She was happy that I'd found the path I was searching for when I called to give her the news.

What I realized is that I like the fact that I'm a talented physician with a bright future in medicine. I've just been in the wrong environment. I wanted to live in the country. At home. And I wanted to help families one-on-one in my community, have a bond and relationship with them. My first sign should have been how excited I was to dive deep into helping Sofia's café. It exhilarated me. I knew I was making a difference in the lives of people close to me.

It's why I decided to finish my residency closer to home and eventually open up my own practice. A small town family clinic. I'm business savvy, and I care so much about Westridge. It's the perfect plan.

The thought of being with Gage might have had something to do with it too.

Okay, so he was a big part of it. A huge part of it.

But let's not feed his ego any more than necessary.

It's hard to argue with him when he's hugging me from behind. His arms feel so warm and protective wrapped around me like this with him at my back. He bends his head down and turns my chin to kiss me again. We haven't stopped doing that since this morning.

At the moment, I'm trying to zip a stuffed suitcase and he won't let go of me.

"We can get home faster on the jet though. I'll find someone to pay to bring my truck back," he all but whines.

I pat him on the forearm but roll my eyes at the same time. "The only way we get home faster is if you stop hugging me and help me pack," I laugh.

"I swore I wouldn't let you go again."

I close my eyes and lean my head back onto his chest. It's tough to take in a deep breath because he's squeezing me so tight.

"I'm not going anywhere. Now, you just have to let me breathe," I choke out.

"Fine." He gives in like it's the last thing he wants to do. Not before turning me in his arms, lifting me in the air, kissing me, and squeezing my butt first though. I pinch his butt back, and he jumps and chases me around the room while we both laugh.

It feels good to laugh again.

* * *

I feel a gentle rub on my shoulder and lean into the strong hand, nuzzling my chin onto it.

"Blythe," he whispers. "We're home."

I move the blanket farther down in my lap and sit up, rubbing at the sleep in my eyes. When we started the drive home, I planned to stop at a few places to sightsee and spend time with Gage. Instead, I slept the whole time while he drove and rubbed my back and shoulders.

The same tension and stress in my muscles that was there when we first met has all but disappeared. But he hasn't been able to keep his hands off me anyway, whether I needed a massage or not.

I blink a few times and see the front gate to the ranch come into view. I wasn't sure if he'd drop me at my parents' house or bring me straight here, but I'm happy with his choice. It's what I would have chosen.

As the headlights beam ahead of us, I recognize the entrance to the long driveway. But there's a new sign above the gate. Two massive logs hold up a fancy metal sign high in the air and there's a cutout in the middle.

Prairie Rose Ranch.

I touch the necklace around my neck and whip my head in Gage's direction.

"You—" I choke on the tears, "you did this?"

He puts the truck in park once we're off the main road and nods his head.

"I did it for us. This place means everything to me, just like you do. It was Sterling, or S, Ranch before. But I want it to be ours, not just mine. I named it for you and I'll do everything else in my life for you too if you'll let me."

Every word out of his mouth is confident. But his eyes tilt at the edges, hovering right above desperation. Just waiting for my reaction.

I could say what I feel and what I know he needs to hear, but actions speak louder than words. So I show him as I lean over and kiss his big soft lips. He holds my face in both of his hands and pulls back an inch.

"I *love* you, Blythe Farrow," he whispers, lingering on the word love with more assertiveness.

He's never seemed so sure. And I've never felt so *home*.

"I love you," I whisper back.

Epilogue

Six months later

"Margaritas? This is a step up for the bunkhouse," Warren laughs.

"Don't worry, there's still plenty of beer to go around," Tripp reassures him. He slides across the hardwood floor in his socks and slams into the pool table where Gage and Heston have a game going. Beer intact.

I smile as I look down at the texts on my phone.

Kee: I'm so glad you got your plane ticket for my birthday! We're going to have so much fun on the beach. I can't freaking wait, miss you! xoxo

Kee: Also please tell Tripp that if he's going to continue recording thirst traps in his bathroom and posting them on his story, he can at least clean the toothpaste off the mirror.

I type out a reply and then continue salting the rims of the glasses in front of me. The boys refused for the longest time to drink anything but beer or whiskey, but we're working on it.

"We should make jungle juice sometime. Now that'd be a

party," I say.

"No thanks. Getting sick off that shit in college once is enough for me." Tripp twists his face in disgust and waves a hand in front of him.

"Sorry," I shake my head. "Did you just say you went to college?" I snort a laugh and squeeze some fresh lime juice into the pitcher of tequila and sweet & sour mix.

"Hey, I'm smarter than y'all give me credit for," he defends himself.

I make eye contact with Heston and he shakes his head but smiles.

"Alright, it was only one semester. But still."

We all burst into a fit of laughter, so much so that I have to wipe the tears from my eyes.

Things have been hard around here dealing with another year of drought on the ranch and figuring out how to handle my work schedule as a new resident. But the people in my life have made every bit of it worth it.

Gage walks over to the kitchen island, sets his pool stick down, and stands behind me. I melt into him as his arms wrap around my waist. Instinctively, he lifts my left hand to his mouth and kisses right where the ring he put there sits.

I wish I could say it was a romantic proposal.

But he had the ring custom-ordered a few months ago. When it arrived, he was so excited, that he couldn't keep it a secret from me. He burst into our house at almost a full sprint holding it out in front of him for me to see.

It was a blur of him sliding it on my finger, asking me if I'd stay with him forever, me crying, and him ripping all of my clothes off.

Of all the decisions I've made in my life, saying yes to him was the easiest one.

We still come to the bunkhouse all the time. Gage spends breakfast over here a few days a week, we all grill out together on the weekends, and still have parties of course. We may have moved out, but it's still home to us just as much as our house on the other end of the ranch is.

With so much time spent at the bunkhouse, I've grown almost as close to Tripp and Heston as I am with my own brother. I couldn't ask for a better group of guys as my fiancé's best friends.

"Did my Dad text you back yet?" I ask.

Gage nods while still nuzzling the side of my neck. "He said they'd love to come over this weekend, and that they'll bring the dessert."

"And have you convinced Mom to let you give the café to her yet?"

"Nope," he laughs. "Which is awkward since I already drew up the paperwork."

"I know it's your way of taking care of my family," I smile. "And I love you for it. But they seem perfectly happy with the way things are."

"*Our* family," he corrects me.

I turn in his arms to face him. His blue eyes meet mine. My hands slide up his chest and eventually cup either side of his face. I pull him down so that our noses touch, and his hands settle on my lower back.

"Yes. *Our* family," I repeat with a smile.

I lift on my tiptoes and press my mouth to his. I'll never get over his deep moan when I kiss him. Every time.

He pulls away enough to bury his face back in my hair. "I changed my mind about hanging out here tonight. Can we go home now?" he growls in my ear while locking his hands together in a tight squeeze around my back. I laugh and wrap my arms completely around his neck, letting him lift me off the ground.

He spins me around, and when my line of vision passes by the TV, my brow furrows. I tap Gage's shoulder to put me down. He sets me on my feet and gives me a questioning look while I pull my phone out of my back pocket. I scroll to the TV app and turn up the volume.

"Look," I say.

A familiar face flashes across the screen just as Warren comes trudging back into the room. He's scowling at his phone, but the name on the TV grabs his attention, and he snaps his head up.

"Local attorney Savannah Chase was escorted out of the courthouse this morning in handcuffs," the news anchor reports. In the corner of the screen is a professional headshot of a woman with a mega-watt smile. Her hair is blown out and curled to perfection, her makeup looks like it was done by a celebrity artist, and she's wearing a light caramel suede blazer on top of a crisp white blouse. She's stunning.

"Her arrest followed a physical altercation on the premises and," the news anchor pauses and squints at the prompter to make sure he's reading it correctly, "alleged indecent exposure."

Tripp snorts and my jaw drops.

A video of a frustrated Savannah whipping her hair out of her face and storming from a building with two cops flanking her now plays in the corner of the screen. She's positively irate, and very clearly shouts *"FUCK!"*

There's no audio to the clip, but it's pretty easy to lip-read when you're that animated. The video goes on to show the cops placing her in the backseat of their cruiser, and then driving away. Several cameras flash and a crowd of onlookers stare in shock at the scene.

The screen pans back to the studio and a suited man starts talking about the weather. I turn the volume back down and take a drink, deep in thought. Finally, it dawns on me where I recognize this girl from and I snap my fingers.

"Hey, am I crazy or is that the girl you went on a date with a few weeks ago, Warren?"

Gage's eyes widen and he looks to Tripp and Heston, but they just shrug.

Warren sets his phone on the table. He puts both hands in his pockets, looks up to the ceiling, and blows out a labored breath.

"That's her."

The End.

Author's Note

"I have a world of creativity to offer, and instead of running away from it, I'm going to embrace it and make it into something special." (Me to myself every night, in the throes of self-doubt and imposter syndrome)

The bunkhouse boys have finally been shared with the world. They've lived in my head for over a year, and they just wouldn't go away. Writing about them has been the thrill of a lifetime.

Putting yourself out there in the form of authorship can feel a lot like emotional warfare. For me, it certainly did. Every bit of it was worth it, though. Since I've struggled with being a serial quitter, this is really the first time that I'm experiencing what it feels like to not give up, and boy is it a sweet feeling! I'm really looking forward to continuing writing and hopefully improving and learning as much as I can along the way.

I am over the moon starting to write the rest of the books in this series for Warren, Tripp, and Heston. I've smiled more in the last few months while readers tell me who their favorite is than I have in a long time! These characters are so special to me. I can't wait to bring them all to life even more with their own love stories.

I want to personally thank a few people who helped make this possible. First and foremost, my husband, who never once made me feel like this was a silly idea. He never let me cry too long, always encouraged me, and brought dinner to my writing cave more times than I can count.

Dani Galliaro - you are such a talented author/editor and I enjoyed every second of working with you. The amount of times I had to clutch my stomach from laughter while reading your notes! It's a good thing that you said you love The Bunkhouse Boys because we have three more books to work on soon! Cheers!

Sonia Gx - thank you for your patience, kindness, and incredible art. When I say I would rather stop writing this series than not have you do all of my covers, I'm completely serious. You're stuck with me!

Sam - I'm the luckiest girl in the world to have stumbled into your orbit. You are special and I treasure you! I wanted to quit so many times when I first started sharing about my book, but I didn't because of you. Thank you.

Ansley - I love your writing, your advice, and your friendship! Thank you for being my first author friend and helping me so much. I'm proud of you and so grateful for you.

Amanda - you should consider professional developmental editing. I love your heart and I'm so glad that we became friends. You have no idea how much I respect your opinion and love our book talks!

Kennedy - The fact that you carved out time to verify the medical school, residency, and career references in my book WHILE in medical school?! Simply amazing. I wanted so desperately to write an authentic female main character with accurate career details. I might be biased, but I LOVE Blythe, and you and your intuitive suggestions made her a better character than I could have ever imagined. Thank you so much, and I know you are going to make an absolutely incredible doctor one day.

Readers - Thank you for your excitement, encouragement, and support. I hope you enjoyed Gage and Blythe, and look forward to the rest of the series! Thank you from the bottom of my heart for giving a debut author like myself a chance. I hope you never stop supporting debut and indie authors! Love you all to the bunkhouse and back.

Content and Trigger Warnings

Explicit Sexual Content
Choking
Drugging/Kidnapping
Guns/shooting
Stabbing
Murder in self defense

About the Author

Lainey Lawson is a romance author living in a small southern town with her own cowboy and their two children. She writes rural setting love stories, always with a flair of unexpected twists and turns. Even when she isn't typing away at her laptop, she's still a homebody. Her favorite things outside of writing include sharing a comforting home cooked-meal, adult beverages served in dainty teacups, reading, spinning records, and time spent with her little family.

Follow Lainey on her Amazon author page, Instagram @laineylawsonromance, and look for her website and newsletter sign-up in the near future!

Printed in Great Britain
by Amazon

47794785R00179